CATHERINE - A HUNDRED YEAR LOVE STORY

CATHERINE - A HUNDRED YEAR LOVE STORY

John Legget Jones

Publisher's note: This is a work of fiction. Names, characters, places, and incidents either are the product of the author's imagination or are used fictitiously. Any resemblance to actual events, locales, or persons, living or dead, is entirely coincidental.

Printed in the United States of America
Edited, formatted, and interior design by Kristen Corrects, Inc.
Cover art design by Laura Duffy Design

First edition published 2016
10 9 8 7 6 5 4 3 2 1

Legget Jones, John
Catherine – A Hundred Year Love Story / John Legget Jones
p. cm.
ISBN-13: 9780997329636
ISBN-10: 0997329637

CHAPTER 1

Catherine loved Sunday afternoons. Every Sunday since she could remember, her family had promenaded through Central Park with the other socially prominent families of New York City. The ladies wore their finest clothes and the gentlemen wore formal suits with tall hats. The promenade was the same every week: her father, Joseph Dawson, and her mother, Martha, walked arm-in-arm followed by Catherine and her brother Howard. Occasionally, the family stopped to chat with friends or to browse the sidewalk vendor displays. They slowly wound their way through the park and eventually ended up at a sidewalk café. The older people stayed in the cafés for the afternoon while the younger ones circled through the park with their friends.

On Sunday, June 11, 1916, it was a perfect spring day. The weather was warm, the flowers were blooming, and the park was exploding with color. The promenade would be different for twenty-year-old Catherine that day because her cadet was going to be there. Cadet Harrison Richardson finished his third year at West Point and arrived home the day before. He would escort her for the promenade and the lavish party that night to announce their engagement. This event was highly anticipated by New York society. All the rich and powerful would be there.

Catherine and Harrison met three years earlier in Paris at a masquerade party at the American Embassy. They were spending the summer there polishing their French and experiencing the culture. Both had led sheltered lives, as most wealthy children of New York do, so neither one had a serious relationship before. The first several times they were together in Paris, they were shy and hardly spoke to each other. But Catherine soon fell for the charming young man. She wrote notes to him and asked him to parties and different outings. He wrote back and secretly started to visit her at a park near where she was staying with friends. Soon the relationship blossomed. When they returned home, the courtship began under strict rules with chaperones and monitored visitations.

Catherine had planned the day for months. She couldn't sleep due to the anticipation of promenading with her cadet and the announcement party. Her mother let her stay home from church in order to make sure her hair and clothes would be perfect.

The plan was for them to meet at the park at precisely one o'clock. Catherine and Harrison would lead the promenade followed by her family, then his parents and his brother and sister.

At promptly one, Catherine and her family arrived at the park in an open, horse-drawn black carriage. Joseph exited first then helped Martha.

Catherine's father Joseph was the typical New York society businessman. He was average height, overweight, and had a full beard. He always wore a dark business suit with a vest and gold watch chain. Joseph was excellent at business and he worked with his father, Douglas, at a glass company. Martha was pretty, slim, and tall with light brown hair and light blue eyes. She looked much younger than she was. Martha was from an upper-class English family. She still had her accent and she rigidly followed the Edwardian traditions in her manners and dress. Her dresses were typically high-necked, long sleeved, ankle length and shaped by a tight corset. She was always impeccably dressed with never a single hair out of place, and that day was no exception.

Catherine had long, wavy light brown hair and light blue eyes, but she was well past pretty and beautiful didn't do her justice either. She turned all men's heads wherever she went. She was tall and graceful with a lovely figure. She was confident, intelligent and thought of herself as a modern woman who didn't follow old-fashioned customs and dress. Her clothes were significantly different from her mother's. The dresses were shorter, the colors were brighter and the necklines lower. Mother and daughter often disagreed over Catherine's clothes.

Catherine stepped from the carriage with her father's help and saw Harrison. He was standing at attention. He saw her and immediately marched over with his family following then stopped in front of her mother.

Cadet Harrison Richardson was a strikingly handsome young man, six feet tall with coal black hair. He had a lean face and a square chin with a nice smile, a hearty laugh, a strong handshake, and was calm in every situation. He was fit and trim, as a future Army officer should be, and looked ready for a parade with his crisply ironed uniform and highly shined black boots. The buttons on his coat sparkled in the sun.

He removed his hat then extended his hand to Mrs. Dawson. She did as well. He gently took her hand and made a slight bow. Harrison said, "Good afternoon, Mrs. Dawson. It is always a pleasure to see you."

She smiled and replied, "You too, Harrison."

Harrison turned to Joseph. "Good afternoon, Mr. Dawson. It is a pleasure to see you as well."

Joseph said, "It is good to see you again. I trust everything went well at the academy."

"Yes sir, it did."

"I'm sure your parents are proud of your accomplishments thus far."

"I believe they are, sir," Harrison replied. "I have been looking forward to today for quite some time."

Joseph responded, "We have as well."

"Sir, may I have the pleasure of escorting your daughter this afternoon?"

"Yes, you may."

Joseph stood next to Martha and put his arm around her. Harrison turned to Catherine, who was smiling and waiting patiently for him to address her.

Harrison beamed as he asked, "My dear Catherine, I would be honored to escort you today if you permit me to do so."

Catherine looked at him with the confidence she always displayed. "I would be honored." She smiled and looked at her parents, who smiled back.

Harrison held out his hand as she removed her white glove and extended her hand. He bowed and kissed it. He stood by her side as she replaced her glove and she put her arm through his. Their promenade through the park began.

Catherine looked stunning in her custom-made dress, a pale yellow confection with white accents. The neckline was low but modest. The dress was gathered at the waist and extended to mid-calf. The sleeves reached her elbow and were embroidered with tiny white flowers. She wore an ivory broach on a delicate gold chain. A sparkling clasp with studded citrines gathered her hair at her neck then cascaded down her back. She was carrying an open, yellow parasol with streaming white ribbons. Her white walking boots had arrived the previous day from Italy.

They were a handsome couple as they strolled through the park. With her cadet by her side, Catherine wanted everyone to see them together. Many of her friends and their families passed by. Several prominent families stopped them to chat. They arrived at an open-air café and their families stayed to have tea with friends. Catherine and Harrison left to walk through the park. They stopped in front of a large, cascading water fountain.

Harrison turned to Catherine. "Finally, we're far enough from our families that I can say what I want to say. My dear, you are absolutely gorgeous!"

She looked up at him and smiled. "Thank you."

"I have to admit; I'm the last person that should comment on fashion, being dressed almost always in West Point grey, but I love your dress!"

Catherine blushed from all his compliments. "Thank you again! I had it made for you. I was so worried because I thought it wouldn't be ready in time."

"I love the color."

Catherine swished her dress around her legs. "It's one of my favorite colors and I know you like yellow as well."

"All cavalry men love yellow."

She looked at his attire. "Harrison, you are so handsome in your uniform!"

"I had thought about wearing my new suit but I thought you would like to see me in my uniform."

"I'm glad you did. It makes me proud to see you in it," she said.

"I'm happy we could get away together for a while. I was surprised no one said we needed a chaperone."

"So was I! I thought for sure Mother would say something but she was busy talking."

"May I kiss you?" he asked.

She looked around at the people near them and replied, "I would love you to, but not here. There are too many people around. Let's go to the flower garden. It's secluded there."

"I'll race you there."

"No you won't, young man! I'm not running in my new boots." She lifted her dress a little and showed him her boots.

"Those, my dear, are also pretty. I have a suggestion. There's a lemonade stand near the bridge. Let's have some lemonade and then we can walk through the flower garden."

She smiled, "That sounds delightful."

They walked arm-in-arm to the stand. Harrison bought them each a glass of lemonade. They sat under a large shade tree on a wooden bench and talked, laughed, and watched people go by. They walked over a bridge then browsed casually through the garden for nearly an hour. Three times during the walk, he kissed her when no one was near.

"Harrison, we should get back soon to the café or my father will send the police to find me."

"One more kiss and then we can go back."

Catherine looked around quickly and whispered, "Just one more."

He made it a long kiss and she had to pull back from him.

"Harrison, you're going to get us into trouble."

"I hope so," he said mischievously.

As they walked back, Harrison asked, "Did you and your parents agree on our wedding date?"

She stopped, turned toward him, and with a concerned look on her face, she took his hands and said, "I wanted to talk to you about that. I have argued with my mother many times about the date. As you know, she is from England. She gets these terrible letters from her family on the horrors that are occurring in the war. Two of my cousins are now widows. She is afraid that I might become one. She wants me to wait and see if we will enter the war. My parents believe it will be a short war if America gets involved and they would prefer we wait until it is over but I don't want to wait. I want to get married after you graduate next June."

"I agree with your parents," Harrison replied. "If we go to war, we will end it quickly. However, there are no assurances that we will. President Wilson has said clearly we will remain neutral."

"Yes, he said that at a dinner I attended. However, my grandfather believes it is inevitable that it will happen." Catherine's hands tightened with worry.

"He could be right, but if the war occurs, I'll be fine. I'll be an officer next year and I have received the finest training to keep my men and myself safe. With our men and resources, I can assure you, we will end the war quickly."

"Oh Harrison, I pray every night that we don't go to war. I don't want anything to delay our wedding."

"Neither do I." He brushed his hand against her cheek. "There's another reason why I'll be fine even if the war does happen. This week, I learned my uncle requested a transfer for me to his cavalry division once I graduate. He is an experienced, battle-tested officer and he will be looking out for me."

"That's wonderful news! I'll make sure my mother knows. Tonight, my father won't announce a wedding date. Will that make you upset?"

Harrison replied, "No, I understand. I don't want you to worry. I'll graduate next year and we'll get married. I don't see anything coming to change our plans. I'll have a good assignment somewhere in the world and you'll be with me. We'll stay in the military if we like it or I'll work for my father's brokerage firm. We'll have a wonderful life together."

"I know we will." She squeezed his hand.

They arrived at the crowded café. Catherine's grandfather, Douglas Dawson, whom she absolutely adored, was there along with a number of family and friends.

Douglas was a well-educated and successful businessman who invented a process for making window glass. His company, the Dawson Glass Company, was the country's largest glass and mirror manufacturer. Douglas worked with his son Joseph, Catherine's father, there. Douglas loved inventing things but he hated being in the office. He had no patience for entertaining customers or bankers so Joseph ran the day-to-day business.

Douglas wasn't like the other gentlemen of New York in looks, manner, or dress. He was clean-shaven and in excellent shape for a man of sixty-five. He was nearly six feet tall with brown hair that had a touch of grey. He always dressed like a safari or Western hunting guide. Today, he was wearing khaki pants and a hunting jacket with a white, open-collared shirt and brown walking boots. Under his jacket, he had a pearl-handled revolver in a shoulder holster that, according to him, he had used before to protect himself. No one would ever guess that he was one of the wealthiest men in America.

Douglas had experienced many exciting adventures, which he enjoyed describing in detail. He had been across the world trying to find better ways to make glass and to investigate what he called the great mysteries of life. He dug for antiquities in the sands of Egypt, lived with the aborigines in the wilds of Australia, searched for the fountain of youth in Central America, and prayed with the monks in Tibet.

He was always willing to be the first to try something new. He was one of the first in New York City to use electricity and the telephone. He loved motorcars and tinkered with them often. His latest model was parked outside the café.

Douglas was tough, hard-charging, loved to play poker, was reckless at times, and often used off-color language, but he had a soft spot and that was Catherine. They were kindred spirits and they truly enjoyed each other's company. He was always willing to give her anything she desired. However, she never asked him for anything but his time, which he gladly gave. When they were together, he was not the larger-than-life, famous, and wealthy man, but instead a kind and loving grandfather whom she called Papa.

Douglas stood and hugged Catherine, "My dear, you are the prettiest woman in New York."

"Thank you, Papa! I can always count on you to make me feel special."

Douglas commented, "That is also a pretty dress, I love yellow."

"Thank you! I always think of spring when I see yellow," replied Catherine.

"I do as well. Now, how has this soldier been treating you?"

Catherine turned, looked up, and smiled at Harrison as she said, "He has been a perfect gentleman."

"I'm glad of that. If not, I'll have him tossed into one of my batches of glass. I always say a little meat in the batch makes better glass."

Everyone laughed except Martha, who had little patience for her father-in-law's frequent rough language and manner.

Harrison said, “Sir, it’s good to see you. Someday, I would like to see how glass is made.”

“I can always use an extra hand at the plant. Why don’t you work at our Long Island factory this summer? I guarantee you one summer at the hot ovens would make you want to be a better officer.”

“Sorry sir, but I will be with the cavalry this summer for maneuvers.”

Douglas was surprised and quickly asked, “The cavalry? You’re in the cavalry?”

“I will be assigned to the cavalry when I graduate.”

“Do you mean horses?”

“Yes sir.”

Douglas paused as if he was carefully considering what he was about to say. “I don’t know much about war but it is clear to me that horses shouldn’t be used in battle any longer. They are obsolete; machines are taking their place on the battlefield. The Germans slaughtered the British and French Cavalry.”

The women were surprised at what he said and looked away.

Mr. Richardson asked, “Harrison, is that true?”

Harrison started to speak but Douglas interrupted him. “Of course it’s true. They were slaughtered. Our boys will be too if we don’t learn from the English and French mistakes.”

Joseph was angry and he interjected, “Father, now isn’t the time or the right company to discuss the war.”

"Oh, I'm sorry! Joseph and Martha tell me that I'm too crude around people. Joseph never lets me around customers or bankers; he's afraid I'll upset or shoot someone." He opened his coat to show his revolver.

Joseph, in an exasperated voice, admonished his father, "I told you before you shouldn't wear your gun! We're in New York City; you don't need it here!"

Douglas waved the back of his hand at him and dismissed what he said. "I wear it *because* we're in New York City! I feel safer in the jungles of New Guinea with the head hunters than I do here!"

Martha stepped in, having heard the rising tension between father and son. "Gentlemen, let's change the subject away from guns and head hunters!"

"I agree. Catherine, will you save me a dance tonight?" asked Douglas.

"Yes Papa, it's always fun to dance with you."

CHAPTER 2

The engagement party was at the best hotel in the city. Three hundred guests from high society, business, and politics were invited, with cocktails at six and dinner promptly at seven.

The dining room was elegant with white Italian marble floors and brightly lit by elaborate, crystal chandeliers. Floor-to-ceiling windows decorated with exquisite sapphire blue silk drapes framed both sides of the room.

By six, everyone had arrived and the party was in full swing. A small orchestra played softly while waiters in white coats and gloves scurried about, serving the guests. The men were in black tie and the women wore their finest gowns in a variety of spring colors. The military men were in formal dress uniforms with all their medals and ribbons prominently displayed.

At six-thirty, Harrison and Catherine stood at the door of the dining room.

Harrison looked at Catherine and stated, “You look a little nervous.”

"I'm scared to death. This is the first time we will be seen formally as a couple. I'm not sure quite how to act."

"You act like the prettiest and most engaging woman in the room because you are," he said.

"How do I do that?" she asked.

"You're always so friendly and intelligent that everyone will see not only your outward beauty, but what I love about you most—the real you."

Catherine smiled and felt more at ease.

They entered the dining room, walking arm in arm. Harrison was handsome in his formal dress cadet uniform and Catherine was breathtaking in her shell pink Parisian evening gown. They mingled with the crowd and often stopped to chat with the high-ranking military officers. They acted as if they had done this many times before. The occasion was festive and happy.

At seven, the orchestra stopped and a waiter with a small chime announced dinner. The guests took their assigned seats at the tables. Weeks of effort by Catherine and her mother went into planning who would sit at each table. A table near the head table was the favored position.

The fine English bone china was pearl white with a delicate, red rose pattern. The fine Italian crystal was trimmed with a wide gold band. Only the best French wine was served.

At eight-thirty, Joseph Dawson stood at the head table and made the engagement announcement. Afterwards, Harrison and Catherine led the guests down the hall to the ballroom where they danced the first waltz.

The ballroom was the largest and grandest in the city. Three ornate crystal balls and many crystal chandeliers hung across the ceiling. Large glass windows were on either side of the room and a French door was in the middle of one wall. The door opened to a spacious terrace overlooking a large, meticulously manicured garden. A wide, ornate marble staircase led to a large water fountain. A winding brick sidewalk began to the right of the fountain. The sidewalk had dense, tall, well-trimmed shrubs on both sides. Several small cascading fountains were positioned along the walk and everywhere there were colorful flowers.

After several dances, Harrison and Catherine walked out on the terrace then down to the garden. The evening was warm and many couples were strolling about. The couple walked through the garden and whenever they were alone, they kissed. They stopped and sat in a large, white gazebo.

Harrison asked, "The party is going well, don't you think?"

"Absolutely." Catherine beamed. "Everyone's told me that they're having an enjoyable time."

"I was right about what I thought earlier. Without a doubt, you are the prettiest woman here!"

Catherine felt the blush that colored her cheeks. "Thank you…and you are so handsome! I keep watching all the girls look at you. Ester walked into a table staring at you."

"You're teasing!"

"No, I saw her do it. I'm so proud to be with you—a West Point cadet—and with that striking dress uniform. I love a man in uniform!"

"Once we're married, maybe I won't wear pajamas to bed. I'll wear a uniform."

She laughed and responded, "That'll be fine with me."

Harrison pulled her close for a kiss deep with passion.

Harrison pulled back and asked, "Have you thought about not having a big wedding and running away to get married?"

Catherine smiled and said, "Oh yes I have, many times. Just now, I was thinking about how nice it would be for us to be together."

"So was I."

"I think it would be wonderful to go somewhere romantic and get married," Catherine said wishfully.

"I know planning this engagement party has been stressful for you and your mother."

Catherine sighed. "Yes, it has been. I dread what the wedding will be like. We had to worry over so many little things. Will there be enough china settings and silverware? Does it match? Mother and I had to worry if this person or that person could sit together. Did you see that old cow, Mrs. Ferguson, who got so upset earlier this evening?"

"No, what happened?"

"She was insulted because she was sitting four tables from the head table. She felt a fourth row table wasn't fitting for a person of her position. Her *position*! Her husband is a dry goods merchant—and it's not a big store! Luckily, we had a couple at a better table that couldn't attend, otherwise she would have had a hissy fit. Mother stepped in and took care of it. Papa said we should kick her and her skinny husband out. He said he would do it for us."

Harrison laughed, "I bet he would too."

"I know he would!"

Harrison got serious and asked, "Why don't we do it?"

"You mean elope?"

"Yes. I don't have to go to maneuvers for a few weeks. We can leave tomorrow and go to Niagara. There's a romantic chapel there. We can get married and be together before I have to leave."

"My mother would die if we did that."

Harrison's eyes widened in excitement; he thought Catherine might be interested in his idea. "Yes, but think about it—all the wedding stress would be over. No more worries about our parents and the guests. We would be together finally."

"Are you serious?" asked Catherine, unbelieving.

"Yes."

Catherine stood and took a couple of steps away. She held onto a rail with her back turned to him. "Where will we live? With what money?"

"I have some money but not much. Do you have any saved?"

She turned to him and said, "I have a little. My trust fund from my grandmother doesn't become mine until January. Let me ask you a question. I thought cadets couldn't be married?"

"You're right; cadets can't be married, so we'll hide it for a few months. I've heard rumors that other cadets have secretly done it."

Catherine shook her head. "Harrison, we should slow down some. This is the passion talking."

"I want to be with you now, not next year."

"Yes dear, I know, but we should wait till you graduate."

"Don't you feel what I feel?" asked Harrison pitifully.

"Yes, but I don't want you to lie and give up your future if we get caught. We should wait."

Harrison hung his head. She walked to him and gently lifted his chin, "Please don't be sad. We will be together every minute until you go to summer maneuvers. After that, we will go to your parents' country home for a week. We will also be together for the holidays. Before you know it, you'll be back, summer will be here, and we will be together forever."

"I guess you're right. I love you so much and I want to be with you."

She said, "I know, I want that too. Nothing will get in the way of our marriage when the time is right."

He stood up, reached for her, pulled her close, and kissed her again. After the kiss, she gently pushed him back and reminded him, "Now Harrison, that's what got us down this path."

Harrison smiled and said, "I like this path."

"Men always do!"

They laughed.

She said, "We should go in before Mother comes looking for us."

They held hands and walked to the ballroom. When they entered, her grandfather was waiting for them.

Douglas smiled and asked in a cheerful voice, "Now, young lady, where is my dance? I must be seen with a pretty young woman tonight in order to make the old women jealous. The evening is not ending without us having at least one dance. Harrison, may I take your fiancée for a spin?"

"Yes sir, you may."

Douglas reached out for her and they waltzed away.

"Do you remember when we used to dance at my home when you were little?" Douglas asked as they danced.

"Oh yes, I loved doing that. The times with you and Grandmother are my best memories."

"Do you remember when we went to Long Island and camped on the sea shore?"

Catherine thought for a moment. "It was fun until it started raining. The three of us got soaked to the skin while you were trying to put up the tent during the storm. Grandmother was upset with you. She told you it was going to rain before we left and she wanted to wait."

"Yes, she was mad for a bit but she got over it. Once we got the tent up and got a fire going, it was better."

They continued to reminisce over the good times they had together—and there were many. After the third dance, they stopped and had a drink.

"Papa, you are so handsome in your evening jacket."

"Thank you, my dear."

"I never see you dressed up like a gentleman. Mother says you always dress like a cowboy."

"Dear, your mother has never seen a real cowboy. I've seen many and I don't dress like one. I dress for comfort."

"Why don't you wear a mustache or beard like the other gentlemen do? It's fashionable, you know."

"I don't care about fashion. Your grandmother liked me clean-shaven. She said mustaches and beards tickled her."

Catherine paused. "I miss her so much," she said quietly.

"I do too."

"I loved all those times I stayed with you and Grandmother. I always had so much fun."

"Those were the best days of my life!"

Catherine inquired, "It's been five years since she passed. Have you thought about getting married again?"

"No dear, your grandmother was my only love."

"All the eligible women are watching you, you know."

"You mean all the old ones."

Catherine laughed and said, "Well, I should say the mature ones."

"Dear, the old cows here tonight strut around as if they want a man but they only want companionship. The young heifers want to save themselves for some young bull but the young bulls don't know what to do with them. This old bull knows what to do and I'm ready to get the job done."

Catherine blushed then laughed, "Papa, you say the funniest things at times. Mother would simply faint away if she heard you say that."

"My dear, your mother is always trying to get me to see this old woman or that old woman. I told her exactly what I told you and she didn't speak to me for weeks. She says my language is vulgar."

"Maybe your words come out a little coarse at times but you don't mean any harm. You're only being you."

"I can't change who I am at this late date."

"The women I know who are interested in you wouldn't want you to change because being unique is what they like about you. You aren't like other men. I know Mrs. Wiggins is definitely interested—she's told me so."

Alarmed Douglas said, "Please tell me that old hen isn't here. She turns me to serious drinking whenever I'm near her."

"Yes, she is. She is across the room watching us right now!"

They looked across the room and Widow Wiggins waved to them. She was a large woman, overly jeweled and flamboyant in her dress and manner. Her corset was tight and attempted to shape her body into her expensive purple gown, but it was only successful at making her large bosom more prominent and her ample bottom wider. A gaudy diamond hair clasp held a large purple ostrich plume in her long, unnaturally red hair. The sleeves of her gown extended to the elbow and there were diamond and gold bracelets on both arms. Diamond rings adorned every finger and there was an exquisite ring on her left ring finger with many diamonds circling a round, violet sapphire.

Catherine waved to Mrs. Wiggins but Douglas didn't acknowledge her. Mrs. Wiggins smiled then started to walk around the crowded dance floor toward them.

Douglas exclaimed, "Oh no! It looks like she's headed this way!"

Harrison approached them and Douglas said hurriedly to him, "Thank goodness the cavalry has arrived! Catherine, I'll return you to Harrison and make my retreat before Mrs. Wiggins captures me. Harrison, you're the sentry on watch now."

Catherine laughed.

Douglas kissed Catherine on the cheek and walked quickly outside to the terrace.

"Your grandfather seems to be in a hurry," Harrison observed.

"Yes he is. Do you see the woman walking across the room in the purple dress?"

Harrison snickered. "Oh my, she is quite a spectacle, isn't she? I've never seen a woman with so much jewelry… and her hair certainly makes her stand out in a crowd."

Catherine laughed. "Yes, she's unique to say the least. She's interested in Papa. I think she's going to try and chase him down."

They watched as the woman walked rapidly out the door to the garden. Unfortunately for Douglas, he couldn't outrun Widow Wiggins, who for her size was remarkably quick on her feet. She caught him and pulled him back to the dance floor. They danced several waltzes together and she stayed glued to his side for the remainder of the evening.

CHAPTER 3

In the sleepy town of Wooster, New York, north of New York City in the Hudson River valley, Mr. Richardson owned a large farm. For the past five generations, the farm had been in his family. Boasting over a thousand acres of the best farmland in New York State, the land was home to horses, cows, sheep, and other domestic animals. There was a large apple orchard and hundreds of acres of corn and hay. A foreman and his family lived in a small home on the property and they ran the day-to-day operations.

The Richardsons' homestead had five bedrooms, three modern bathrooms, a large country kitchen, a formal dining room, and a living room with a river rock fireplace that covered one entire wall. The two-story house was built with Pennsylvania Bluestone, giving it a royal and sturdy appearance. The house, which had a wraparound porch, was nestled under several large shade trees. It sat on a hill overlooking a winding stream that eventually emptied into the Hudson River.

The Richardsons visited the farm often, and every year they vacationed there during the county fair. The fair was the largest one in the state and always a source of entertainment for the family.

Catherine arrived on Friday evening. Harrison planned to arrive on Saturday after finishing his maneuvers. Catherine didn't communicate with Harrison during the previous few weeks because during maneuvers, the cadets don't have time to write home. She was anxious to see him. She had gotten up early on Saturday and was ready long before it was time to leave for the train station. She tried to pass the time reading but all she could think about was Harrison. The morning seemed to drag by.

The Richardsons didn't seem to be in any hurry to get to the station. She was worried that they wouldn't get there in time and Harrison would be waiting for them. Catherine asked Mr. Richardson twice if they would be late. He assured her they would be there on time. To Catherine, the carriage ride to the station seemed to take forever.

They arrived as the train was pulling in at its scheduled time of twelve o'clock. Catherine hurried out of the carriage. The station was crowded so she stood on a bench in the back.

Harrison was the first one off. She waved to him across the platform and yelled, "Harrison! Harrison!"

He heard her and saw her standing on the bench waving at him. He pushed through the crowd, dropped his bags, and lifted her off the bench. He twirled her around then kissed her.

He pulled back from the kiss and said, "I have missed you so!"

"So have I," she said gleefully.

"Are my parents here?"

"Yes, so are your brother and sister. They're waiting in the carriage."

He asked in a hopeful voice, "So no one's watching us?"

"Just all the people on the platform," said Catherine, breathless.

"I don't know any of these people." He pulled her close and kissed her again. She didn't resist and he held her close.

The crowd around them started to applaud. Embarrassed, Catherine hid her face in Harrison's shoulder.

Harrison announced, "I'm not ashamed to show people that I love you."

She looked up at him, smiled, and said, "Neither am I, but I don't want to give them a show. Let's get to the carriage."

Harrison picked up his bags with his right hand then he took Catherine with his left. They walked out to the carriage. His family warmly greeted him and then they got in. Two sleek black horses pulled the open red carriage. Mr. and Mrs. Richardson were in the front, Catherine and Harrison were in the middle seat, and

Harrison's younger brother and sister sat in the back. The weather was clear and hot, as was usually the case for late August in southern New York.

The fairgrounds were several miles outside of town and there was a long procession of riders on horses and people in carriages, wagons, and motorcars headed there. The procession barely moved because a motorcar had broken down and blocked the road. The people on horses and in horse-drawn carriages shouted good-humored comments about going back to a horse to the motorcar's driver as they went by. Several people stopped in other motorcars to try to help, which added to the restriction in the road.

Once they passed the roadblock, the rest of the trip went quickly. They parked the carriage in a large field and tied up the horses.

A large red circus tent dominated the fairground. The tent was at least a hundred yards long and several stories high. Six large poles, equally spaced, poked through the tent's top and held it up. Each pole had a large flag on top that flapped in the breeze. At one end of the grounds was a large Ferris wheel advertised as being the tallest in the world. The fairground was crowded with people. The barkers were out on the midway trying to pull people into the various sideshows.

Catherine and Harrison walked the midway among the games and played a few. Harrison tried the hammer contest and easily rang the bell, which won Catherine a small, white bear. Harrison tried to get her to go to a sideshow, which advertised a two-headed boy and the world's strongest woman, but she refused.

The two walked through a large tent that had many vendors selling everything from furniture to iceboxes to health cures. Catherine took her time browsing through the goods and told Harrison what items she wanted in their home. They also sampled the various foods. Catherine loved the taffy apples and Harrison preferred the cotton candy.

Mr. Richardson had sheep entered in a competition beginning at three o'clock. Mr. Richardson took great pride in his sheep herd and spent a lot of money to make sure he always had the best stock available. Two of his sheep won blue ribbons that day.

The day's main event was the harness racing. Mr. Richardson loved the races and the betting, and that day he won three races. After the races, they headed home before it got too dark. They were tired but everyone agreed that it had been a lot of fun.

The following day was Sunday, so they went to the Catholic church in downtown Wooster. After services, they stayed in town for lunch, which was a big social event every week. They had lunch at an outside café. The Richardson family was well known and many families stopped by.

After lunch, the family walked along the Hudson River on the edge of town. Harrison's family continued to walk while Catherine and Harrison sat on a bench and watched the river.

Harrison asked, "How do you like it here?"

She said excitedly, "I love this town and your family's farm. The people are friendly and the pace of life is so different. There's always the hustle and bustle in the city but here it's quiet and peaceful."

"Now that I know you like it here, I must tell you some good news. Remember when I told you my father might leave me the farm?"

"Yes."

"He talked with my brother and sister about it. They don't like spending time in the country. They prefer the city. This morning before breakfast, Father said he will leave the farm to me."

Her face lit up with pleasant surprise. "Oh, that's wonderful! We can now always look forward to this being our home. I can see us with our own family coming to the fair and having lunch here on Sunday. It makes me feel secure knowing that we'll have a place of our own."

"I love the stone house. It looks like it was built to last forever, and the tall shade trees make the porch a cool place to sit and relax."

Catherine agreed. "I love the house too. In particular, I love the tall ceilings, the oak floors, and the large kitchen where everyone can come in while dinner is prepared."

"Tomorrow our cook will be back from her holiday. She'll make a large breakfast with eggs, biscuits, potatoes, gravy, ham, and bacon. For lunch, there's another large meal and the same thing for supper. She's used to cooking for farmhands so there's always an abundance... but do you know what I have found?"

"What?" she asked.

"Before every meal, I'm always starved. It must be because we're always busy when we're here. No matter how much she makes, we always eat everything she serves."

"I remember visiting my aunt in Vermont. She cooked the same way. Every meal was a feast; I loved going there."

"Tomorrow morning, I promise you by six o'clock, you'll wake up because of the wonderful smells."

"Harrison, please stop talking about food, we just ate and you're making me hungry again!"

"This place does that to you."

"I have a wedding coming up next year so I can't go back home as fat as a pig."

"For this week, please enjoy yourself and the food. You have the whole winter to get ready for the wedding."

"I'll enjoy it. I didn't get to ask you—how were the maneuvers this year?"

Harrison's face became serious. "It was different this year. The High Command is preparing us for war. All the exercises were deadly serious with no mistakes tolerated. They kept reminding us that small mistakes take men's lives."

Catherine's countenance darkened. "Do you think we will go to war?"

"The politicians keep saying no but the military men say it's coming."

"Do you think our wedding is safe for next summer?" Catherine asked, her brows knitting with worry.

"Yes. We will be fine. I'll graduate in June and nothing will happen before then to affect our plans."

"I hope so."

"I know so, but I'm still willing to elope if you are."

Catherine stated firmly, "*No!* We've been down this road before."

"I know. I'm teasing. Our wedding isn't far off now."

Catherine said, "I still don't have the date yet. I'll eventually wear my parents down and we'll agree to a date. I want the wedding immediately after your graduation. I'll work out the details with my parents over the winter."

"I'll leave all that to you. Now for the rest of this week, we have a family picnic planned tomorrow. On Tuesday, we'll take a boat ride up the river. It's fun and peaceful. On Wednesday, we'll go back to the fair. There's pie judging then a pie auction for charity. Of course, we eat the pies. There's a stock auction my father attends and a rodeo. On Thursday, I'm taking you fishing."

"Harrison, I've never fished before."

Harrison grinned. "I plan to teach you."

"I'm not sure I want to go fishing."

"Don't worry, you'll like it."

Catherine asked, "I think the serpent said the same thing to Eve in the Garden of Eden, didn't he?"

"Probably," said Harrison. They laughed.

"What happens on Friday?"

"I'm not sure, but I think some shopping for you would be in order as long as you go fishing on Thursday."

Catherine asked with a smile. "Are you trying to bribe me?"

"Yes."

Catherine considered for a moment then said, "I'm willing to be bribed. This sounds like a fun week for us."

"It will be."

Catherine leaned forward and kissed him.

CHAPTER 4

CHRISTMAS IN NEW YORK WAS always special for Catherine. The lights, the window displays, and the decorations on every light post made it feel festive, but in December 1916, it was a somber time. Since the end of the summer, the wishful thinking that America wouldn't enter the war had ended. War was near and people felt this would be the last Christmas before America's men would be fighting in Europe. People wanted to enjoy one more Christmas before it happened.

The use of electric lights on Christmas trees was new and popular for people who could afford them. This would be the first year Catherine's family would use electric lights. In years past, they used candles. Last year, Douglas had used electric Christmas lights and they were the rage of their social circle; many families had visited to see them. Douglas had cautioned Joseph that the new lights were finicky and he could help him with them but Joseph said he could do it on his own. So far, in three frustrating attempts, he couldn't get the lights to work. It was Christmas Eve and he was confident the lights would work for the dinner planned that evening with the Richardson family and his father.

Harrison's train was scheduled to arrive in the afternoon and he would remain at home until after the New Year. Mrs. Dawson agreed Catherine could meet him at the station if her brother would be the chaperone. Reluctantly, Howard agreed to accompany her.

Catherine was excited because she hadn't seen Harrison since Thanksgiving. A cab picked Catherine and Howard up at their house for the ride to the train station.

As soon as they settled in, Howard declared, "Catherine, I have other plans for today. Once Harrison arrives, I'll leave you with him."

Catherine's brows furrowed. "Howard, Mother will be upset if she finds out you left me alone with Harrison!"

"Mother won't know unless you tell her." He gazed out the window, uninterested.

"People may see us together and there will be talk!"

Howard shook his head and said gruffly, "People always talk and I have to go somewhere."

"Where?"

"You don't need to know," he mumbled.

She pouted, "You're going to get me in trouble on the first day Harrison is back."

"Mother won't ask anything, but if she does, you should say we got separated in the big crowds after we found Harrison. You had coffee then came home."

"But I wanted the three of us to walk in the park today before it gets dark," she protested.

Howard turned around angrily and said, "Go ahead and go for a walk! Why do I have to waste my afternoon walking behind two people who don't want me there in the first place?"

Catherine insisted, "You have to because it isn't proper for us to be alone!"

"I trust you and Harrison will not do anything improper. I'll meet you at the apothecary at six then we will walk home together."

Catherine squared her shoulders; she said indignantly, "I don't like this!"

Howard smiled, "Harrison will."

"No he won't! He knows it isn't proper for us not to be chaperoned."

"Rubbish! Harrison will be delighted to know he has you alone for a few hours."

Catherine adamantly said, "If Mother finds out, I'm telling her you abandoned me."

"She won't."

Catherine stifled a sob. This was exactly the type of thing Howard did, she thought. She knew he sneaked out frequently to be with his friends. She had seen him leave immediately after their parents went to bed and return late at night. She didn't want the dinner disrupted by Howard doing something foolish.

The cab took them to the station and they walked down to the platform. They arrived as Harrison's train was pulling in. Harrison was the first to exit and he saw Catherine immediately. He hurriedly walked over, picked her up, and twirled her around then kissed her, a long and passionate kiss. When they separated, Howard was gone.

Harrison asked, "Where did Howard go?"

"I don't know." Catherine couldn't help but allow the anger to show. "He was supposed to be our chaperone today but he told me during the cab ride that he had to leave. I suspect he will be with his friends somewhere." She huffed.

Harrison grinned. "Well, bully for him! I didn't want a chaperone anyway!" He kissed her again and this one was even more passionate.

Catherine gently pushed back from the kiss and said, "That's why we need a chaperone! You won't behave!"

Harrison asked, "Do you really want me to behave?"

She smiled and replied, "No, but I don't want to get in trouble with our parents on your first day home if someone sees us kissing in public."

"Maybe we should go where we can kiss in private."

"I can tell I'm going to have trouble keeping you in line."

"I'm so happy to see you that I have to admit, I will be out of line from time to time…but in a caring and gentle way," he amended.

She patted him on the chest. "I'll rely on your word. Now I had planned for us to go for a walk in the park before dinner. With the overnight snow, it will be so picturesque…but without Howard, I don't think we should go."

"We can still go."

"Surely someone will see us." She looked worried.

"We will be careful, and if anyone asks, we will say our chaperone broke through the ice on the lake and we couldn't save him."

She laughed and muttered, "I feel like pushing Howard into the lake."

"I'm happy he's gone. Now I have you all to myself."

She looked up at him and smiled wryly. "Yes, but that worries me."

They left the station and took a cab to Central Park. When they arrived, Harrison paid the driver to deliver his luggage to his home. He and Catherine bundled up and walked arm in arm. They admired the park's winter splendor.

As they walked, they occasionally stopped and kissed. The time alone was good for them. They caught up on what had been going on in their lives. Even though Catherine wrote him every day, she seemed to have an endless list of things to share. He enjoyed listening to her chatter.

The day was getting colder and they stopped to have some coffee to warm themselves. They sat at a table at their favorite café and soon they heard a familiar voice behind them.

"Does your mother know you're out on the town with a young man without a chaperone?"

They turned to the voice. It was her grandfather.

Catherine blushed and replied, “Papa, let me explain!”

Douglas smiled and said, “Dear, you don’t have to explain to me. I’m happy to see you.”

Harrison and Catherine stood. Douglas gave her a hug then shook hands with Harrison.

“We had a chaperone but he disappeared,” explained Catherine.

“He disappeared? That sounds familiar.” Douglas paused. “Let me guess, was it Howard?”

“Yes, how did you know?” asked Catherine.

“He disappeared on me too,” Douglas said. “Last month, he called me and asked to meet for lunch at the club. I was happy he thought of me. He showed up for ten minutes then he said he needed to go somewhere. In a second, he vanished. I figured he was seeing a girl somewhere.”

“We’re supposed to meet him at the apothecary at six then we will walk home together. Are you coming to our house tonight?”

“Yes, I’m looking forward to it. Let’s have some coffee and you two can tell me what’s going on in your lives. I’ll take you in my motorcar to pick up Howard. I want to see his face when I show up.”

“Me too,” said Catherine.

They spent the rest of the afternoon talking and drinking coffee. Douglas had recently returned from a trip to South America and he told them an exciting tale of his recent adventure on the Amazon.

Harrison asked, "In your travels, what is the most interesting thing you've seen?"

Douglas got serious, his face darkened and he answered, "I was traveling in Italy and I heard about a mystical glassmaking process. I went to the town where the process was supposedly done. I asked many people about it but only one person would talk to me. He was an old man and he only whispered to me about it because he was afraid people might overhear. I learned from him the name of a man who knew about the process. I found him and saw his amazing glass."

"What was so amazing about it?" asked Catherine.

"I promised not to tell what it does, but in simple terms, it allows you to see into a different world."

Harrison sat up straighter then asked. "What do you mean?"

"I lived with some holy men in the mountains of China and Tibet for a few months. They believe there are different worlds or dimensions that exist at the same time while we are living in this world. I didn't believe them until I saw a different world when I looked into a mirror that the man made."

Catherine looked confused. "I still don't understand what you mean."

"Let me put it this way. Imagine if you could look into a mirror and be able to see your grandmother living as if she had never died."

Catherine thought about it. "It sounds wonderful but also scary."

"It was both, and that is why many people consider it taboo. I was scared when I first saw it but I quickly realized how special it was."

"I don't understand how anyone could do what you say," said Harrison.

"Some things are hard to explain or understand. This is one of them...but that's enough on that topic. I've already said too much." Douglas leaned back in his chair. "I can't tell you more because I made a promise. Let me leave it this way: Someday I want to make the glass, and you two can see it. Now, it is getting late and we need to pick up Howard."

Howard waited inside the apothecary for Catherine and Harrison. A look of surprise washed over his face when Douglas walked in with them.

"Please don't tell my parents," he begged before even a hello.

Douglas looked smug. "I won't, but I expect something in return."

Howard looked on expectantly.

"You have to go to lunch with me and agree not to leave."

Relief fell over Howard's face. "Deal," he replied.

The four went to the Dawson home and soon after their arrival, the Richardson family arrived. After pleasantries and warm cider, everyone gathered around the Christmas tree to light it for the first time. Joseph plugged in the lights and they flickered for a second then nothing happened.

"What's going on here?" he muttered angrily. Joseph started to diagnose what went wrong but soon became frustrated.

"Here, son, let me." Douglas quickly fixed the problem to the chagrin of Joseph. Douglas plugged in the lights and they immediately came on.

A collective gasp flooded the room. The tree, with its electric lights, was dazzling.

After dinner, they exchanged gifts. Catherine received an exquisite silk scarf from Harrison. He received from Catherine a rare book. Douglas winked at Catherine when he gave his gift to Martha, who was surprised when she unwrapped a large oil painting of a cowboy from a well-known Western artist. The cowboy was standing next to a horse and was wearing authentic cowboy attire, which looked nothing like what Douglas wore day-to-day. Catherine laughed to herself because she knew why Douglas gave it to her.

During the remainder of the Christmas holidays, Catherine and Harrison spent most of their time together but unfortunately, for Harrison, there was always a chaperone with them. After New Year's, Harrison returned to West Point with no plans to return home until Easter. Catherine focused now on planning their wedding.

CHAPTER 5

It was Wednesday, February 7, 1917. The Great War in Europe had been raging for the past three years with no end in sight. America was close to entering it. The newspapers described the ongoing carnage in the trenches in France as well as the other fronts in the war. German submarines, known as U-boats, continued to sink ships across the North Atlantic and in the Mediterranean. Germany had recently announced it would attack any ship in the waters around Europe. The United States ended diplomatic relations with Germany and war was imminent.

Against this backdrop of war, the plans for the wedding moved ahead. The date was set for June 30, 1917. Everyone agreed the wedding would be postponed if the United States entered the war.

Martha and Catherine were having afternoon tea in the parlor when the front door bell rang. The maid answered the door. It was the postman with a special delivery.

The maid brought the letter to Catherine. It was from Harrison. Catherine opened it and immediately she could see there was a problem. He always started his letters with the words “My dearest Catherine,” but not this time. This letter was short—less than a paragraph, as if he was in a terrible hurry—and it was dated two days ago.

> *Catherine, I received news today that our graduation date will be accelerated to April 20. We expect to ship out to France soon after graduation. I pray we can move our wedding date up. I will be coming home in two weeks for a visit. We can discuss the date then. Love you deeply, Harrison.*

Catherine started crying and handed the letter to her mother. Martha read it.

Catherine, in tears, pleaded, “Mother, we must move the wedding date up.”

“Dear, he is going to war. We have talked about this. You should wait until he returns.”

A sob escaped her. “I can’t wait; he may be away for years.”

“Yes, I know.” Martha moved closer to Catherine to comfort her. “You agreed if we entered the war that you would wait.”

Catherine shook her head indignantly. “I know, but I didn’t expect this to really happen.”

"You know what is going on in Europe. More men have died in the war than any other war before. He may never return from it."

Catherine sobbed. "Mother, don't say such a thing. It is bad luck!"

"Catherine, you know it could happen."

"Yes, but as I told you before, he will be behind the lines with his uncle."

"Hopefully he will be, but anything can happen in war," Martha stated honestly. "An artillery shell killed my niece's husband in a hospital. He was a doctor and he was several miles behind the lines."

Catherine's sobs quieted. She was silent and took a few moments to recover from her tears. She stood and walked to the window. "You tell me these awful things all the time," she said in a still quivering voice. "I can't let myself think about it."

"You have to, darling," Martha insisted. "You can't lie to yourself. He is in the military and he is going to war."

Catherine turned around; she felt the tears rise again. "I know that. I love him and I want to marry him before he goes."

Martha sighed. "I know the feelings you are experiencing. I know the desires of being a young woman. I don't want you to become a war widow."

"I would rather be with him for a short time then never be with him if something happens."

"It will be harder to remarry later if you are a widow."

Catherine stood behind a chair. Her white-knuckled hands grabbed the fabric. "Mother, stop it! I don't want to think about being a widow. That is a wretched thought!"

"I'm not trying to make you upset. I only want you to know the reality of what is coming."

The tears flowed from Catherine's eyes again. "No, you shouldn't say it that way. You talk as if his death was a certainty. You should say what might come."

"Yes, you're right," Martha conceded.

"Can we please move the wedding date?"

"I need to talk to your father about it."

Catherine paused then asked, "So you are agreeing we can move the date?"

"No, not yet, I need to talk to your father first."

"When will you talk to him?"

"I'll talk to him tonight before dinner."

Catherine turned to her mother and pleaded, "Mother, you must persuade him. We have to get married before Harrison leaves."

"Dear, I understand."

"I need to write back to Harrison immediately so he knows we are discussing it."

Catherine ran up to her room and quickly wrote a letter. She gave the letter to her lady's maid, Louise, who rushed it to the post office.

That evening, Joseph arrived home from the office promptly at five-thirty, as normal. The maid was standing by the front door waiting. When he came in, she took his hat and coat. Martha was dressed in dinner attire and was waiting in the parlor as she did every evening. She sat on the couch reading a book. Her red wine and his scotch were on the table already poured. Joseph walked to the couch.

Martha put her book down, "Good evening dear."

"Good evening to you."

He kissed Martha on the cheek then sat next to her.

He picked up his glass and so did she. They lightly touched the glasses together then sipped their drinks.

Martha inquired, "How was the office today?"

"It was a good day! We've been worried that orders would slow down due to all the war talk but so far, business is holding up well. How was your day?"

She sighed. "Catherine got a special post from Harrison today. His graduation date has been accelerated and he expects to ship out to France soon after."

Joseph's expression remained unchanged. "I'm not surprised. Our boys will be fighting there soon."

"Catherine wants to move the wedding date up. I was hoping the war would end and Harrison wouldn't have to go. Now I don't know what to do. You've read the letters from my family in England. You know what's happening in France. I don't want Catherine to be a war widow. You are going to support me and tell her she should wait till he comes back, aren't you?"

"Catherine is of age now. If she wants to get married, there's nothing we can do." He took a sip of his drink.

Martha's expression hardened. "No, there is a lot we can do! You can say no and we can have your father talk to her. He is against us going to war."

Joseph stated bluntly, "I know his feelings about the war, but President Wilson is correct on changing his position."

"I agree with your father. Wilson is wrong! There is no reason for our boys to die in that terrible European war. Germany can't hold out much longer. We should provide the war supplies they need but not our children."

"I know your view on the war. We've had this discussion many times. What do you want me to do about Catherine?"

"Talk to her. Maybe you can talk some sense into her. She won't listen to me."

"I will try, but Catherine has always been strong-willed like her grandfather," he said with a tone of resignation in his voice.

"She still lives under our roof. She should follow our rules," Martha said firmly.

It was clear he'd lost this battle. He said without conviction, "I'll talk to her, but this is the twentieth century. Young women are different now. The world is changing fast."

"I hate the way things are now. When I grew up in England, the world was kinder, gentler. I always had happy parties to look forward to and fun things to do. Now the world is harsh and cruel. I believe it now when people say that the devil rules this world."

"Yes, the world is changing and not for the better. Please ask Catherine to come down and I'll talk to her."

Martha left and went upstairs. Joseph finished his drink and read the evening newspaper as he waited. Catherine came down dressed for dinner in a green dress.

The words tumbled from Catherine's lips as soon as she entered the room. "Thank you for talking to me. We must move our wedding up; I hope you agree."

"Catherine, when we agreed on the wedding date, your mother and I thought we wouldn't enter the war. Now with that happening, we need to reconsider the timing of your wedding."

"But why? Harrison was always going to be an officer and we would likely face this sometime in the future."

"Yes," Joseph began, "but you know Harrison is probably not going to be a career officer. Going into the military was to help season him and prepare him to be a businessman."

"Yes that's true, but things have changed. We are going to war. We need to support him."

He asked, "Why does marrying him now or later affect the way we support him?"

"He needs to know there is someone here who loves him and wants him back no matter what happens."

"Catherine, my Aunt Belle married a young man before he left for the Civil War. He lost a leg at the Battle of Gettysburg. He always felt they should have waited because their marriage and lives were so affected by the war."

"I met Aunt Belle. I wonder how she felt about that. She always seemed happy to me. After the war, they had six children, so apparently being in the bedroom with Aunt Belle was the part of being married that Uncle Matthew liked."

Her father's face paled with surprise. He cleared his throat, "My point is anything can happen. War today is so deadly; I urge you to wait."

"You urge me to wait but you are not saying no." Tears began to fill her eyes.

"I am saying no."

Tears rolled down Catherine's cheeks and her chin crumpled but she had to show him that she would not accept no as an answer. "Father, I have always followed your word but I will not in this case!" She stood up straighter in order to deliver her message as forceful as she could. "As you know, Grandmother Helen left me a large trust. The money became mine when I turned twenty-one this year. If I don't receive your permission, I'm prepared to elope with Harrison and live on my own if I have to."

Joseph set his drink down, he raised his eyebrows. "Catherine, you can't do that! It will look to our friends as if there is something wrong and you had to get married."

Catherine sobbed but went on. "I don't care what people think. I want to be with Harrison."

"Dear, please stop crying! I'll think about this more."

Catherine's sobs abated for a moment. "Are you saying you give me your permission?"

"I'm saying I need to reconsider your view. I'll talk to your mother about it."

Catherine looked up hopefully. "When?"

"I'll talk to her tonight after dinner. Now you go upstairs and wipe those tears away. I hate to see you upset."

"I'm sorry for crying, but this is important."

"I know, dear." He kissed her on the cheek.

Soon Howard and Martha come down for dinner. Ten minutes later, Catherine arrived. Normally during dinner, there was a lively discussion, but the tone at the table was subdued.

After dinner, the family always retired to the parlor for brandy but Catherine and Howard went to their rooms. Martha and Joseph sat on the parlor couch and the maid poured them a brandy then left.

Martha asked, "How was the conversation with Catherine?"

He looked down and said softly, "She started to cry when I told her I was against them getting married now."

"I expected she might. You were firm with her on your decision, weren't you?" asked Martha with a hopeful tone.

Joseph, his head still down, admitted, "No, I wasn't. She said if she doesn't get my permission she will elope. She has my mother's trust fund and she said she will live on her own."

Martha sighed then stated forcefully, "I knew your mother giving her that fortune would haunt us someday!"

He held up his hand. "Let's not start that argument again. My mother loved her and they were close."

She exclaimed, "Your mother's had too much influence on her and she hurt my relationship with Catherine!"

Joseph stated in a stern voice, "We are not discussing that again!"

She paused, then in a softer tone apologized, "I'm sorry. You're right. The issue now is the wedding." She reached out and took his hand, "If Catherine elopes, all of our friends will believe something's wrong. You know the gossip will start."

He nodded, "I told her that. I can see the men at the club asking me if she's with child, especially James McCarthy. He has been a detractor of mine since we were in primary school."

"Yes, and his old hag of a wife would love to spread this kind of gossip. What are we going to do? I don't want her to elope but I don't want her to get married."

"I don't see we have much choice, but I do have an idea. I'm having dinner with Senator Stratton next week. He is going to run for reelection and he needs contributions. I'll ask him to intervene on our behalf and get Harrison assigned to a staff position in London or Paris. He will be far away from the front and will be safe."

Hope lit up Martha's face. "That's a wonderful idea. Do you think he has enough influence?"

"I know he does," he said confidently. "He was responsible for getting Robert Buford's son a new assignment away from convoy escort duty, which is so dangerous."

"What will we tell Catherine?"

"Let's ask Catherine to invite Harrison here for dinner to discuss moving the date after I've had the dinner with the senator. If the senator agrees, which I'm sure he will, we can agree to an earlier wedding date."

CHAPTER 6

THE FOLLOWING WEEK JOSEPH MET with Senator Stratton for dinner and the senator readily agreed to help with Harrison in return for a generous donation. With this agreement in hand, Mr. and Mrs. Dawson had dinner with Catherine and Harrison and agreed the wedding would take place on Saturday, May 5, 1917.

Martha and Catherine immediately started making the changes in the wedding plans but there were two problems: Catherine's wedding dress and their honeymoon location. The original dressmaker couldn't meet the earlier date and a new dressmaker was required. This was a significant emotional issue for Catherine but the new dressmaker quickly allayed her fears by promising that her dress would be exactly what she wanted and would be ready on time.

They had planned to honeymoon in the Hamptons on Long Island, but the early May date was before the season started and their hotel wouldn't be open. Harrison's father had a friend who owned a newly built estate in the Hamptons. The friend offered the estate and all the service staff. Catherine and Harrison would in effect have a hotel to themselves.

As the date drew near and the plans for such a large and elegant wedding became known, people started to comment in such gloomy times the size of the wedding was inappropriate. Several women spoke to Catherine directly about their concerns. However, Catherine didn't shy away from their comments. Catherine told the women her wedding was exactly what people needed. She felt people needed to get away from the depressing war news. She made it clear this was her wedding and if they were uncomfortable then they shouldn't attend. Not surprisingly, all the women who expressed concerns still decided to come. Catherine made sure none of these women were located near the head table or sat together.

On the wedding day, it was warm and clear. A large, closed, white coach with two white horses brought Catherine and her family to the cathedral. When the coach stopped in front, her father and mother stepped from the coach and walked arm in arm up the stairs on a blue carpet.

Two bridesmaids were in the coach and helped Catherine step down. The bridesmaids smoothed out her wedding dress and train. Her dress was white silk with wrist length sleeves. The dress was tight in the waist and the skirt was full with a long train. The neckline was designed to show her grandmother's exquisite diamond necklace. Her hair was up and she had a full veil. The bridal train flowed down the carpet as she walked. She carried a bouquet of yellow roses wrapped with white ribbons. The two hundred guests were standing as she entered. Harrison and his eight groomsmen were in formal dress Army officer's uniforms with parade swords on their sides.

The cathedral had large stained glass windows with a grand pipe organ. The afternoon sun shimmered through the stained glass and cast vibrant colors onto the wedding scene. An organist and a large choir provided wonderful music before and after the ceremony. At the end, the couple kissed to celebrate their marriage, and then the priest introduced the couple to the guests, who applauded loudly. The groomsmen exited quickly and set up four on each side outside the cathedral doors. The bride and groom walked down the aisle together and stood by the door to greet the guests. After the guests filed by, Catherine and Harrison walked out under an arch of swords, their hearts bursting with nervous excitement. The guests tossed flower petals as they walked down the steps and entered a small white coach with a single white horse.

The coach started a slow ride through the city in order to allow their guests enough time to travel from the cathedral to a hotel where they were having the reception. In the carriage, a bottle of champagne cooled in a silver bucket.

"Catherine, when I saw you start down the aisle, I thought my heart was going to stop. I actually gasped because you are so beautiful!"

She smiled, "Thank you! All those officers with you on the platform were so regal. You were the handsome one!"

"Your dress is the prettiest wedding dress I have ever seen. So many people commented on how elegant it is."

"As you know, I had a difficult time getting a new dress made in time. I think the dressmaker did a wonderful job." She smoothed her hands over the fabric.

"I have never seen that stunning necklace before."

Catherine touched it and said, "My grandmother Helen gave it to me."

"It looks wonderful on you. You look like a princess!"

"Yes, and you are my prince." They kissed and Harrison didn't want to stop. She laughed and pulled back.

"Harrison, now please stop! We will have time for that later!"

Harrison nestled into Catherine's neck. "I think we should go on out to the Hamptons now and skip the reception. No one will miss us."

Catherine pushed Harrison away playfully. "Our parents will and we will have people waiting for us. It wouldn't be proper not to show up!"

"I don't care if it is proper. Soon, I'll leave for France. I want to spend every minute with you."

She squeezed his hand and said, "Now Harrison, I know what you mean, and once the reception is over, we will be together. For now, let's enjoy the ride and have some champagne."

After a leisurely ride, the carriage arrived at the hotel and the guests were on the steps waiting for them. Harrison stepped out first then assisted Catherine. The bridesmaids were there and helped her with her dress. The officers were a few feet away from the carriage with the arch of swords ready. They walked through the arch on a red carpet to a room where they prepared for the reception. Mrs. Dawson, the bridesmaids, and Louise removed the long train and touched up Catherine's hair and makeup. Quickly, they were ready and stood at the entrance to the reception hall. After nearly an hour in the receiving line, Catherine and Harrison took their seats at the head table and dinner began. The dinner was magnificent with several courses of food and wine.

After dinner, Catherine and Harrison led the guests to the ballroom. A full orchestra was there and the music began. Catherine and Harrison had the first dance and they smoothly moved around the floor. Halfway through the dance, Catherine's father stopped them and he danced with her. Harrison then danced with his mother. The song ended and couples filled the floor, dancing a classic waltz.

At midnight, Catherine and Harrison retired to the honeymoon suite on the hotel's top floor. The suite was large with two master bedrooms and a large living room. Louise was waiting for her. She helped Catherine remove her jewelry, the dress and corset then packed them. She helped Catherine with her hair and nightclothes. Catherine changed into a white silk nightgown and robe.

While Catherine changed, a large bouquet of blush red roses and a bottle of champagne on ice that Harrison ordered, arrived. Harrison opened the bottle and made sure the flowers were properly displayed. He went to the other bedroom and changed into navy blue silk pajamas with a matching robe.

Louise left and Catherine walked from her bedroom to find the large arrangement of roses and the champagne.

Catherine asked, "Harrison, are you here?"

"Yes," answered Harrison from the other bedroom.

"These roses are beautiful!"

Harrison walked out from the bedroom and put his arms around her. He smiled then said tenderly, "No, you are the beautiful one!" He kissed her and held her close.

Her voice had a tremor as she said, "Thank you!" She giggled nervously. "I love your pajamas."

"These are a gift from my mother. She said I needed to wear something special tonight. Would you like some champagne?"

"I would love some."

She noticed his hands shook as he poured the drinks. He handed her a glass and he took one. He raised his glass and she did as well.

He toasted, "To us!"

They touched the glasses together then sipped. Catherine sat on the couch and watched Harrison pace back and forth with his champagne.

She observed, "You seem a little nervous."

He stopped and turned to her, "I am. I'm afraid I might do something wrong tonight."

She smiled and asked, "Like what?"

"I don't know, but something foolish."

"Come and sit beside me." She patted the couch next to her; he walked over and sat.

She softly said, "Tell me what you're feeling."

"I feel awkward and a little unsure of myself. I have never done what I hope we will do tonight. I'm afraid I'll do something wrong, or I might hurt you."

She smiled, "I'll help you. If anything hurts, I'll tell you. You'll have to be gentle to start."

He replied tenderly, "I'll always be gentle with you."

"I know you will and that's one reason why I love you. You're always respectful of my feelings."

He took his hands, cupped her face, and kissed her gently then said, "I will need you to guide me."

"I will. And you'll have to tell me what you need."

They started to kiss and their desire soon overtook them.

Catherine whispered, "Let's go to the bedroom."

Slowly, they lay back on the bed and the passion rose higher. Harrison was gentle with her. Catherine guided him to understand her body and he guided her with his. It was a wonderful night of discovery for them.

The following morning, Harrison woke first and lay in the bed looking at Catherine. He admired how pretty she was sleeping. He took his hand and gently stroked her hair. Slowly, she woke up, opened her eyes, and saw him looking at her.

He said quietly, "I awoke to find a princess in my bed."

"You did? How did a princess get into your bed?"

"I'm not sure, but she is so pretty and she didn't bring any clothes."

Catherine immediately pulled the sheets around her. Her face was a deep crimson blush. Harrison gently pulled the sheets back.

"I was enjoying what I was looking at and I need to see more."

Catherine's shade darkened even more. "A gentleman should not be peeking at a lady lying in bed."

"Maybe not, but a husband would." He pulled her close and kissed her.

After the kiss, Catherine said, "I must not have done a good job last night. You seem ready for more."

"My dear, I never thought my wedding night could be so wonderful. I hope I didn't hurt you."

She offered a sweet bashful smile. “No dear, not at all.”

“I need to be with you again if you don’t think I’m a brute or something.”

This time her smile was wider. “No, I want you too.”

As they kissed, their desire took over once more. Until late morning, they enjoyed each other.

After lunch, they left for thc Hamptons. The estate, which had over thirty rooms, was recently completed and designed to look like a French chateau. Their master suite was elegant with a balcony that overlooked the ocean. The estate was secluded on a hundred acres of lush green meadows with flowering trees and colorful gardens. A long pier jutted out into the bay with a sailboat moored at the end. The stables were new and several horses were available to them.

Their stay was like a fairy tale. Their love for each other grew as their journey of discovery continued. Each evening was blissful and each morning they stayed in bed late, never once having an early breakfast.

Every day, they did something different, touring the area, shopping, sailing, riding horses, walking along the ocean. They spent a lot of their time talking about the future. They made plans for after the war. They discussed having children and where they would live. Too quickly, their honeymoon ended.

On their last evening, they went to the master suite immediately after dinner. They stayed up late talking and making the kind of passionate love that happens when a couple expects to be apart for a long time. They never wanted the evening to end, but it did as they fell asleep in one another's arms.

CHAPTER 7

HARRISON'S SHIP WAS SCHEDULED TO leave at noon on Sunday, May 20, 1917 from the New York Harbor. The destination was a secret but the suspicion was Liverpool. Early that morning, Catherine and Harrison had breakfast then gathered the staff together and thanked them for their kindness during their stay at the estate.

Catherine wore a special dress she had made for the occasion. She wanted Harrison to remember how she looked on that day. The elegant silk dress was a deep sky blue. It had a delicate, white lace collar, long sleeves, and a flaring skirt that stopped at mid-calf. She wore white shoes. Harrison wore his Army officer's tan doughboy uniform. On the ride to the ship, she gave him an exquisite pocket watch and inside was a picture of her in the dress. They tried to be happy but the ride was solemn with them holding each other close and occasionally kissing.

Both of their families met them at the dock and Harrison's mother started to cry immediately. Tears ran down her face quietly the entire time and Harrison's father was somber. Martha also started to cry, which deepened Catherine's sorrow.

The boarding whistle blew. Harrison shook hands with the men and kissed Martha on the cheek. He hugged his mother, kissed her on the cheek, and told her goodbye. She immediately started to sob, turned to her husband, and buried her face into his shoulder.

Catherine and Harrison walked slowly to the gate; he stopped near it, reached into his jacket pocket, and removed a small black box. He opened it and inside was a gold necklace with a locket. He opened the locket and showed her a picture of him in his dress Army uniform. He closed the locket and put it around her neck.

"This is perfect, thank you." The corners of her mouth turned down and she forced the sobs back.

"I love you so much," said Harrison.

Catherine, in a desperate voice, said, "I'm trying to be strong but I can't any longer. All of this is hitting me now. I finally see that you are leaving me but you can't go. Our honeymoon has to continue for a while longer. Take the next ship or the next ship after that. You can't leave me!"

"I can't do that. It's too late."

She pressed him, "It's not too late. We can run away. We will tell them you missed the ship. You were sick. I was sick. We will think of something. Please, please don't go."

"Catherine, what's wrong? You have always been the strong one."

Tears flowed down her face and she whimpered, "Our engagement, wedding, and honeymoon have been a romantic fairy tale. Everything has been perfect. I planned to see you off and be strong but my heart is breaking. I have never felt like this before. I have a knife in my chest and the pain is unbearable. You are such a part of me that I can't bear to let you go."

Harrison had tears running down his face. "I know my heart is breaking too. I haven't told you this but I'm scared. I don't know what will happen when I leave here. I hope for the best but I have doubts." A quiet sob escaped him; he looked down, ashamed.

"You should have told me!"

"I'm a West Point graduate, I'm supposed to be fearless and strong but I'm not."

Catherine begged, "Please stay, please stay!"

The final whistle blew; Harrison grimaced and said, "Catherine, I have to go."

She begged again, "Don't go, please stay. If you love me, you will stay!"

Harrison's face was torn with emotion. "Don't say that. You know I love you."

Seeing his face made her tears flow even more. "I'm sorry for that. I don't want you to leave me."

"I don't want to go but I must. Remember when I wanted to elope? You said, 'Before you know it I'll be back.' It's the same thing here. Time will go by fast and I'll be back. We will spend the rest of our lives together."

He kissed her one last time. "Please go with my parents to our farm whenever you can. I want to think about you being there waiting for me."

She tried to suppress her sobs but they only seemed to worsen. "I will. We will go there when you return. Please stay safe."

He embraced her one last time. "I'll see you soon."

He turned and faded into the crowd of soldiers in tan uniforms filing into the ship. Catherine stood there crying. She looked for him but couldn't see him since there were hundreds of soldiers on the large ship and they all crowded the rails. Soon the ship pulled away from the dock.

That night she wrote the first of many letters to him.

Harrison's ship made its way out to sea and sailed northeast along the coast with a Navy destroyer escort. The ship would be one of a large convoy of military and merchant ships that would gather off the coast of Nova Scotia. Once all the ships had assembled, the Navy destroyers would guard the convoy on the voyage. Harrison's ship was a converted passenger ship. Grey camouflage paint and black painted windows tried to hide the luxury ship's elegance but the fine chandeliers and ornate woodwork were still there.

The ship was faster than the convoy. Fast on the ocean in times of war meant safety because a quick ship could outmaneuver a German U-boat. Any ship in the convoy that couldn't keep up was doomed because a straggler was an easy target. Recently, a freighter lagged behind a convoy off the coast of Ireland. Torpedoed by a U-boat, it sank in minutes with all hands lost.

Beginning the first day, the lifeboat drills started. It was evident to Harrison there were not enough lifeboats and rafts for all the soldiers. Soon the soldiers realized the same thing. Each man developed his own plan on what to do if the ship started sinking.

The closer the convoy got to the coast of England, the more anxious the troops became. The Irish Sea was a favorite hunting area for the U-boats. Twice the alarms sounded, but no attack occurred. There was a large celebration when the convoy entered the safety of the port.

The ship docked at Liverpool then the troops took trains to a camp near Dover, England. The men stayed in Dover until they were ferried to France in late June 1917.

CHAPTER 8

HARRISON AND HIS REGIMENT WERE the first American Expeditionary Forces to land in France. Their job was to set up training camps as well as communication and supply networks for the large Army, which was coming. Harrison was part of the nucleus of General Pershing's new army. The British and French command wanted the American troops put into the trenches immediately. However, General Pershing knew the American troops were not prepared to go to battle. His plan was to gather his Army, train them more, and then send them in as one American Army, not as replacement troops for the British and French.

The first few months in France, Harrison was busy helping set up the logistics. Eventually two million American soldiers were coming to France along with their equipment and supplies. The time to put this all in place was short and required a tremendous amount of coordination. Soon, troops and supplies started to arrive.

From the beginning, Harrison made sure his superiors knew when the time came that he wanted to be on the front line. His superiors made it clear that when the battles began, he would be in headquarters far from the front. His training in logistics and war strategy was far more valuable than leading troops into battle. This frustrated Harrison because he was a West Point graduate and all he was doing was chasing down fresh meat and vegetables for the troops. However, he was an exceptional soldier and he did his job without any complaints.

In the beginning, Harrison's letters to Catherine were optimistic, but their positive tone slowly faded. His view of the war changed after he spent some time at the front. Several command officers and Harrison spent time in the trenches observing the British and French troops in battle and learning their strategies. After this, Harrison no longer felt that the war would end quickly. He wrote to Catherine that the war was a stalemate between two great armies. The lines seldom moved much and the same filthy trenches were lost and regained repeatedly. He described the terrible smell of rotting horses and men lying in the fields. Horses and men wounded in the no man's land between Allied and German trenches were left there because snipers shot anything that moved. The cries of the wounded horses and men were horrifying. Sometimes, the men would shoot the dying horses, only to become targets for the snipers.

Harrison learned officers died quickly at the front lines. Officers were easy to spot because they dressed differently and carried pistols instead of rifles. Many officers would dress and arm as regular soldiers when they were in the trenches. Harrison was shocked at how appalling the conditions were, and he shared his observations with his Catherine.

One morning in early October 1917, a letter arrived for Catherine from Harrison. She opened it and learned Harrison was now in a front line infantry unit assigned to the French 18th Infantry division. The plan was to get battle experience for some of the American troops. Harrison wrote that he was pleased that he would be in the thick of things. In his new role, he would be a liaison officer with the French Army.

Catherine realized Harrison was now in imminent danger. Horrified, she immediately spoke to her parents and her in-laws about his change in assignment. Mr. Dawson hurriedly sent a telegram to Senator Stratton and demanded he investigate the change in Harrison's assignment.

The next few letters from Harrison were more like notes than his typical long letters. The stationary was dirty and the ink smudged. Harrison wrote about the horrors he saw in the trenches. Constant bombardment, explosions, and death surrounded him. His troops were scared and he admitted he was as well. The trenches were cold, wet, and dark. Rats were everywhere; they were as large as cats and were brazen, chewing on everything including wounded men and horses. Harrison's letters had a desperate tone to them. He said he missed her and he looked at her picture in the watch often. He complained that her letters to him had stopped and he hoped she was well.

Catherine wrote to him every day and she was upset her letters were lost. She tried to keep her letters to him optimistic. She kept him up to date on what was occurring at home and with their families. She often wrote about her grandfather and his most recent adventure because she knew Harrison liked to hear about him. She wrote that Douglas took her on a long motorcar ride into the country and explained how much fun they had. His parents often saw her. She had visited the farm several times and she went to the county fair with them. She wrote extensively about what they did together. She also wrote about the Broadway shows she saw and she would write the songs' lyrics for him.

In November 1917, Harrison's letters stopped. The newspapers reported the first Americans had died in battle and the Germans had captured others. American casualty lists were published in the papers. Catherine anxiously waited for the morning and evening newspaper to see if Harrison was on a list. She could do nothing but wait.

On Saturday, December 1, 1917, the front door rang. Catherine and her parents were in the parlor having coffee. They were expecting the Richardsons for lunch.

Catherine opened the door and was surprised to find a young man standing there. He was wearing the uniform of a telegram carrier. It was a cold day so he was bundled up well.

He removed his wool hat and scarf. He had a somber face and said in a downcast voice, "I have a telegram for Mrs. Richardson."

"I am Mrs. Richardson. Please let me get some money for your tip."

"No madam, a tip isn't necessary."

Catherine was surprised; carriers always expected tips. He handed an envelope to her and quickly walked down the steps.

Catherine closed the door and opened the telegram. She frowned. It was from the War Department.

> *Mrs. Harrison Richardson, we regret to inform you that your husband, Lt. Harrison Richardson, is missing after a battle near the town of Bathelémont, France in early November. As new information becomes available, we will inform you.*

Catherine sunk to the floor and dropped the telegram. She murmured, "This couldn't be real—could it?"

"Catherine, what's wrong?" her mother asked as she and her father rushed to her then helped her to the couch.

Her father picked up the telegram, read it and sadly handed it to his wife as Catherine cried. All three were at a loss for words.

A few minutes later, the Richardsons arrived. After reading the telegram, Mrs. Richardson started to sob. They spent the rest of the day trying to decide what, if anything, they could or should do.

Over the next several days, Catherine was in despair, as was everyone else. With the war raging, getting accurate information was nearly impossible, which heightened anxiety even more. She didn't know whom to contact to get more information. Joseph and Mr. Richardson tried to leverage their political contacts for news. Martha sent telegrams to her family in England hoping they could help. However, all of their attempts to learn more were in vain. No credible news was arriving so they had to rely on the newspapers and the rampant rumors for information. Christmas went by without any news and the sadness Catherine felt grew daily. She felt as if she were standing on the precipice of a great deep pit, one that could swallow her up at any moment. She felt out of control and terrified.

On New Year's Eve, Mr. Richardson received a telegram from Senator Stratton. It said wounded men from Harrison's unit would arrive in New York on January 3. Mr. Richardson and Catherine decided to meet the ship to see if they could learn anything new on Harrison.

It was a cold and rainy day when the ship arrived. The pier was crowded with families, friends, and newspaper reporters. A black and white list of casualties in a newspaper was one thing, but watching in person as men were loaded into ambulances like cordwood was sobering. The people on the pier at first quietly watched the procession of stretchers file pass, then an old woman stopped one. She asked about her son. Soon dozens of people lined up and asked about their relative or friend. As bad news was shared, people scurried away sobbing.

The stretchers were coming out in two lines. Catherine and Mr. Richardson each stood in a line and asked about Harrison.

Catherine saw a man pass by on a stretcher that she recognized. "Stop," she shouted. "Stop!" She chased after it. She got near and saw that the man was a groomsman from her wedding.

Catherine asked, "Alfred, is that you?"

The man was wounded in the chest and missing his left arm. He weakly nodded. "Catherine," he whispered.

She was shocked at how severe he was wounded and she struggled to find the words. "I'm sorry you are hurt."

"It has been hell but I'm so happy to be home."

The bearers set the stretcher down. Catherine kneeled next to him and held his hand.

He asked, "Have you seen my parents? They should be here."

"Not yet but I'll certainly tell them I saw you."

"Tell them I'm going to the Brooklyn Army Hospital."

"I'll tell them that." She pressed forward, eager to change the subject. "I haven't heard from Harrison. Do you know anything about him?"

"Catherine, I shouldn't be the one to talk to you about this."

The breath caught in Catherine's throat. Her voice rose and she pleaded, "What do you mean? I only know he is missing but there's been no news for weeks. If you know something, you must tell me!"

Alfred sighed and pressed his lips together briefly before speaking. "We were assigned to a French Infantry company. It was supposed to be a quiet area on the front but the Germans learned the Americans were there. They shelled us then attacked. In the first wave, I got hurt. During a lull in the fighting, Harrison carried me to the aid station and then he went back. I learned later there was a huge explosion near him and he disappeared." He swallowed roughly, as if swallowing a lump in this throat. "I don't think he made it."

Catherine could hear her heartbeat thumping loudly in her ears, though she didn't believe her heart could still beat after hearing the news. Her next words came out so quietly that Alfred could barely hear them over the surrounding clamor. "Are you sure?"

"I asked the men who were there about him but no one saw him again."

A flare of hope rose in her chest, and she clutched on to it with her life. "So he could be alive. The telegram I got said he was missing."

The next words out of Alfred's mouth crushed her hope and smashed her heart. "Catherine, I'm sorry to tell you this but missing often means the body can't be found. The explosions are so horrible that men simply disappear. A man can be there one minute and gone the next. The Germans took our position and no one came back."

"But you didn't see him dead," she stammered. "So he could still be alive?"

"I saw so many things that I thought weren't possible. So I guess he could have survived but I don't know. Catherine, I'm so sorry to tell you this."

Catherine didn't give a moment's thought to accepting that Harrison might be dead. It couldn't be so. "Alfred, thank you for telling me," she said as if she were discussing the Sunday brunch. "Let's have these men get you to the hospital. I'll get word to your parents."

The men picked up the stretcher and walked away. Catherine searched for and found Alfred's parents. They were grateful and left for the hospital immediately. She found Mr. Richardson and told him the story. He had also heard a similar one from a wounded senior officer.

Cold and wet, Catherine and Mr. Richardson sadly went home to tell the families their story. On the ride home, the reality sank in: Perhaps Harrison really was dead. Catherine felt hopeless.

CHAPTER 9

THE NEWSPAPERS CONTINUED TO REPORT how appalling the conditions were at the front and the rumors about poor care of American soldiers in front line hospitals were rampant. According to the papers, the large number of men wounded in battle and ill from various trench-borne diseases were overwhelming the field hospitals. Rumors spread fast about Americans being shuttled from field hospitals to hospitals in French towns then becoming lost. Weeks passed with no news on the wounded or missing so people were desperate for information. Some wealthy families decided to take matters into their own hands. Many of them left for Europe or sent people to find and care for their men.

Atlantic travel was dangerous due to the German U-boats. It was still possible to get to Europe but it was expensive and the conditions were harsh. For the wealthy and politically connected families, they could pay the high prices for a berth on a merchant ship in a convoy to

England. This was the shortest route but the most dangerous because the U-boats were hunting the convoys.

A safer route existed but it was much longer. People traveled by train to ports in the Southern states then took ships to Havana, Cuba. From Havana, they took ships from neutral countries to Spain or France. From there, the families took trains to the front.

However, even this route wasn't entirely safe. The Germans boarded even the neutral ships. The Germans would sink any ship that carried war material no matter how small the quantity.

At a dinner, Catherine heard a story about a man, a friend of her father, who went to France to search for his missing son. The son had joined the Canadian Army and went missing in early 1917. After months of no news, the father decided to go to France and search on his own. After three weeks of visiting hospitals and aid stations along the front, he found his son in a small French hospital. The son was shell shocked, which was a common injury. The massive concussion from an artillery shell can knock men out or kill them but their bodies often show little outward signs of injury. The shell-shocked men were often seen wandering about in the trenches and on the battlefield. The son had no identification papers and didn't remember who he was or where he was from. The father moved him to a private hospital in England.

After the dinner that night, Catherine couldn't sleep because she kept thinking about the man going to France to find his son. She thought about Harrison maybe lying unknown in a decrepit hospital with no one to help him. She cried herself to sleep.

The next morning, she decided to talk to Louise about it. Catherine always confided in Louise about whatever problem troubled her.

Louise arrived to help Catherine prepare for the day. She entered the room, went to the curtains and opened them to let in the morning light. Catherine was in bed. Louise, who was French and had a pleasant, soft accent, said, "Good morning madam, I hope you slept well."

Catherine moaned, "I did not."

With a concerned look, Louise asked, "I'm sorry to hear that; why didn't you sleep well?"

"I heard something at the dinner last night that kept me up."

"What did you hear?"

Catherine sat up in bed, after rubbing her eyes, she told her the story.

"What an amazing story! Do you think the same thing happened to Harrison?" asked Louise.

"I don't know," Catherine said, "but I admire the man for going and looking for his son."

"I do as well. That was a brave thing to do."

Catherine thought for a moment then announced, "I was thinking I should go to France and search for Harrison."

Louise gasped. "No! No! Madam, it is too dangerous to go there. As you know, my family is still in France.

Even though they are in Paris and not near the front, the conditions are terrible there. There is little food and no fuel for heating. There is nothing but disease, misery, and death at the front. There is also the danger that the Germans could advance any time."

Catherine stared off in the distance. "Yes, I know, but someone needs to do something. He could be lying somewhere alone and needing our help."

"I know what you are feeling. My Pierre is also on the front lines with the French Army. I worry about him all the time."

"I know you do, but if he went missing, what would you do?" Catherine asked.

"I don't have the money to do anything if that happens. My only way of helping him is to pray he stays safe."

"I have the money. I could go there. If you were me, would you go?"

Louise walked to the window and looked out. She stood there for a minute then she turned to Catherine. "Madam, I shouldn't tell you this but if your love for Harrison is as deep and strong as my love for Pierre, I would go if I had the money. No one could stop me!"

Catherine offered a small smile. "Thank you for being honest with me."

Louise looked nervous. "Please don't tell anyone we discussed this, especially your mother."

"I won't."

"So are you going to search for Harrison?"

Catherine didn't hesitate, "Yes." It would be a hard journey, she knew, but it must be done. "I have to talk to my parents."

Catherine thought for the rest of the day about the way she should discuss it with everyone. She decided to have a dinner with her family, her grandfather and with Harrison's parents to talk to them about it. She asked her mother if she could have a dinner for everyone that week.

On Friday evening at promptly six o'clock, Mr. and Mrs. Richardson and Douglas arrived for dinner. The maid brought them to the parlor and after a few pleasantries, they each had a glass of wine. They sat in the parlor and enjoyed the wine.

Mr. Richardson asked Catherine, "My dear, how are you holding up?"

Catherine shrugged. "It depends on the day. I knew everyone was coming for dinner tonight so mother and I were busy today. However, on most days, I spend the day worrying about Harrison."

Mrs. Richardson agreed, "So do I! I read the paper the first thing in the morning to see if there is any news. Whenever the doorbell rings, I worry about getting a telegram or post with bad news."

"So much bad news is arriving by telegram that the younger telegram carriers often refuse to deliver any from the War Department. The older managers deliver them," said Mr. Richardson.

Catherine said, "Yes, the young man who delivered the telegram about Harrison was sad. I'm sure it's hard on them."

"Yes, it's so sad anymore. There's never any good news," remarked Martha.

This was her chance. "I heard some good news," Catherine said. "I'm sure you all know George Levinson. He went to France to look for his son who was missing. Did you hear what happened?"

"No dear," answered Mrs. Richardson.

"Mr. Levinson found his son in a hospital in France. He had been shell shocked, had no papers and he didn't remember who he was or where he was from."

"Oh thank God!" said Martha.

"George Levinson told me at the club he was going to search for his son. I told him he was a fool to go. By golly, he proved me wrong!" said Joseph.

Catherine pressed on. "Mr. Levinson moved his son to a private hospital in England where he is recovering."

"That's good news! I didn't think old George had enough backbone to take such a risk," said Douglas. "He always seemed a little sheepish to me. I always thought his wife wore the pants in the family. I would never shop at his store because I didn't respect him. I have a completely different view of him now."

"But going to Europe is dangerous with all those U-boats. I wonder how he got there?" asked Mr. Richardson.

Catherine answered, "He traveled to Cuba then took a Spanish ship to a port in northern Spain. He then took trains to the front."

"That had to have been an exciting trip. I envy the man," said Douglas.

Catherine had been waiting for the right time to tell her news. She took a deep breath then blurted out, "I would like to do the same thing he did. I want to go there and look for Harrison."

There was silence for a few seconds as her news sunk in.

Then her mother exclaimed in a loud voice, "Do I understand this correctly? You want to go to France."

"Yes."

Douglas got up and walked to the window. He kept his back to everyone.

Howard, who was sitting on a chair in the corner, jumped up and walked to her. "Catherine, I'll go with you."

A wave first of surprise, then gratitude washed over Catherine. She stood and hugged him. "Thank you," she whispered into her brother's shoulder.

Her mother said angrily, "Howard, don't get involved in this foolish plan!" She turned to her husband. "Joseph, *do* something!"

Joseph opened his mouth, then closed it again helplessly.

Howard turned to his mother and stated, "Catherine will need a male companion. It's logical that I be the one to go with her. If I don't go with her then I plan to do what my friends are doing and join the Army."

Martha put her hand over her heart. "Howard, this is the first I have heard about you going to the Army. We can discuss that later. Now please stay out of this!"

Howard sulked back to his chair.

Martha turned to Catherine. "Now Catherine, I forbid you to go to France!" Spittle flew from her lips. Catherine realized, as everybody else did in the room, that Martha was stricken with fear.

"I am going even if I have to go alone," responded Catherine defiantly.

Mrs. Richardson leaned forward in her chair and said, "Dear, I know you want to help Harrison, but the best place for you is here. A lady shouldn't go to the front, especially someone of your breeding. Lower class women go there to be nurses and do other things but not a lady!"

Catherine replied firmly, "Mrs. Richardson, I disagree! Women of all social classes are going there to help. Women are helping in the war not only as nurses, but as drivers, and doctors."

Mrs. Richardson was surprised at her response. "Those women are rough and crude. You are not—or at least I thought you were not!"

"Those women are brave and they are willing to help," Catherine rebuked. "We should be supporting their decisions, not looking down on them!"

Her father seemed to have finally found his voice. "Dear, what you are thinking about doing is dangerous.

Harrison could come home while you are gone. Then what?"

"I'll come home." She said it quickly; she hoped they didn't sense the nervousness in her tone.

Her father stated firmly, "You should stay here and wait. Mr. Levinson was damn lucky he found his son."

Catherine didn't back down. "Yes, he was lucky, but Mr. Levinson did *something*! He didn't stay at home debating the risks." The adrenaline was flowing through her; she stamped her foot without realizing it. "He went there when people told him he shouldn't go. If he had not gone there, what would have happened to his son? Now his son is getting better care; he will recover and come home."

She paused for a second, her face softened then she said, "Maybe Harrison is also shell shocked. Alfred, his friend, said there was a large explosion, and then Harrison disappeared. He could have wandered away and right now be lying in some decrepit hospital. I need to try to find him!"

"What will you do, Catherine?" Her mother's tone was harsh. "Do you intend to just show up in France then go from camp to camp?"

Catherine hesitated, then plunged ahead. "I don't know. I'll talk to Mr. Levinson and see how he did it." She wondered how she'd do it, but she couldn't back down and abandon her Harrison.

"This is a childish and naïve idea," her mother pressed. "You haven't thought this through. This will be dangerous."

Catherine replied, "Dangerous, yes. I know it will be."

"Catherine, I insist you stop this foolishness now! You can't go! I will not let you go!" Her mother pointed her finger at Catherine.

Her father added, "I agree. Harrison isn't here to say this so I will. You cannot go!"

Catherine knew she was her own person and that the final decision was up to her. But she was hoping for more support. She looked around the room nervously. Douglas was gazing at her. She asked, "Papa, what do you think?"

He looked at his son and his daughter-in-law then at Catherine and paused for a few seconds. He said, "Catherine, I think you should go and I'll go with you. I have traveled throughout Europe. You will be safe with me."

Catherine breathed an audible sigh of relief. She went to him, hugged him, and said, "Thank you Papa!"

Mrs. Richardson looked like she was going to faint and leaned back on the couch.

Howard asked, "What about me? I want to go!"

Douglas replied, "Why not! You could use a little seasoning. You would be welcome!" He slapped Howard on the back.

Joseph was furious and stood to confront Douglas. "Father, no! There is a war going on! The Germans are torpedoing ships nearly every day now. You aren't taking my children to be killed!"

Martha also stood. "Douglas Dawson!" she began forcefully. "You have trampled on us for the final time. Helen always got between Catherine and me, now you are doing the same thing! I'll not stand for this. You have to support us on this!"

"Joseph and Martha, your daughter wants to find her husband. I think it is a courageous thing she wants to do. Catherine convinced me I should do something as well. I'll go even if Catherine and Howard don't go."

Joseph shrieked back, "Father, you can't be serious! This isn't one of your escapades so you can tell your friends at the club what an adventurer you are. These are terrible times with people getting killed every day."

"I know these are bad times." Douglas narrowed his eyes. "I don't support this war. I told President Wilson to his face we should stay out of it because it's a European war, not an American war. But Catherine could be right—Harrison could be in one of those French hospitals now, wounded and alone. We should at least try to find him."

Mrs. Richardson started sobbing.

Mr. Richardson said loudly, "I think our job is to stay here and wait. We shouldn't be nosing into our military's business. Our military leaders are trying to win a war and keep our men as safe as they can. I have faith they will find him and bring him home. Catherine, I don't approve of you going, but I can't stop you. We are going home! This conversation is too upsetting for us!"

The conversation had taken a dreadful turn; one Catherine didn't expect or want. Catherine begged, "Please don't leave! I'm sorry this came out the way it did."

Mr. Richardson asked, "Are you saying you will stay home?"

Catherine shirked back as if he had slapped her. "No." She forced her voice to remain level. "I'm saying I wish I had talked to you about this in a different way."

"We're leaving," stated Mr. Richardson. He helped his wife stand then they walked quickly to the front door, got their coats and left.

Martha complained, "Catherine, see what you've done? You have insulted your husband's parents and our guests!"

Catherine closed her eyes and tried to make her threatening tears go away. "I didn't mean to insult them... but I want to find my husband."

Martha was livid. "Douglas Dawson, you leave my house this minute! You cannot return until you apologize to me for getting involved in my family's business."

"Martha, hell will freeze before I apologize to you for helping my granddaughter find her husband." Douglas walked to the front door and took his hat and coat from the closet. He put them on and said, "Catherine, please come to my home tomorrow for lunch and we will make plans for Europe. Howard, I'm proud of you and you are welcome to come tomorrow as well."

Douglas opened the front door then slammed it behind him as he left.

Martha ran upstairs crying.

Joseph cursed, "I need a real drink, not this damn wine but whiskey!" He walked to the liquor cabinet, poured a double shot, gulped it down then went upstairs.

Howard and Catherine were alone in the parlor.

Howard grinned. "This has been exciting! I'm going to have some whiskey. Would you like some?"

Catherine replied, "No thank you. I'll have some wine, though. I didn't know you drank whiskey."

"I drink whiskey on special occasions and this is a special occasion!"

"Does Father know?"

Howard responded, "He knows about the brandy that we have as a family. He doesn't watch the whiskey so I occasionally have one. I like it."

He got a drink for himself and Catherine a glass of wine. They sat on the couch.

"Catherine, I'm proud of you. You stood up to everyone. You gave me the courage to tell them something I have been holding back."

The worry line on Catherine's forehead lessened. "I was surprised by your news."

Howard smiled with pride and stated, "Many of my friends are already in the Army. I'm eighteen and I can join without Father's permission."

"That's a big decision."

"Yes, it is. When I finished school, I wasn't ready to go to college. I felt that too many things were going on in the world. I didn't want to be locked away in a dusty old classroom with my head buried in a textbook. I've had time to think about what I want to do and I believe the Army is an excellent choice for me. Before I join, I think this trip with you would be exciting. Do you mind if I go? I kind of forced my way into your plans."

Catherine reached out her hand and squeezed his, "Not at all, I thought it was thoughtful and kind of you to volunteer."

"That's good, it sounds exciting. I'm starved. Let's have dinner."

"Do you think Father will mind if we eat?"

Howard shrugged. "Probably, but I can smell the food. I know it's ready." He walked to the kitchen and asked the maid to serve dinner for two. Brother and sister took seats at the dining table.

Catherine asked, "Howard, I have been seeing you come in late at night."

"You have?"

"Yes, where have you been going?"

He looked around to make sure they were alone. He asked, "Do you promise not to tell Mother?"

"Yes."

He whispered, "I'm seeing a girl."

Catherine smiled and asked, "Why do you need to keep it a secret?"

He whispered again, “She is a store clerk and she’s Protestant.”

Catherine laughed then caught herself, “Mother will die when she hears this!”

He laughed too and pleaded, “Yes I know, so please don’t tell her.”

“I won’t. Do you love her?”

He declared, “Yes, but it’s so hard to see her. Her parents don’t want her to see a Catholic boy.”

“You have a real problem on your hands.”

Howard smiled. “Yes, but it’s a good problem. She is cute and smart. You would like her.”

“I’m sure I would.” Catherine leaned forward. “What are you going to do?”

“I don’t know yet. I’ll continue to see her even if Mother finds out.”

“Well, I hope she doesn’t discover this anytime soon. I don’t know if she can handle any more stress.” Catherine grinned.

CHAPTER 10

LATE MORNING THE NEXT DAY, Catherine left to visit her grandfather. He lived a short cab ride away but instead of taking a cab, she decided to walk. It was a cold morning, but the sun was shining and it would be warmer when she returned. As she walked, she thought about the past day's events and she felt comfortable with her decision.

Douglas' home was a pillared, limestone mansion on millionaires' row on Fifth Avenue. His neighbors were the most prominent families in New York. Douglas didn't want to live there at first. He felt the mansions were more like palaces than homes. However, his wife wanted to make their home there. He reluctantly agreed to build if the home was simpler. Mrs. Douglas worked with the best architect in New York and succeeded in building the type of home Douglas agreed to. People felt it was elegant but not pretentious.

Unlike the other mansions on Fifth Avenue, which crammed as much as possible onto the property, Douglas' home stood back from the street with a garden in front. A wrought iron gate and fence protected the property but allowed the people passing by to see the flowers. His gardener rotated the plants to make sure there was always color, even in winter.

Catherine arrived at his house before noon. She walked up to the porch and rang the bell. The maid greeted her.

"Miss Dawson, we have been expecting you. I'm sorry, I forgot, you are now Mrs. Richardson. Please come in."

Catherine stepped in, "Miss Keyes, it is good to see you again. Is Papa home?"

"Yes dear, he is. He has been up since dawn getting ready for you. He had the cook go to the market early this morning to get your special sweet rolls. Let me take your coat."

"I didn't want him to go to any trouble for me," said Catherine as she removed her coat and handed it to Miss Keyes.

"You being his only granddaughter, he would do anything to make you happy." Miss Keyes smiled. "The happiest times in his life were when you used to come here and spend the weekends with him and Miss Helen."

"I loved coming here. They always had sweet rolls, and those special Swiss chocolates were always in the cookie jar."

"He got the chocolates for you too."

Catherine's hand flew to her mouth. "Did he?"

"Oh yes, you are special to him."

Behind her, Catherine heard someone walking up. She turned and it was her grandfather.

"Catherine, thank you for coming!" He kissed her on the cheek. "Please come into the parlor. We will talk until lunch."

"Please excuse me, I'll get lunch ready for you," said Miss Keyes, then she left.

Catherine and Douglas walked into the parlor and sat on the couch together.

He asked, "Is Howard coming?"

"No, some things happened this morning. Last night after you left, my parents went upstairs and never came back down. This morning at breakfast, there was a big discussion about my trip. They were still upset over my decision but they were especially upset over what Howard announced. They never expected he was considering the Army. Mother cried and begged him not to go on the trip. She said she couldn't bear having her children go on such a dangerous endeavor. He agreed not to go if I approved. Since I knew you were going, I told him he could stay at home. They are still trying to convince him not to join the Army. My parents are happy Howard is staying but they are still upset with me. I have to tell you that Mother is infuriated with you."

Douglas guffawed. "I know your mother and she will forgive me when we find Harrison. Mr. and Mrs. Richardson were also upset."

Catherine looked down. "Yes, I feel badly about that. I wrote them a letter apologizing for the way it happened. However, I made it clear that I was going."

"Bully for you! You have had a full day already."

"Yes, I feel like I know what to do now. Are you still willing to go with me?" she asked hopefully.

Douglas lit up. "Absolutely! This morning, I called my friend to start the travel plans. She thought I had been drinking when I told her we wanted to go to Europe to search for Harrison."

"Papa, you have to admit it, this trip does sound a little crazy."

"No dear, it's daring! I love doing daring things. My friend has made trip arrangements for people who needed to travel to Europe during the war for business and family reasons. She has helped a wine merchant travel to France every year during the war without any issues. She intends for us to follow the same route that he took."

Catherine smiled hopefully. "That's good to hear."

Miss Keyes walked into the room and announced, "Lunch is ready."

Douglas exclaimed, "Excellent! I hope you're hungry. I got the sweet rolls you like."

"Thank you for that. The sweet rolls always make me think of Grandmother."

"It makes me think of her too." Douglas sighed. "I haven't had sweet rolls for a while and I remembered how much you liked them."

They rose and walked to the dining room. He pulled out her chair for her. They sat down for lunch.

"Dear, I have been thinking about our trip and there are a few things I want to talk to you about. I know you have been to Europe before, but this trip will be different. We won't be on a modern, luxury passenger ship. The voyage across won't be easy; it will be uncomfortable and maybe dangerous at times. We will be on merchant ships and the crews on these ships are...." He trailed off, pausing to think. "The crews can be a little rough. They aren't used to being around ladies."

"Yes Papa, I know it will be different."

"In particular, I don't want you to dress as a wealthy New Yorker. You have to travel as a plain woman who is traveling with her grandfather. The clothes you wear here will be out of place for this trip. Once we get to Europe, we can buy the clothes you normally wear."

Catherine nodded. "I understand."

"Also, we must travel lightly because I don't know what we will encounter. You can only bring two trunks."

She laughed, "I had six when I went to Paris. I bought two more when I was there. I can do that."

"Also, I have something you must learn how to use." He reached into his coat and took out a small revolver. He put it on the table near her.

Catherine stared at it, "Papa, I've never held a gun before. I don't like this." She pushed it back toward him.

"Dear, we need to be able to protect ourselves." He pushed it back to her.

Catherine leaned back in her seat, crossed her arms and declared, "I'm afraid of guns."

"That's because you don't know how to use one. I'll take you out behind the glass plant and teach you how to use it."

Catherine shook her head. "I don't know about this."

"You must be able to take care of yourself if something happens. You have to learn to do this." His eyebrows rose high on his forehead. "Once you've shot it a few times, you will become comfortable with it."

"Papa, Mother will use the gun on *you* if she finds out about this."

Douglas smiled and said, "It will be our secret."

"I don't like this but I'll do it. I didn't expect to have to become Annie Oakley to travel with you."

He laughed and stated, "I want you to be safe. Now tomorrow, we will go out to the plant. I'll keep this for you until the trip. How soon can you be ready?"

"I can buy the clothes I need quickly." Catherine inquired, "Is a week too long?"

"No, that's fine. It will take a few days to confirm our arrangements. We will plan to leave in two weeks. I expect the trip will start by taking a train somewhere south."

"Mr. Levinson went to Havana. Have you been there?"

"Oh yes, I've been there twice. It's a tropical paradise." Douglas went on to tell her about his journey to

Cuba and they spent the afternoon talking, laughing, and planning their trip. The next day, he took her to the plant and taught her how to use the gun. She got comfortable with it quickly. After a second trip to the plant, she began to develop into a respectable shot.

Douglas spoke to a few of his friends about the trip he was planning and he learned the Americans were now sending their sick and wounded to English hospitals. Since it had been awhile since Harrison was reported missing, they would search the hospitals in England first for him, then go to France if they had to.

Douglas knew, because of his political connections, that he could easily get berths for them on a merchant ship in a Navy-escorted convoy. However, he felt it was too dangerous because of the German U-boats. He decided their travel plan would be to take a train from New York to Charleston, South Carolina then a ship from there to Havana. From Havana, they would take a neutral Spanish ship to the port of Bilbao on the northern coast of Spain. From there they would take a smaller ship to England. He had heard the Germans weren't stopping the smaller Spanish ships and those ships made frequent trips to England.

Catherine and Douglas made their final preparations for the trip. Catherine filled two trunks with clothes and accessories. She didn't pack any of her fancy dresses except one, the blue dress she wore to the dock when Harrison left. She wanted him to see her dressed as she was that day as if he had never left.

CHAPTER 11

The relationship between Catherine and her mother was strained. Martha talked to Catherine only a few times after the disastrous dinner with the Richardsons and the conversations were short and abrupt.

Joseph eventually spoke to Catherine and they made up. He still didn't like the thought of her going to Europe but he had accepted her decision. Joseph insisted that Martha talk to Catherine before the trip so they could resolve their differences.

Martha went to Catherine's room the day before she was to leave. Catherine and Howard always had breakfast later in the morning so she knew Catherine would be with Louise getting dressed. Martha knocked on the door.

"Come in," said Catherine.

Martha opened the door. Catherine was sitting at her dressing table and Louise was brushing her hair. "I would like to talk to Catherine for a few minutes."

"Yes, madam." Louise put down the brush and left.

Hanging on the closet door was a dress that Catherine would be wearing on the trip. Martha walked up to it, examined it closely, frowned, and asked scornfully, "Where did this awful dress come from? It looks like something a clerk or village girl would wear."

"I bought it for the trip. The travel to Europe will be difficult and I can't wear my typical clothes."

"Did you buy others like this?" She started to walk over to a trunk but Catherine was nearby so she quickly sat on it.

"Yes, I bought several. They are comfortable and will wear well on the trip."

Her mother put her hands on her hips and scoffed, "I hope none of our friends see you in your peasant clothes."

Catherine sighed. "I know the clothes are plain but I can't dress like I normally do on the trip."

"Why not?"

"I won't be on a luxury passenger ship or staying in nice hotels. I'll be on merchant ships and staying at cheap inns. I don't want to call attention to myself."

Martha, with her hands still on her hips and her chin raised, said, "I could never do that!"

"Yes Mother, I know." Sarcasm oozed from Catherine's voice.

Martha pointed her finger at her. "Catherine, I don't like the tone of your voice. I will not allow you to talk to me in that manner!"

"Mother, I know you don't approve of the trip but I have to go. I'm leaving tomorrow."

The gravity of the situation seemed to slap Martha back into reality. "You don't have to go. You and your grandfather have this romantic notion of this trip but it is dangerous!"

"If you came in here to try to persuade me, you are only making me more determincd to go."

Her daughter's reaction only served to light Martha's fuse again. She took a few deep breaths to relax before she spoke.

She offered calmly, "Yes, I did want to talk to you about going. I have been thinking about this. You should stay home and let your grandfather go. He's used to this type of thing."

"Harrison may need me."

"A nurse can provide anything he needs. Your grandfather can easily find one there."

"I am his wife. I can provide his care."

Martha was losing her patience. "You can't even take care of yourself. You have a maid who does everything for you including your hair." She waved at the closed door as if motioning toward Louise. "How can you can help him if he needs medical care?" She put her hands on her temples and her frustration showed. "This trip is simply a romantic childish notion! Can't you see that?"

"I'm sorry you think so little of me. I'll have to prove you wrong."

Mother and daughter glared across the room at one another in a battle that stretched far below the surface of this disagreement.

"I don't think little of you," Martha replied. "I admire you but I'm worried sick over this." She started to cry.

Catherine stood up and walked over to her.

"Mother, don't cry, please don't cry."

"Catherine, please don't go."

"I have to go."

Martha's crying changed to rage. "No you don't! You are being stubborn like your grandmother! She taught you to be independent; I hate her for that!"

"Mother, don't say that!"

Almost shouting, Martha ranted, "I do hate her! She has always been a shadow between us. She and I were never close. She told me once when we disagreed over how I was raising you that I was too English. She said I was always too formal and proper and needed to be more American! She always wanted you to be with her on weekends, holidays, and during the summer. She wanted to be your mother. You loved her more than me!"

"Mother!"

"Catherine, I'm pleading with you. Please don't go!"

"I have to go. I have to try to help Harrison."

Martha stormed out and slammed the door.

Catherine walked back to her dressing table and sat down in a daze then she started to cry. After a few minutes she stopped and looked in the mirror. She had remembered what her mother said about her not being able to take care of herself. She stared at her hair.

She got up and walked to the door where the bell cord was to ring for her maid. She pulled it twice; she returned to her dressing table and stared at the mirror. Louise soon opened the door and walked in.

“Madam, you have been crying; is something wrong?”

Catherine wiped her eyes. “I had a fight with my mother.”

“Was it about the trip?”

“Yes.”

Louise bowed her head. “I’m so sorry. I was hoping she was finally going to accept your decision.”

“She hasn’t, and I’m not sure she ever will. I have made a decision. Louise, I want you to cut my hair.”

Shock covered Louise’s face. “No! No! Madam, you have beautiful hair!”

“I need my hair to be easier to take care of on the trip. I want it bobbed like Kathleen Lawrence’s hair.”

Louise was hesitant. “Are you sure?”

“Yes, I’m sure.” Catherine nodded.

“Your mother will be upset with you and she will be upset with me too.”

Catherine handed her a pair of scissors. “Yes, but I need to do it. I’ll make sure she knows it was my idea.”

“Yes, madam, but I don’t want to be here when she finds out.” Louise took the scissors and started to cut.

An hour later, her hair was ready. It was now short, fashionably short. It was a startling difference.

Catherine beamed as she looked at her hair. "Louise, I love it. It will be much easier to take care." She got up and hugged her.

"I hope your mother likes it."

Catherine laughed. "She won't. I don't want her to see me until Father comes home. I'll stay here and make sure everything is ready for the trip. Will you please bring lunch here when it's ready?"

"Yes, madam."

Louise brought her lunch then returned at five and helped her mistress get dressed for dinner. Catherine picked her father's favorite dress, which was pink. When Catherine came down for dinner, her parents and Howard were sitting at the dining room table. As she entered the room, her father and brother saw her first. Her brother smiled and her father choked on some water he was drinking. Her mother turned to see her and immediately had a look of disapproval. Catherine sat next to her father. There was a long awkward silence.

Howard finally broke the silence. "So Catherine, anything new with you?" He smiled widely.

She smiled. "No, how about you?"

"I was thinking about getting my hair cut in a different style but I think I'll wait for a while. I don't think Mother can handle both of us changing our hair. Mother, do you agree?"

Martha ignored him and said to Catherine sarcastically, "So you did this to spite me, didn't you?"

"No, you told me this morning I couldn't take care of myself. I thought I should cut my hair so it would be easier to care of during my trip."

Martha remarked, "I loved your long hair. I don't think Harrison will like it short."

"Harrison will understand why I did it."

Martha said, "This is another example of you being childish. You're trying to hurt me."

"No, I'm doing what I think I need to do."

Howard interjected, "I love it. It's so fashionable."

Catherine smiled and said, "Thank you!"

Martha glared at Howard and commanded, "Howard, stay out of this!"

Howard reasoned, "Mother, it does look nice and it will be easier for her to take care of." Martha continued to glare at him and he smirked back.

Joseph changed the subject and asked, "Catherine, what time will you be leaving tomorrow?"

"Papa will pick me up at ten."

He revealed, "I worry about you going but I know you will be in good hands with my father. Dear, do you have something to say about Catherine's trip?"

Martha glared at him, "No!"

"Are you sure?"

"Yes!" she confirmed with an angry look.

For the rest of the dinner, Martha was quiet. Howard and her father asked about the trip and Catherine told them their plans. After dinner, normally the family retired to the parlor for brandy but Martha went upstairs without saying a word. Catherine, Howard, and Joseph stayed up late talking about the trip.

CHAPTER 12

Douglas arrived promptly at ten on Saturday, March 9, 1918. Their train was at noon. Everyone gathered in the parlor to say goodbye but it was an awkward situation. No one was talking because everyone knew Martha's feelings about the trip. Finally, Joseph nudged his wife.

Martha stepped close to Catherine and apologized, "Dear, I'm sorry we have had a difference of opinion about your trip. I want you to know I love you. Please be careful and don't take any chances you don't have to."

"Mother, thank you, I'm sorry too." Catherine swallowed. "I should have tried harder to smooth things over."

"Dear, I could have too. I do like your hair." She tucked a stray lock behind Catherine's ear.

"Thank you, I needed to know you like it."

Catherine hugged her and Martha kissed her on her cheek. Catherine blinked rapidly to hold back tears.

Martha turned to Douglas and stated firmly, "Douglas Dawson, you had better take good care of my baby girl!"

"I promise, I will."

The cab driver finished loading the luggage and they were ready to go. The final goodbyes were said then Martha hugged Catherine one last time.

The cab driver drove them to the station. The train trip to Charleston was uneventful and they arrived on Sunday with their ship scheduled to leave on Monday. They checked into a stately old hotel near the harbor. Charleston was a busy port and even on Sunday, the streets were crowded with trucks and wagons hauling goods to and from the ships.

It was a warm day; Douglas walked to the harbor offices for the steamship company to get their tickets while Catherine stayed at the hotel. He arrived to find a long line. As he waited, he learned that their ship to Cuba was damaged in a recent storm and wouldn't be ready for several weeks. Douglas rebooked on a different ship leaving in three weeks. He was upset about the change in plans and debated whether they should return home. He decided to check on a different steamship company or leave from a different port. He spent the afternoon searching for an alternative but he had no luck finding one.

Discouraged, he stopped for a drink at an empty dockside tavern. He sat at the bar and asked the bartender for a beer. Douglas struck up a conversation with him and told him about his troubles.

"There's a ship at the run-down part of the harbor," the bartender volunteered. "The *Majesty*," he added. "The captain mostly hauls cargo but will take passengers on occasion. But be careful—the captain and crew are a rough-and-tumble bunch. There are rumors that the captain smuggles rum from the Caribbean Islands."

Hope lit up Douglas' face. Douglas thanked him for the information, paid for the beer, left a generous tip, and walked down to the ship following the bartender's directions.

Only one ship was at this end of the harbor. The area had several abandoned buildings and warehouses. Douglas walked to the ship's gangplank and he yelled from the dock, "Is there anyone on board?"

A large, dark, tanned man with a full beard and long black hair pulled into a ponytail appeared from below. He had on black pants and no shirt. "Who wants to know?"

"My name is Douglas Dawson and I'm looking for passage to Havana."

The man stepped to the rail. "I'm Captain Lapointe; come on board."

Douglas walked across the gangplank onto the ship. Captain Lapointe walked up to him. He had dark evil eyes and two gold front teeth.

The captain questioned, "Why do you want to go to Havana?"

"I have business there."

The captain looked him over closely and probed deeper, "What kind of business?"

"I'm in the glass business."

The captain rubbed his beard. "I have been thinking of making a trip south. For the right price, I would be willing to go to Havana. Who will be going and how much baggage do you have?"

"It will be me and my granddaughter plus three trunks."

The captain stared at him, spit over the rail and offered, "The price is five hundred in cash."

"I'll pay you three."

The captain thought for a second and countered, "I'll take four."

Douglas replied, "I expect two cabins and three meals a day for that price."

The captain said gruffly, "The food is edible and there are no rats in the cabins."

"When can we leave?"

"You pay me now and we will leave on Tuesday at high tide."

Douglas nodded. "I'll pay you one hundred now and the rest when we dock in Havana."

The captain stared at him with narrowed eyes but Douglas didn't change his expression. The captain grunted, "Deal."

Douglas paid him and returned to the hotel, happy with his plan.

On Tuesday at noon, Catherine and Douglas arrived at the dock. Catherine didn't like the look of the captain, the crew, or the ship. The ship was an old, two-masked schooner with a shallow draft and badly needed paint. Douglas told Catherine the ship could operate in shallow waters, which was important for smugglers who needed to drop off or pick up cargo near the shore.

The crew of seven was dirty, loud, and vulgar. Douglas warned them to stay away from Catherine and he showed them that he was armed. The first mate was a young man in his mid-twenties, slender, tanned, with tattoos and long blond hair. He ignored Douglas' warning about Catherine. He watched Catherine closely and tried often to speak with her. Whenever Catherine came on deck, the first mate followed her everywhere.

The weather for the first two days was clear and they made excellent progress. The third morning, a storm blew in and the sea was rough. The storm raged through the day and night; by noon the next day, the sky cleared and the sea was calm. That night, the crew was drinking heavily and Douglas was playing cards with them. The first mate quietly left the game and snuck to Catherine's cabin. Being the first mate, he had access to all the keys. He quietly unlocked Catherine's door but it wouldn't open so he pushed hard against it.

Douglas had instructed Catherine to push a heavy dresser against the door each night, which she did. She was in bed but not asleep. She bolted upright on the mattress when she heard a soft creak. She listened closely and realized the dresser had moved an inch. She got up quickly and put on her robe.

She took the gun from under her pillow and quietly walked across the room. She stood behind a chair across from the door. Her room was dark but the hall outside her door was bright from a large lantern. The door was open a couple of inches now. She saw a hand on the door.

The first mate pushed the door open enough to get in. He had no shirt and shoes. He was sweating heavily and had a hungry, scary look. She wasn't more than six feet away from him. From the hall lantern light, he saw her behind the chair and smiled at her. She raised the gun and aimed at his chest. He stopped smiling.

"Sir, I think you have the wrong room!" Her voice wavered.

"My lady, I want to talk to you."

Catherine gulped a breath of air. "If you want to talk to me then we can talk in the morning, on deck."

The man gave a sly smile. "This is something we can only talk about privately."

He stepped toward her.

The gun wobbled in Catherine's hand. "If you take another step, I will shoot you."

She pulled back the hammer on the gun and it made a loud click. He froze.

He smiled and questioned, "My lady, you wouldn't shoot me, would you?"

As her answer, Catherine aimed the gun a little to the left of him and pulled the trigger. In the small room, the gun made a terrible roar, and the mirror in the chest burst into a thousand pieces. The first mate jumped back, alarmed. Catherine calmly pulled the hammer back again.

Now with more courage, she declared, "I will not miss next time."

The first mate turned and bolted from the room. Catherine quickly closed the door, locked it, and stood against it.

Douglas and the crew heard the shot. They ran quickly to her door. Douglas yelled for her and beat on the door. She let him and the captain in. Out of breath, she told Douglas and the captain what happened. The gravity of the situation hit her and wracking sobs escaped her throat. Douglas wrapped his arms around her consoling her.

"Go on!" Douglas' loud voice bellowed to the captain. "Go get him!"

The captain and crew searched the ship and they found the first mate hiding under a bunk. The captain locked him in the cargo hull. Douglas stayed with Catherine and slept that night in the chair.

The next day, a sailor told Douglas he didn't know ladies carried guns. Douglas told him all New York ladies wear them in their garter belts at all times—and the sailor believed him. For the rest of the trip, the sailors stayed clear of Catherine.

After arriving in Havana, it would be a week before the ship arrived to take them to Spain. Douglas took Catherine across the island sightseeing. The weather was warm, the island was a paradise, and the people were friendly. Catherine and Douglas enjoyed the sunny weather, knowing it was the calm before the storm.

Their Spanish ship arrived in port on schedule. The ship was new and designed to haul cargo but it also had several comfortable passenger cabins. Douglas examined the cargo to make sure no war materials were included. The cargo was only rum and sugar. The voyage was uneventful until they reached the Spanish coast.

It was near dawn when Catherine and Douglas woke to alarm bells ringing. Across the ship, sailors were running about and the officers were shouting orders in Spanish. The ship's engines shut down and the vessel slowed to a stop. In their robes, Catherine and Douglas walked from their cabins to the rail to see what was happening.

Not far from the ship there was a German U-boat. The Germans were going to board the ship.

Catherine and Douglas rushed back to their cabins and quickly dressed.

Douglas went to Catherine's cabin. Catherine asked him in a nervous voice, "What do we do?" She shoved her hands in her armpits to stop them from shaking.

Douglas instructed, "The first thing we do is hide our guns." He handed her his gun.

Catherine asked, "Where?"

"Hide them inside your dress."

"Are you serious?"

"Yes."

She took his gun and got hers. She turned her back, opened the front of her dress, and poked the guns into the fabric's folds.

"Now what?" she questioned.

"We do whatever they say. We must act as if we meet Germans every day. However, under no circumstance do you go with them anywhere. You stay next to me. If they try to separate us, quietly hand me my gun. Do you understand?"

"I understand, but Papa, I'm really scared."

"I know, dear, but we will be fine."

They waited in Catherine's cabin and listened intently for any noise.

The Germans boarded the ship. They yelled orders, pushed around the Spanish sailors, and showed their guns. The sounds were muffled but that didn't make them less terrifying.

Someone banged on their door; then, before either Catherine or Douglas could rise, in burst four German sailors. One had a pistol and he waved at them to stand near the door. Papa and Catherine stood and walked to the door; both feigned confidence. Two sailors started to search the room. The one with the gun kept it aimed at them while another sailor searched Douglas. He finished with Douglas and he turned to Catherine and smiled a wicked grin. He stepped toward her.

Douglas quickly stood in front of him and insisted, "You are not touching her!"

The German sailor laughed and slapped Douglas hard across the face. Douglas stumbled against the wall but quickly regained his footing and stepped back in front of Catherine. The sailor laughed and muttered something in German. He stared at Douglas for a few seconds, who looked at him directly in the eyes without showing any fear. The sailor stepped past him and helped the others search the room. The sailor with the gun continued to point it at Douglas and Catherine. They finished ransacking Catherine's room then huddled together and talked quietly.

After a minute of discussion, one of the Germans ordered in guttural English, "Go to the bridge."

The sailor followed Catherine and Douglas as they walked. The ship's captain and a German officer were there. The German officer spoke to the German sailor then he left.

The officer, in perfect English, stated in an arrogant and condescending tone, "My name is Lieutenant Berger. What are your names and where are you from?"

"My name is Douglas Dawson and this is my granddaughter Catherine Richardson. We are from New York City."

"Where are you traveling and why?"

"Her husband is an American Army officer and he is listed as missing in France. We haven't heard any news about him for months so we are traveling to Europe to search for him. We believe he may be shell shocked and is in a hospital somewhere in England or France. We are going to Bilbao then on to London."

"How do you know he is in England?" the officer asked skeptically.

"We don't know for sure. If we don't find him there, then we will go to France."

Still skeptical, the officer inquired, "Madam, why did you come and not send someone to find him?"

"He is my husband. He may need my help if he is injured."

He looked at her. "How long have you been married?"

"Since last spring."

"I see." The German barked a laugh. "You are a newlywed. Do you know we shoot spies on the spot when we find them?"

Catherine's face paled. "I'm not a spy."

"Is this old man a spy?"

"No, he is my grandfather. We are only trying to find my husband."

The officer looked at her for a few seconds and his demeanor softened. He concluded, "A woman who travels this far to search for her husband is special. Madam, you have my deepest respect." He removed his hat and bowed to her.

"Thank you, sir." The knot of stress in Catherine's shoulders eased some.

The officer remarked, "I went to school in Boston and I have family there. I like it there. Maybe after the war, I will go back. Mr. Dawson, have you traveled to Boston?"

"Yes sir, many times."

The officer promised, "I will contact the U-boats in the area and I can guarantee your safe passage to Bilbao. Madam, I hope you find your husband."

Catherine said, "Thank you."

"You may return to your cabins."

They made their way back to Catherine's cabin. Once they were inside, Catherine breathed a heavy sigh of relief, as if she had held it since the bridge. "I was scared to death."

"I was too." Douglas collapsed into the chair.

"Papa, you were so brave to stand up to that sailor."

"I didn't want him to touch you—plus, if he had found our guns, they may have shot us."

Catherine turned her back, opened her dress front, and removed the guns. She handed him his.

"I was praying I wouldn't have to walk much more because the guns were about to slip out of my dress."

They laughed nervously.

Soon the ship got underway. The next day they arrived at the Port of Bilbao and checked into a downtown hotel. Douglas searched for and quickly found a ship for London. They stayed in Bilbao for two days. The voyage from Bilbao to London was uneventful.

One month after leaving New York, they arrived in London. They telegraphed home to announce their arrival and asked if there was anything new on Harrison. They received a telegram the next day from home telling them there was nothing new. After resting for a day and buying the proper clothes for Catherine, they were ready to begin their search.

CHAPTER 13

Douglas and Catherine began their search at the American Army Headquarters, which was located in a mammoth building in downtown London. They spoke to several people and finally found an officer who helped them. He checked a list of casualties. "No, there is nobody by the name of Richardson here," he said. He looked up at their disappointed faces. "But the list isn't accurate and it is possible that he could be in an English hospital." He rummaged through some paperwork and gave them a list of hospitals.

They immediately visited hospitals in and near London, finding the hospitals were overflowing. As a result, American soldiers were often placed in nearby private homes and estates which they also visited. Many of the soldiers were ill with Spanish influenza. The soldiers brought the disease from France and it was now an epidemic in England.

The number and severity of the soldiers' injuries was soon too much for Catherine. In particular, the men who were burned or injured so severely that they had no faces haunted her. She prayed that Harrison wasn't one of these faceless men. She was depressed and skeptical that they would ever get any new information. Catherine wrote home keeping them informed on what they were doing. The longer they were in England, the more despondent her letters became.

The last hospital on the list was in Portsmouth, which was on the coast of the English Channel. They didn't find Harrison but they learned of a British officer, Captain Reese, who kept more up-to-date files on the American soldiers. The officer was in the British Army Headquarters in London.

They visited the British Army Headquarters and a guard escorted them to Captain Reese's office. Captain Reese was a six-foot tall Scotsman with red hair and a long, red mustache, waxed at the ends. The Captain was reading a document when Douglas knocked on the door.

"Captain Reese, I presume?" asked Douglas.

"Aye, that's me," replied the captain as he stood.

"My name is Douglas Dawson and this is my granddaughter Catherine Richardson."

"Americans, hey?"

"Yes, we are from New York. We are searching for Catherine's husband who is listed as missing in France."

"That's what we do here. Before this assignment with the Yanks, I was responsible for all the British Army personnel records. We have kept records on every

British soldier since before the North American colony rebellion."

Douglas had to bite his tongue when the captain said *rebellion* but he let it pass. Douglas commented, "That's an important service to provide."

"Aye, it is. We can tell you the history of every British soldier. We take pride in the accuracy of our records. We never close out a file. Sometimes we learn new information years, maybe even decades later. We follow a strict process and we always strive to know where our men are. We report frequently on them. We started recently doing the same thing for the Americans. Frankly, the Americans were arrogant and unorganized when they first arrived. They thought they would show up in France and the Germans would surrender. They learned quickly the Germans are determined to fight it out. We are teaching the Yanks the proper way to record where their boys are by using precise records and discipline. Now what is the lad's rank, name, and unit?"

Catherine answered, "My husband is Lieutenant Harrison Richardson; he was with the 16th infantry, 1st Infantry Division. He was last reported to be near the town of Bathelémont, France in early November."

Captain Reese wrote the information on a card and offered, "It's nearly tea time; please go downstairs to the café and have a cup. Return in about an hour and I'll report to you what we know."

An hour later, Captain Reese greeted them with a smile.

"I have good news for you. Lieutenant Richardson is in a hospital in Dover, England. He has been there for two weeks. You can take a train from the London station directly to Dover. You can be there by late this afternoon."

Catherine's heart squeezed in her chest. She felt as if she were about to faint, cry, and jump in the air all at the same time. "Oh my, you found him! I had almost given up hope of finding him in England." She rushed to the captain and hugged him. "I was hoping we wouldn't have to go to France," she babbled on. "Thank you, Captain Reese, thank you!"

He blushed and said, "You are quite welcome, my dear. I'm normally the bearer of bad news; I'm glad I could help you."

Douglas' eyes brimmed with tears. "Sir, you have given us hope." He shook Captain Reese's hand vigorously.

"I wish you the best of luck. I hope you find him recovering well."

Douglas and Catherine could hardly control their glee. As they left the headquarters, it started to storm. Douglas didn't want to travel in the bad weather but Catherine was anxious to see Harrison. He talked her into staying in London that night. The plan was to leave the next morning for Dover.

The next day, Douglas went to her room and knocked but she didn't answer. Douglas found a maid, who let him in. Catherine was still in bed. Douglas talked to her and felt her forehead. She had a fever. He immediately had the hotel manager find a doctor, who examined her. He said Catherine should remain in bed and was hopeful she would be fine in a few days. Douglas found a nurse to stay with her, and reluctantly traveled alone to Dover.

He took the one o'clock train, putting him at the hospital at three-thirty. The last train back to London was at five so he had to hurry. The clerk at the hospital reception desk did have Lieutenant Harrison Richardson registered, which was encouraging. A nurse brought him to the officers' ward on the top floor. Harrison was in bed number five and the curtain was drawn. Nurses were attending to someone behind the curtain.

The nurse opened the curtain and stepped in. She came out, closed the curtain, and said, "Please have a seat. The lieutenant's dressings need changing."

She went back in. He overheard the nurses talking as they tried to console the person behind the curtain. He was moaning and crying out in pain.

Douglas was uncomfortable sitting there. He got up and walked to the hall.

After a few minutes, the nurse came out. "He is ready now."

She took him to the curtain and opened it. She said, "Lieutenant Richardson, you have a visitor. There is a Mr. Dawson from the States to see you."

The lieutenant was lying back in the bed. Douglas could see the young man had lost his left leg and had bandages on his left arm…but there was something wrong. The man didn't look like Harrison.

Douglas asked, "Are you Lieutenant Harrison Richardson from New York?"

"Yes sir."

"You were assigned to the 1st Infantry Division?"

"Yes sir."

"You were stationed at Bathelémont."

"Yes sir."

Douglas turned to the nurse and asked, "My dear, may I have some time alone with Lieutenant Richardson?"

"Of course; if you need anything please ring the bell."

The nurse left then Douglas said with a low angry voice, "I know you are not Lieutenant Harrison Richardson from New York! Who are you and where is Lieutenant Richardson?"

The man, after a few awkward seconds, looked down and said with shame, "You're right. I'm not Lieutenant Richardson."

"Where is he?" Douglas demanded

The man still didn't look at him and replied softly, "He is a prisoner of war in Germany."

"Why are you impersonating him?" asked Douglas, his voice rising.

The man looked at Douglas and pleaded, "Sir, don't get upset, I'll tell you what happened. Please have a seat."

Douglas sat next to his bed.

"Lieutenant Richardson saved my life. I was assigned to the French 18th Infantry division. My company was in a forward trench. A battle began and soon we were under orders to pull back. Several of us ended up in a support trench with Lieutenant Richardson. His orders were to hold the line against the Germans. We fought back an attack then the battle eased. He took several wounded men back for medical care. He returned and the Germans attacked again. It started with a large artillery barrage. Shrapnel tore through my arm and leg, which left me helpless. The barrage ended then the Germans charged and soon the fighting was hand-to-hand. The Germans retreated and there was a lull as both sides reassembled. We were short on men and ammunition. Lieutenant Richardson was worried we were going to be overrun. He gave me his officer's overcoat, his tunic, and his identification documents. He said I would get better care if I was captured as an officer. He took my coat and documents."

"I see, he traded places with you." Douglas reached out and put his hand on the fellow's arm.

"Yes sir, he did. Soon the shelling started again. Their artillery was accurate and deadly. A large explosion knocked me out. When I awoke, I was on a hospital bed in a German field hospital. Lieutenant Richardson was next to me unconscious and he woke up on the second day. His left arm was broken and he had some minor wounds. We were next to each other in the German hospital for four days. He was sent to a prisoner of war camp for enlisted men in Germany. I asked a German medical officer where he was going. He wrote the name of the prison for me and it is in my wallet—sorry, in his wallet. I went to a hospital for officers. I got an infection in my leg then a high fever and I was sick for a long time. A Red Cross doctor toured the hospital and saw me. He negotiated with the Germans to get me back to England as part of an injured officer prisoner exchange. When I arrived here they tried to save my leg but couldn't and it was removed a few days ago."

Douglas sighed, disappointed that this man wasn't Harrison but empathetic for his story. "You have an amazing story and you have endured a great deal."

"Yes sir but if I hadn't been listed as an officer, I'm sure I would have died. I didn't know what to do once I got here so I continued to be Lieutenant Richardson."

"So what is your real name?"

"I'm Corporal Tom Madrigal of the 16th infantry regiment, 1st Infantry division. I'm from St. Louis."

"Corporal, are you absolutely sure he was captured?"

"Yes sir, he was with me. He gave me a letter and asked me to hand deliver it for him when I got back home. I gave him one too. His letter is addressed to his wife, Catherine Richardson."

"She is my granddaughter."

"Hand me that satchel on the dresser; the letter and his wallet are in it."

Douglas handed him the satchel. He searched through it, then gave Douglas a letter and a wallet.

Corporal Madrigal continued, "The officer camps are better than the enlisted prisoner camps. When he gave me his identity, he may have given up his life. I'm so thankful for what he did. I lost my leg but I'll go home to my wife, children and my job as a bookkeeper. He may never make it back. I ask you and his family's forgiveness for taking his identity."

"Corporal Madrigal, Harrison knew what he was doing. You didn't take his identity; he gave it to you."

Corporal Madrigal smiled. "I haven't thought about it that way."

"Thinking about your situation, you should tell the people here that your memory cleared up as a result of my visit. You remember now that Lieutenant Richardson changed places with you. They will believe your story because so many men have been shell shocked. Go live a full life. Harrison will want to know you are well."

Corporal Madrigal looked up at Douglas. "Mr. Dawson, you have given me a way out of this situation. I'm thankful to you. When you see Mrs. Richardson, please tell her that her husband was a brave man."

Douglas gently patted the man's arm. "I will. Son, you take care of yourself."

Douglas left and went to London. When he arrived at the hotel, Catherine was sleeping, hot with a fever.

The next morning, Catherine's condition had not improved. Douglas decided to tell Captain Reese what he had learned and see how he could get more information on Harrison. He left Catherine with the nurse and he went to the British Army headquarters. Douglas knocked on the door of Captain Reese's office.

The captain looked up, stood, and commented, "Mr. Dawson, you have returned so quickly. I presume you have some news for me."

"Yes sir, I do. I visited the young man yesterday. He is not Lieutenant Richardson. The young man there is Corporal Tom Madrigal. He is shell shocked and recovering from serious injuries."

Captain Reese listened and made notes.

"Our Lieutenant Richardson traded places with the corporal so he would get better care in an officer hospital. When the corporal woke up in the German hospital, the papers on him showed he was an officer. He didn't remember who he was until our discussion."

"Aye, I have heard of many lads losing their memories and at times, it takes something simple, like a conversation, to jar them back to reality. Let me have someone look up the records for Corporal Tom Madrigal."

The Captain walked out to a clerk. They talked for a moment then they walked across the floor together to a file cabinet and opened it. They searched through it and found a file. Captain Reese read it, wrote down some information, and then returned.

Captain Reese reported, "Corporal Tom Madrigal is from St. Louis; he is Lutheran, married with two children, and twenty-five years old. He was in the 1st Infantry division and was captured in November near the town of Bathelémont, France. He was wounded and was sent to a German medical hospital. He recovered then went to the Wittenberg prison camp. The Red Cross reported in December that he was in good health. No other information is available."

Douglas looked relieved. "The Wittenberg prison camp is the one that a German officer said he was going to. So our Lieutenant Richardson is alive but is a prisoner of war."

"Yes sir."

"Thank God for that." Douglas exhaled.

"Mr. Dawson, the Red Cross visits the camps periodically and provides updates on the prisoners. I'll contact you if anything new becomes available."

"This is my card with my address in New York." He handed Captain Reese his card. "Thank you for your help." They shook hands.

"I'm glad I could be of service to you," said Captain Reese.

That evening, Catherine was well enough to hear the news about Harrison. Douglas told her everything he learned. She was sad to hear he was in prison but happy to know he was alive. Douglas gave her the letter from Harrison and sat down next to her.

My dearest Catherine,

You probably know by now that unfortunately my service to my country has ended for the moment. Times have been difficult but I will get back home to you soon

and we can start our lives again. I think often of our wedding, our honeymoon, and the day you were with me at the dock. You look for me because I will be home one day and we will be happy again.
With all my love, Harrison.

Catherine cried as she read the note. She asked, "Papa, do we know where he is in Germany?"

"Yes, he is in Wittenberg, which is in Northern Germany."

Catherine's eyes widened. "I'll look it up on a map so I can have a better idea where he is. I know he will be fine. The war will end soon and he will come home to me. I'll be waiting for him in New York."

Douglas reached over and squeezed her arm. "I know you will, dear. Now you need to rest so you can get better."

In a soft, tearful voice, Catherine whispered, "Papa, I want to go home. Will you please take me home?"

Douglas held her hand and patted it ever so gently. "Yes dear, I will."

"I will see my Harrison again, won't I?"

He nodded. "I promise you will see him again. You two will walk together in Central Park like you did before."

Catherine smiled as a tear rolled from her eye. "I love you, Papa."

Since she was little, Douglas had always teased her by saying, "You know you are my favorite granddaughter." He repeated it now.

She always replied the same way, and followed right along: "Papa, I'm your only granddaughter."

"Yes dear, but you are still my favorite one. Now you rest."

"I'll after I write some in my diary. I want to make sure I write down everything we have learned today. This has been a good day."

"Yes, it has."

Douglas went to bed that night thankful she was improving. He telegraphed home the news about Harrison, telling them Catherine was ill and he planned to stay in London until she recovered.

The next day, a telegram arrived from home. Joseph had arranged through Senator Stratton for passage for them on a hospital ship that would be leaving England for New York in a week.

Catherine's fever returned late that night. In the morning, Douglas moved her to a hospital and several doctors saw her but offered conflicting diagnoses: one doctor said it was cholera and another insisted it was pneumonia. Catherine's temperature rose to 103 degrees; she had a cough and had trouble breathing.

Desperate, Douglas went to an American military hospital in London and found an Army doctor who agreed to examine her.

"I've seen her symptoms in many of the American soldiers coming from France," the doctor concluded in a quiet meeting with Douglas shortly after examining her. "She has the Spanish influenza. There is no treatment for it. If she can make it through the high fever, she will recover."

The nurses redoubled their efforts to try to bring her fever down using cold towels and ice. They gave her aspirin and cinnamon powder mixed in milk. They used every method they knew to get her temperature down.

Douglas stayed at her side, comforting her as best as he could. She woke from time to time and each time she asked if there was news on Harrison.

Three days before they were to set sail for home, Catherine passed away at six o'clock in the evening while Douglas held her hand. He stayed there weeping late into the night.

Not only were people dying across Europe from the terrible war, they were now dying from a pandemic. The first wave of Spanish influenza had spread across Europe and Catherine was one of its victims.

CHAPTER 14

THE NEXT MORNING, THE AUTHORITIES came to take Catherine's body. A near panic had moved across England due to the large number of people dying from influenza. The authorities didn't know how the disease spread so they were acting quickly to remove the dead and bury them. Douglas didn't want to lose control of Catherine's body so he immediately arranged for her cremation. He took her blue dress from the hotel and had her changed into it. The last time he saw her was at the funeral home. It was only grandfather and granddaughter in a lonely, cold room. He cried over her as the attendants closed her coffin.

He now faced one of the most difficult things he had to do in his life: telling his son and daughter-in-law that their daughter was dead. He dreaded sending the telegram knowing it would change their lives forever.

The telegraph office was two blocks from the funeral home; the walk was long for him. The office was on the corner and it was empty except for the operator, a thin, tall, older man with white hair and round, gold wire glasses.

Standing at the counter, Douglas tried several times to write a message but he tore up each one.

The operator was watching him. "I can tell you're having trouble writing what you want to say. Do you need some help?"

"I have some bad news to tell and I can't find the right words."

"What happened?"

"My granddaughter died."

"I'm sorry for your loss. Who are you sending this to?"

"Her parents."

The operator leaned back in his chair. "Sir, no words will ever console them. They will have some peace if they know she didn't die alone and she passed peacefully if she did."

Douglas reflected on what the operator said. "Thank you sir, you have helped."

Douglas wrote down a message and handed it to the operator. The operator read it, nodded his head, then sent it. The telegram read:

> *It breaks my heart to tell you that last evening Catherine passed away in her sleep from influenza. The doctors did everything they could. I was with her every minute and she passed peacefully. I will return with her ashes*

soon. I am in total despair about her and because I did not keep you better informed. With my deepest sympathy and sincere apology, Douglas.

Douglas paid for the telegram, thanked the operator, left him a generous tip, and walked to a park down the street.

A mother and a daughter were in the park. The little girl was playing on a swing. Douglas sat on a bench and watched her, and tears filled his eyes as images of Catherine as a child flooded over him—the trips to the circus, walks along the ocean, the promenades in Central Park, and the many weekends she stayed with him and his wife. He remembered the motorcar ride they took recently in the New York countryside. She was so happy during the trip. But now she was gone. The only true joy left in his life was gone. He started to sob.

The skies darkened and rain was about to fall. The woman and the girl hurriedly left the park. Douglas sat there as the rain poured. After a few minutes, he was soaked to the skin and cold. He got up and walked slowly to the hotel.

The following morning, Catherine's ashes arrived in a plain tin box. Douglas opened it. His beautiful granddaughter was now only cold, gray ashes. He sat down with the box and cried. After a few minutes of uncontrolled sobbing, he looked at the box and exclaimed, "Catherine cannot be in something so plain and ugly. She must have something that suits her."

Down the street from the hotel was a glass store. He hurried down the half block, his shoulders squared against the rain that still fell. He purchased an expensive, yellow crystal vase. He returned to the hotel and put her ashes in the vase. He sealed the top with cork and wax then carefully packed the vase into one of her trunks.

He sent a telegram to the Senator Stratton asking him to get him a berth on one of the convoys. That evening, he received a telegram from the senator, confirming he had booked travel home for Douglas on a merchant ship in a Navy convoy.

On the passage home, Douglas seldom left the cabin; depression covered him like a shroud. He believed that he had been too cavalier about taking Catherine to Europe. His desire for adventure had exposed his granddaughter to a disease she may not have gotten in the safety and comfort of her home. He felt completely responsible for her death.

The night before he arrived home, he tried to sleep but couldn't. He kept thinking of Catherine lying in the bed and dying without him being able to help. The promise he had made to her that she would come home and she would see her lieutenant again haunted him.

He lay in bed and struggled with an idea he had that would help him keep his promise to her. Years ago, he had met a man in Italy who told him about a magical glassmaking process that would have the power to transform Catherine's fate. This man's glassmaking process was a powerful thing—something that would strike fear into the hearts of many. Douglas never thought he would ever want to use it, but now he had no other choice. He decided to try it when he got home.

Late in the afternoon on Sunday, the ship docked in New York. Douglas gathered the luggage then took a cab to his home. The driver helped him with the luggage then left. Douglas opened a trunk and took out the yellow vase and Catherine's diary. He placed them on his desk in the library. He walked to a wall of books and on the third shelf was a red leather-bound book. He had received the book from the man in Italy. The book was about ancient glassmaking techniques.

Douglas opened it and copied down on a sheet of paper a glassmaking process and formula then put the paper in an envelope. Exhausted from the travel, he went upstairs to bed.

The next morning after breakfast, he went to his library. He picked up the envelope and the yellow vase. He asked his house keeper to send Catherine's trunks to her home with a note saying he would personally deliver her ashes later that day. He then drove to the glass factory. The plant foreman met him as he walked to his office carrying the vase.

"Mr. Dawson, what are you doing here today? I wasn't expecting you. I thought you were in Europe."

"I arrived home yesterday. I'm here because we are going to make a new type of glass."

The foreman rubbed his hands on his apron. "I always enjoy it when you make new glass. What do want me to do?"

Douglas took the envelope from his coat pocket and handed it to the foreman. "We will be using this process and formula."

The foreman opened and read it.

Douglas explained, "The Chinese blue obsidian stone is in warehouse 12. You know the stuff."

The foreman nodded. "Yes sir. That stone is expensive. This calls for a lot of it. I thought we had trouble getting it."

Douglas nodded. "Yes, we do. Chinese blue obsidian stone is rare."

"You have had me use some in the past, but only a few pounds." The foreman was hesitant.

"Yes, I know, but this is a special glass. You need to follow the process and formula exactly as it is written."

The foreman gave a brief nod. "Yes sir."

"When the batch has reached 1300 degrees, we will add the stone. Please get me when you are ready to add it," Douglas instructed.

"Yes sir."

Three hours later the foreman went to Douglas' office; he knocked then opened the door. Douglas was at his desk reading his mail.

"Mr. Dawson, the batch is ready."

Douglas took the vase and they walked out to the furnace. The furnace was hot and loud due to the large gas burners heating the furnace.

Douglas yelled to the foreman, "Add the stone!"

The foreman had three men shovel the stone into the oven. As it melted, a thick, blue haze formed over the oven, something they had never seen before. After a few minutes, the stone had melted but the blue haze hung in the air. The molted glass bubbled in the oven and sparks shot up.

Douglas yelled to the foreman, "Okay, it's time to add this."

Douglas handed him the yellow vase. The foreman went to the oven, tossed it in, and walked back to Douglas. Within a few seconds, there was a loud noise that sounded like thunder. Then there was a second one, which was even louder. Large sparks flew from the oven and splattered on the ground. The workers ran for safety, covering their heads. The furnace sucked the blue haze into the molted mass with a deafening whistling sound. The sparks stopped and the molted glass in the furnace settled down.

The foreman yelled to Douglas, "What the hell was that?"

Douglas yelled back, "That's the sound of a special glass being made. Let it cook for another hour then pour and cut it into sheets like you normally do."

"Yes sir."

Douglas went to his office. Four hours later, the glass had been poured, cut into sheets, and stacked.

Douglas went out onto the floor to examine the glass. The foreman observed, "This glass is so clear. I believe this is the best glass we have ever made."

"You did a good job. Let the glass cool for two days then silver it. I want you to cut one sheet into a full-length mirror. Put the mirror into an oak frame and base then have it delivered to my home. I want you to build a special crate for the rest of the glass. Build the crate extra strong to protect the glass. Put the crate into warehouse 12 and mark the crate as *Experimental mirror glass – Do not move without the written approval of Douglas Dawson*," Douglas instructed. "Do you understand?"

"Yes sir."

With the glass made, Douglas returned to the city. On the ride back, he thought about what he needed to do next. His son was expecting him to deliver Catherine's ashes.

Douglas stopped at a china store and bought a new yellow vase before returning home. He took fine ashes from his fireplace hearth and filled the vase. After sealing the top with cork and wax, he put the vase into a box. He called his son and told him he was bringing Catherine's ashes to him.

Joseph met him at the front door. Douglas, standing in a black suit and holding the fake ashes, begged, "Please forgive me."

Joseph took the box and closed the door without saying a word. Douglas stood there with tears running down his face.

Douglas returned home and immediately went to the bar in his library. He opened a bottle of whiskey and he drank until he passed out on his couch.

A week later, hundreds of people attended Catherine's funeral. Her father laid the yellow vase in her casket, which was placed in the Richardson's family plot in a Catholic cemetery in New York City, next to a spot reserved for Harrison. Catherine's mother confronted Douglas immediately after the ceremony at the cemetery. She insisted he was responsible for Catherine's death and she would never forgive him for it. She vowed she would never speak to him again. The funeral's sadness and the confrontation with Martha weighed heavily on Douglas.

The day after Catherine's funeral, the full-length mirror with oak frame and stand arrived and Douglas placed it in a guest bedroom. He checked on it often. If the process worked, the mirror would change color.

One morning weeks later, he entered the guest room. The room was bright from the sunlight as it was every morning. Douglas examined the mirror. It had changed; the mirror had a blue tint. He smiled and watched it.

Within a few seconds, an image appeared. The process had worked. Catherine was in the mirror in her blue dress. She wasn't a reflection in the mirror; the mirror allowed him to see into her new world. She smiled at him.

Tears came to his eyes. "My dear, I have been waiting for you."

She nodded her head and continued to smile.

"I know you can hear me but I will not be able to hear you. I'm not sure why the mirror works this way, but it does."

She smiled and nodded.

Douglas recalled, "I told you in London I would make sure you would see Harrison again. He isn't back yet from the war but when he does return, you will be here. I have prayed the process would work. Now I'm sure you want to know how you got here."

He pulled up a chair and sat. "I told you a little about this process when we had coffee together that day in the café with Harrison."

Catherine nodded, remembering.

"A year after your grandmother died, I missed her terribly and I was looking for a new adventure. I had always wanted to go to the Murano islands outside of Venice, Italy. Glass has been made there for centuries. I visited a number of glassmakers there and learned some new techniques. I also learned of a glassmaker who had a secret process that people there were afraid to talk about. I wanted to talk to him but he never saw anyone. I sent a letter to him telling him it would be an honor to meet him. Apparently, he had heard of me. He replied to my letter and invited me to his shop."

"He was a fascinating and brilliant man. His name was Michael Musso. Michael was a large, strong man with long grey hair, a booming voice, and a fiery temper. He had spent some time in the United States and he knew English. I saw samples of his glass, which were awe-inspiring with the most vibrant colors I have ever seen. We spent the first day we met talking about glass and enjoying some excellent wine. He invited me back and soon we became good friends."

Douglas leaned forward in the chair, getting tense and serious. "One day, we were having some wine. Michael was in a foul mood and he drank a lot. He became dark and started complaining about how his friends had deserted him over something he had done. I asked him what happened. He said he would have to show me."

"He took me to his private workshop. The workshop was in a large windowless building behind his home. A heavy, steel gate protected the door. The building was in two sections—one was where glass was made. It was a typical manufacturing shop that was dirty and filled with equipment. There was a large special glass oven and many unique glassmaking tools. The other section of the building was a display area for glass. The display area was bright, clean, and painted in vibrant colors. The glass there was extraordinary."

"In one corner of the display area, there was a mirror on a stand, covered by a cloth, and near it was a rocking chair. He said the glass in the mirror was blue obsidian glass, also known as capture glass. It was a special blue-tinted glass made from Chinese blue obsidian stone. This stone is found only after volcanic eruptions in remote areas of China. I told him I had heard of blue obsidian glass but I had never heard of capture glass."

"He asked me to stand in front of the mirror and like with you today, an image appeared. He told me it was his wife." Douglas spoke somberly as he recalled the memory. "I must tell you that I was afraid but he calmly told me the tragic story of how Angelica had died and how he used a special glassmaking process to allow him to see his precious wife again. He said that every day, he went there and talked to her for hours. I was shocked at first then I thought it was some cruel trick—but it wasn't."

Douglas leaned back in the chair. "Mr. Musso said that on a trip to China, he met a holy man who gave him a book on ancient glassmaking techniques. From what I understand from Mr. Musso and in reading the book, which was in Latin, the capture glass process somehow opens up a window into time and it captures the essence of a person. When a person is captured in the glass, he or she returns to the time in their life when they were the most vibrant. Mr. Musso's wife died in her late forties but she returned as a woman in her twenties. She was young and beautiful like you are."

"I immediately thought of your grandmother. I wished I had known of this process when she died. Her ashes, as you know, were spread on her beloved Long Island seashore, so I couldn't do it."

Catherine listened intently.

Douglas continued, "Mr. Musso gave me the book because he said he had only one son but the son couldn't be trusted with such a powerful process. I was reluctant to take it but he insisted. He wanted a glassmaker to have it who would keep it secret and I promised him that I would. Several of his friends believed the process was evil. They wanted him to destroy the glass. He wouldn't and he lost them as friends. He cautioned me if I ever used the process that I should only use it in a special circumstance and that people would be afraid of it. We remained friends until his death last year."

Catherine nodded.

"Catherine, when you passed so suddenly, I was so sad. I had promised you would see Harrison again and I couldn't think of any other way. When he comes back from the war, you will be with him again. I hope you aren't angry and you will forgive me for doing this."

Catherine smiled as if she wasn't upset about what he had done.

"From what I understand about the process, it somehow stops time. It is like the movies we see at the theater. You will be safe and you will appear in the mirrors as long as you want to."

Catherine smiled and nodded.

Douglas could see the background behind her. There was green grass, trees, colorful flowers, and a stone country home. It comforted him. He knew she was somewhere peaceful and safe.

Douglas visited with Catherine every day and told her about the events that were going on in the world. He cherished those visits and loved seeing her but he also worried that someone might discover her.

CHAPTER 15

THE WAR FINALLY STARTED TO grind to an end. The newspapers reported that diplomatic discussions to end it were occurring. People felt the Americans would be coming home soon including the prisoners of war. Everyone was looking forward to Harrison returning home.

Douglas' relationship with his son and daughter-in-law was still deeply damaged. Since Catherine's funeral, Martha hadn't spoken to him. Douglas saw Joseph at the office but he talked only about business. Douglas tried several times to talk to him about Catherine but Joseph wouldn't talk about it.

Howard had reached out to him. He didn't hold Douglas responsible for Catherine's death. He knew she would have gone to Europe alone if she had to. Howard told him that his mother was in deep mourning and his father drank heavily.

On a Saturday morning in October 1918, Douglas' front door bell rang while he was having breakfast. The maid answered the door and received a telegram. She brought it to Douglas at the dining room table.

> *Mr. Dawson, we received word from the Red Cross. Corporal Tom Madrigal of the 1st Infantry division died from influenza last winter at the Wittenberg prison camp. I am sorry I do not have better news. Captain Reese.*

Douglas hung his head and sobbed. First Catherine and now Harrison. He knew this news would be devastating to Catherine. Holding the telegram, he got up and started to go upstairs but he stopped and cried aloud, "I can't tell her this! I promised her they would be together someday. If she knows he died, she may lose hope and disappear. I can't lose her again."

He immediately left the house and went for a walk. He ended up, without giving it any thought, in Central Park. Something seemed to pull him there. As he walked through the park, he thought of Catherine. It was a warm, clear day and the park was crowded. There was an art fair there and many artists were displaying their work.

A photographer was taking pictures of a couple, the woman was wearing a white dress and holding a parasol, the young man was in a black suit. He was standing straight with his hat in his hand and jutting out his chest with pride. The photographer took his time making sure everything was perfect.

As he watched the couple, Douglas remembered how Catherine and Harrison looked on their engagement day. They were happy and had their whole lives in front of them. Now they were gone and separated forever from each other. This couldn't be what was supposed to happen to them. They had to be together.

Douglas wondered if he could bring them together in the mirror.

He rushed home, went to the library, and took out the red leather-bound book. He quickly searched through it. In the last section of the book, he found a process and formula to reuse capture glass and to add additional people. The process required more materials and significantly higher temperature for a longer period. The author cautioned about using the process because it was seldom successful and dangerous due to the higher temperature. If the process didn't work, Catherine would be lost—but there was a chance that Douglas could bring them together, and he decided any chance was better than no chance. He would have to go to Germany, find Harrison's body and bring him home to Catherine then capture them in the glass together.

Douglas called Mr. Richardson and told him the news about Harrison. He was devastated and started to sob over the phone. He couldn't repeat to his wife what Douglas had said. Mrs. Richardson took the phone and Douglas repeated the news. She dropped the phone to the floor and started crying. The maid picked up the phone and told Douglas the Richardsons were too distraught to talk any further. Douglas called Joseph and told him the news. Joseph listened and hung up without saying a word.

The following day, Douglas visited the Richardsons to pay his respects. Black banners draped the entrance to their home and Mrs. Richardson was dressed in black. Mr. Richardson told Douglas there would be no closure for them without his body and a service to commemorate him. Douglas assured them that when the war was over, he would bring Harrison home for a proper burial with Catherine.

"Thank you for caring about our son," Mr. Richardson said.

Guilt overwhelmed Douglas. His desire wasn't to bring the body home for them but for Harrison to be with Catherine.

In November 1918, the armistice was signed and the war was finally over. Douglas immediately made plans to go to Germany in the spring of 1919.

The morning of his trip to Germany, Douglas saw Catherine. She was smiling as she always did. He said, "My dear, I'll be going on a trip and I'll be away for some time. I love you and I'll see you soon." Douglas took a cab to the harbor and boarded a ship for Amsterdam.

The voyage was easy now since luxury passenger ships to Europe had started again. He arrived in Amsterdam in early May and boarded a train for the journey to Wittenberg, Germany. A normal trip from Amsterdam to Wittenberg would have taken a day but this trip took three days. The train schedules before the war were always precise but now the trains were often late or canceled with no explanation. The war had ended but the misery for the German people continued. Germany's government was bankrupt and its people were starving. Everywhere he went, he found the living conditions to be horrific with food and necessities hard to find.

Once Douglas finally arrived in Wittenberg, the townspeople were reluctant to talk to him. They were afraid of the famous rich American searching for a dead prisoner of war.

Eventually, he found a well-respected barrister to help him. Douglas employed him to help navigate the language and the bureaucracy to find Corporal Madrigal's grave. The barrister was able to obtain access to the prison records, which confirmed Corporal Madrigal had died during the winter of 1917-1918. Many prisoners died that winter, and due to the fear of disease, some bodies were put in mass graves or into hastily dug unmarked graves. It wasn't possible to determine where Harrison's grave was. Douglas spent three months searching for him with no success.

Douglas would return to Germany twice more to search for Harrison. He was able to find German soldiers stationed at the prison during the war but they didn't remember a lowly corporal who died so soon after arriving there. He had discussions with German authorities to disinter the bodies and try to determine who was buried in the mass and unmarked graves but German politics prevented any progress. Each unsuccessful trip drained more life from Douglas. His health slowly started to fade.

Douglas didn't tell Catherine that Harrison had died in the prison camp and his grave was lost. He was afraid if she knew, she wouldn't continue to wait for him and she would be lost forever. To her, the war was still on and Harrison was still a prisoner.

CHAPTER 16

Douglas' desire for the glassmaking business and for traveling the world ended with Catherine's death. He eventually stopped going to the office and he sold his share of the business to his son, except for the materials in warehouse 12. Joseph only spoke to him when he had to. Martha kept her word and never spoke to him again. However, Douglas continued to see Howard often and they grew close.

Howard didn't join the Army and after the war, he went to college. After graduating, he started working as a stockbroker for Harrison's father. He enjoyed the business and was successful. Howard didn't marry the Protestant store clerk; they drifted apart while he was at college. He married a Catholic girl from a prominent New York family and had two sons.

Douglas spent his time working on and driving his motorcars, playing cards at the club, and talking with as well as worrying about Catherine. Each morning, he would visit with her and tell her what was happening in the world but he continued to lie about the status of the war and Harrison's death.

Douglas felt burdened with putting Catherine into the glass. He thought of telling Catherine's parents about her but didn't because of their strained relationship. At times, keeping the secret of Catherine was overwhelming to him and he wished many times he hadn't captured her in the glass.

During the spring of 1926, Douglas' health began to deteriorate after some heart problems. He started to feel desperate about Catherine. He knew when he died Catherine would still appear in the mirror. He had to have a plan after his death for Catherine to have a chance to see her husband again.

The only person he thought he could use was Howard. But Douglas didn't want to tell Howard about Catherine being in the mirror. He was afraid that if Howard knew about Catherine, it would affect their relationship, which he cherished. Mr. Musso had lost close friends when they learned about the process; Douglas couldn't stand the thought of losing Howard.

The best way, Douglas reasoned, was for Howard to discover Catherine on his own by giving the mirror to him after Douglas passed. He told Howard there was a special mirror that Catherine loved and he asked Howard to put it in his home. Howard agreed to move it when the time came. Douglas told him there might be questions after his death and if he had questions to read his diary.

The key element of Douglas' plan was that Howard eventually would see Catherine when the mirror was at his home. Howard would question how she got there then he would read Douglas' diary. The entire story was there. Douglas carefully detailed in his diary the story of Mr. Musso and the secret glassmaking process. He described the exact process to follow to capture Harrison in the glass. He described everything he knew about Harrison and where he was in Germany. Howard would have everything he needed to have the special glass made. Douglas designed and supervised the building of his crypt to store all the materials needed. The crypt had two rooms. One room was for his coffin and the second room was for the ingredients needed for the glassmaking process.

Douglas had the Chinese blue obsidian stone put into teak barrels that wouldn't rot. The barrels were in warehouse 12 along with the crate of blue obsidian mirror glass. His plan was to move everything into the second room of the crypt once it was finished. Douglas was content with the plan to reunite Catherine and Harrison.

The crypt was finished and it was time to move the materials. On Friday, May 10, 1927, a truck arrived at the glass plant with an order to pick up all the materials in warehouse 12. The security guard read the order and guided the truck to the warehouse. The guard opened the warehouse. He watched the driver and his assistant load the barrels. They had finished loading the barrels and were about to load the crate of blue obsidian glass. The guard saw the instructions on the crate's side that read, *Experimental mirror glass – Do not move without the written approval of Douglas Dawson!*

He told the driver he needed to get a written order from Douglas Dawson to move the glass. The guard went to the gate office, checked the phone directory and didn't see Douglas Dawson's name. The guard was new; he didn't know who Douglas Dawson was and that he no longer worked at the company. The guard told the driver he would have to return. The driver shrugged his shoulders, closed the truck doors, and left. The guard wrote a note to Douglas Dawson asking permission to allow the moving company to pick up the glass. He put the note in an envelope addressed to Douglas Dawson at the main office and sent it via intercompany mail.

The driver took the teak barrels to the cemetery. A worker at the cemetery opened the crypt for the movers, where the teak barrels were unloaded and carefully stacked in the second room. The driver called his office manager and told him the materials were delivered and the office manager called Douglas to tell him the job was done.

The next day, the letter from the security guard arrived at the Dawson Glass Company's main office. The mail clerk saw the letter and put it in a special box for

Douglas Dawson. The mail was delivered to Douglas once a month.

Three weeks later, Douglas passed away in his sleep. A large funeral was held. Joseph Dawson attended but Martha did not. At the cemetery, Joseph remarked to Howard about the size of his father's crypt. He felt it was pretentious and out of character for his father. Neither he nor Howard entered the crypt.

The day after the funeral, the monthly batch of mail from the office arrived. Howard, who was the estate trustee, opened the guard's letter weeks later, but he discarded it as unimportant.

Douglas' estate went to Howard along with his diary, Catherine's diary, lab notes, and books including the red leather-bound glassmaking book. Howard sold Douglas' home and the furnishings except for Catherine's mirror. He had a mover pick it up.

En route to Howard's home, the mover had a minor traffic accident. The mirror in the oak frame was broken. The mover swept up the glass and threw the pieces in the trash. The mover took the oak frame to a glass shop and had the glass replaced.

Howard received the oak frame with the new mirror and put it into one of his guest rooms. He never knew that the mirror had been broken and that Catherine had been lost. His grandfather's diary, Catherine's diary, lab notes, and books were in his library but he never read them.

In late 1948, Joseph Dawson died and then a few months later Martha Dawson passed away. One year later, the Dawson Glass Company was sold. In April 1950, the new owners took the blue obsidian glass in the special crate in warehouse 12 and cut the glass into mirrors for a new hotel in New York City next to Central Park.

CHAPTER 17

IT WAS MONDAY, JULY 11, 2011; Hank Johnson's flight from Cleveland to New York arrived three hours late. He checked his cell phone and had several texts from a customer wanting to know where he was. Each one was more urgent. The last one was in all capital letters, a sure sign of trouble. Hank waited to call until he was in the terminal, which was crowded because of delayed flights due to thunderstorms. Hank waded his way through the crowd to find a cab and called his client as he walked.

The client griped, "It's about time you called! Where the hell have you been?"

"The flight was late, I just landed in New York," replied Hank.

"I got your project manager's report. Have you seen it yet?"

"Not yet."

The client complained, "His report said we'll need to pay ten million more than we expected. He said we made design changes so we're responsible for the additional costs. Let me tell you something, we didn't cause these overruns!"

"I'll see him tonight at dinner and get the details."

"You'd better get a handle on this quickly! I have our lawyers ready!"

Hank shoved down his annoyance. "That's why I'm here. I'll bring the team together and report to you tomorrow by noon Chicago time."

"Why can't you call me today?" the client whined. "It's only five-thirty there."

"It will be six-thirty or later before I get downtown. I have dinner with the project manager at seven."

"I need answers quickly; do you understand?"

Hank replied brusquely. "I understand."

The client hung up. The project was a luxury hotel in New York City. The project had been underway for two years and was three months late. This wasn't unusual because construction projects sometimes get off course.

Hank Johnson was sixty-two, average height, and in good shape with brown hair speckled with grey. He was the CEO and the majority owner of an international construction company. Normally, he wouldn't have been involved this much in a construction project; another executive would have been in charge. However, this was a new customer who had several other large hotels planned, so Hank felt he needed to be personally involved.

The trip to New York was set up hastily and his assistant had overlooked getting him a limo. He went to the cab line but it was long and unmoving. The wait would be over an hour in ninety-degree heat. He knew better than to do this, but he walked up to a freelance driver.

The man saw him coming and asked in a foreign accent, "Need limo?"

"Yes, to Central Park East."

"On curb, black Cadillac, sign says Buson Limo, $60 dollars."

Hank walked out to the limo. The driver put his bags into the trunk. As he collapsed into the back seat, he told the driver, "I have a hotel and I thought I had the name in my appointment calendar. Head for Central Park East and I'll find it. Can you turn on the air conditioner? It's hot in here."

The driver said with a thick accent, "Air condition no work, sorry."

Hank swore. "Great! Another day in paradise!"

"Don't know this Paradise. Do you have address?" asked the driver.

Hank stared in disbelief, "Paradise is not the hotel!" Frustrated, he said, "Just a minute and I'll find it." Hank quickly searched his briefcase as sweat dripped into his eyes.

He finally found the trip itinerary. "I'm staying at the Grand Barker Hotel."

"You want Barker not Paradise?"

"I want the Grand Barker Hotel."

"Okie doke."

Hank shook his head. The limo's backseat was stifling with no air conditioning. He quickly removed his coat and tie, which provided little relief. In desperation, he lowered the back windows and it helped some. The drive in was slow due to the traffic and Hank was miserable. They finally arrived at the hotel. Hank tried to give the driver a credit card.

The driver barked, "No take credit card!"

"Really! You won't take a credit card?"

"No take."

Hank opened his wallet. He had only sixty-three dollars, which would leave the driver only a three-dollar tip. Hank decided to get his bags before he gave him the money. Hank got out and so did the driver. The driver got his bags and put them on the curb.

Hank handed the sixty-three dollars to him. The driver counted the money. He was immediately upset. "Three dollar, you give me three-dollar tip. You cheap!"

"Hey buddy, you don't take a credit card so I can't leave you a big tip. All I have is sixty-three."

The driver started yelling at him in his native language. Hank wasn't sure what he was saying but he recognized several universally known cuss words, and the cab driver's hand signs were familiar.

Hank ignored him, picked up his bags then walked into the hotel. The driver stayed at the curb and continued to curse at him.

Hank had never stayed at the Barker. It was a stately, red brick building with a grand lobby. The first thing he noticed was the cool air, which was comforting. He wanted to get to his room and take a shower before dinner. The clerk at the reception desk was friendly and Hank soon had the key card to room 613.

Hank went to the room, unlocked the door, put his bags on the bed, undressed and then took a shower. After a long shower, he felt better. He wrapped a towel around himself and opened the bathroom door.

In the hallway mirror was a woman, a beautiful young woman dressed in a blue dress. She smiled.

Startled, he jumped back, closed the bathroom door and wondered, "Who is that?"

He thought about the situation for a minute. He cracked the door and yelled out, "If this is some kind of joke, it isn't funny!"

He closed the door and waited for a response but the room was quiet. He slowly opened the door and looked at the mirror but didn't see anything. With the towel still around him, he stood in front of the mirror and closely examined it. The mirror was on an outside wall so no one could be behind it. Quickly, he grabbed some clothes, went into the bathroom, closed the door, dressed quickly, and with his hair still wet, headed to the front desk.

At the front desk, Hank asked the clerk for the manager.

The manager quickly arrived. He was a dignified, tall, African American gentleman in his sixties with short graying hair and was dressed in an expensive dark blue suit, white shirt, and light blue silk tie.

"Hello, my name is Cecil Thomas. How may I help you?"

"Mr. Thomas, my name is Hank Johnson and there's a problem in my room."

"Mr. Johnson, let me see if I can help you. What is the problem?"

Hank looked around to see if anyone was listening and whispered, "I was coming out of the bathroom and I saw a woman in the mirror."

Mr. Thomas asked, "What room are you in?"

"My room is 613."

Mr. Thomas gave a brief smile. "Room 613, I understand now. Please step over here and we can talk privately."

Mr. Thomas and Hank walked a few steps away from the front desk.

The manager said quietly, "Mr. Johnson, the woman you saw is Catherine Richardson. Catherine has been a guest of our hotel for over sixty years now. She comes to certain rooms in the hotel and appears in the mirror. She is looking for her lieutenant."

Hank crossed his arms angrily. "Am I on some sort of comedy show or is this some sort of practical joke? I don't find this funny at all."

"No, sir, there is no practical joke here. Let me tell you her story. During War World One, Catherine married a young lieutenant here in New York. The young lieutenant went to France and never came home. Somehow Catherine came to our hotel and she has been looking for her husband since then. She's harmless and she doesn't appear often."

Hank was skeptical, "Really? You're not putting me on?"

"I'm telling you the absolute truth."

"This is hard to believe!" Hank scoffed.

"Would you like a different room? She probably will not return during your visit."

Hank thought for a few seconds and responded, "Yes, I would like another room."

Mr. Thomas gave a brief nod. "No problem. I'll have the bellhop give you a hand."

"Thank you."

In a couple of minutes, Hank had a different room. The first thing he did was check out the mirror and he didn't see anything unusual. Hank got dressed and went to dinner that night with the project manager.

The next day, Hank had a meeting with his team. The project had some issues but it wasn't a disaster. Hank went to the hotel that night and couldn't help thinking about Catherine and the story Mr. Thomas had told him.

Hank called his daughter in Cleveland and told her about the woman in the mirror. At the end, his daughter, in a joking voice, asked, "Have you been hitting the Jack Daniels?"

He laughed and replied, "No Sarah, this is a true story."

"Dad, it's been three years this month since Mom died," she stated in a serious tone.

Hank sighed. "I know, dear. I think about her all the time."

"Do you think your mind is playing tricks on you? I know you miss her terribly." Sarah sounded concerned.

"I talked to the hotel manager and he told me the story. I didn't imagine that part."

Sarah chuckled. "Okay, I'll give you that, but this has to be a prank. You're in New York and they have a number of TV shows produced there."

"I thought about that and I asked him that question. He said no."

Sarah laughed again. "Well, strange things do happen."

Hank shrugged, but then realized she couldn't see his gesture. "It's a great story, don't you think?"

"It's a sad story. The woman has been searching for her husband since the end of World War One and can't find him. Almost a hundred years."

Hank thought for a moment. "Yes, come to think about it, it is sad."

"When are you coming home?" she asked.

"Tomorrow."

"Baby wants to see you. She asks about you every day. Can you stop by?"

"I will."

Sarah hesitated. "Dad?"

"Yes, dear?"

She laughed, "No more Jack Daniels, okay?"

Hank laughed then answered, "Okay, but I haven't been drinking. Love you."

"Love you too."

The following day, Hank flew home.

CHAPTER 18

Over the weekend, Hank couldn't stop thinking about the woman in the mirror. Her story kept running through his mind. He would be going to New York again to check on the hotel project so he thought he would stay at the Barker and learn more about her.

On Tuesday, Hank flew to New York. This time the trip was smooth, and he arrived at the hotel late in the afternoon. He had reserved room 613. He checked in, went to the room, and after putting his bags away, he carefully examined the mirror. The glass had a blue tint and it was clear without any distortions. There was a chair at the desk so he moved it in front of the mirror and sat down. He waited to see if anything happened. Nothing. After a few minutes, disappointed, he went to the telephone and dialed the front desk.

"Is Mr. Thomas in?" he asked.

"No sir," the voice on the other end answered. "He will be back tomorrow afternoon. May I help you with anything?"

"No, I have a question for him. Please have him call my cell phone tomorrow. You have my number on my registration." Hank gave his name and room number.

"Absolutely."

Hank hung up, walked to the mirror, sat down, and watched it for a while. Still nothing happened. He put the chair away and got ready for dinner.

He had dinner with the project manager and the news on the project was improving. After dinner, he returned to his room.

That evening, he checked the mirror several times but didn't see anything. Later he got ready for bed. Normally, he would undress in the room and change into pajamas but for some reason he felt as if he should change in the bathroom. He laughed and muttered, "Catherine is making me shy."

The next day was busy with meetings and after lunch, he got a call on his cell phone from the hotel.

"Hello, this is Hank Johnson."

"Mr. Johnson, this is Cecil Thomas from the Grand Barker Hotel. You left me a message to call you."

"Yes, Mr. Thomas, may I meet with you for a few minutes today?"

"Of course, Mr. Johnson. Is there something I can help you with?"

"No, I have a couple of questions for you."

Mr. Thomas said, "Every day at four-thirty, I have a reception for the guests in the back lobby. There will be wine and food. May we meet then?"

"That's fine. I'll see you at four-thirty."

That evening, Hank left the construction site and went to the reception. Mr. Thomas was there in the back lobby, which had a large reception area. The ceiling was at least three stories high and a balcony surrounded it.

Mr. Thomas said, "Mr. Johnson, thanks for coming back! I'm having some of this fine California Riesling. Would you like a glass?" He held up his drink.

"Yes, please."

Mr. Thomas poured him a glass.

Hank took a sip. "This is excellent!"

"This is my favorite wine," stated Mr. Thomas.

Hank looked at Mr. Thomas, "Mr. Thomas, I have a question for you."

Mr. Thomas grinned. "Let me guess. It is about Catherine, isn't it?"

"It is. I'm having trouble believing the story."

"I know, but it's true," Mr. Thomas responded. "When she first started appearing in the hotel, no one knew who she was. The original hotel owner eventually saw her and recognized her. He knew her and her family. He told me about her."

Hank sipped his wine. "The story intrigues me. Can you tell me any more about her?"

"I know a little more about her. Let's sit and I can tell you what I know."

They moved to a couch.

Mr. Thomas began, "I believe I told you her name is Catherine Richardson and her maiden name is Dawson. Her family owned a well-known company here in New York. Her husband's family owned one of the original Wall Street brokerage firms. It is one of the few brokerage firms to make it through the Depression. They are still in existence today. Catherine and Harrison were only married for a short time before he went to France. He was reported missing and she waited and waited but there was no news about him. She went to Europe to search for him. Unfortunately, she died during the trip."

Hank's face fell. "Very sad!"

"Yes, it is a sad story. That's about all I know. Have you seen her again in the room?"

"No. Do you see her often?"

Mr. Thomas answered, "I have been here thirty years and I have seen her many times. She is a beautiful lady."

"Yes she is."

"Mr. Johnson, what do you do for a living?" Mr. Thomas asked.

"I am the CEO of a construction company. We're building a new luxury hotel a few blocks from here and, like this hotel, it overlooks Central Park."

"Is it the Skyview International?"

Hank nodded.

"The hotel you're building and this hotel are owned by the same company."

Hank was surprised. "No kidding, now I know why my assistant booked me here."

Mr. Thomas asked, "Have you met Mr. Ackerman? He's the chairman of the company."

Hank shook his head. "I have not. How long have you worked for the company?"

"Almost thirty-one years."

Hank motioned at the room around them. "This is a majestic hotel. It has a lot of charm."

"Yes it does, but unfortunately soon after the new hotel opens, this one will be shut down."

Hank was surprised. "That is a shame."

"Yes, the property is worth so much here that it's better for the company to tear it down. They're planning to build luxury condos here."

Hank asked, "Well, I suppose that's progress. Have you seen the design of the new hotel? It will be the best luxury hotel in New York City."

"Yes, I've seen it."

"The penthouse suites will be the hotel's crown jewels. The rich and famous will all want to stay there."

Mr. Thomas studied him for a few seconds and seemed to be thinking about something. "The suites were designed based on the ones we have here. Let me take you up to the grand suite. I want to show you something."

They walked to the elevator. Mr. Thomas took a special key and used it to access the penthouse suite floor. They arrived on the floor and there were several suites.

One was the grand suite; Mr. Thomas opened it for him. The suite was elegant. It had a sitting room, a dining room, a kitchen, and a large master suite.

"Mr. Thomas, this is magnificent! The grand suite at the new hotel has almost an identical layout plus there is a second large master bedroom."

"That would be this one."

Mr. Thomas led him to a door with a lock on it. He used a special card key to open it. The bedroom was large and faced west, offering a view out the windows down on Central Park. The drapes were open and the room was sunny. There was a king size bed in the middle and a door led to an elegant marble bathroom. On both sides of the room were mirrors like the one in Hank's room. Ten mirrors were in the room, five on either side.

Mr. Thomas said, "This is Catherine's room."

"Catherine's room? You mean the Catherine that I saw?"

"Yes, years ago the original hotel owner had these mirrors moved here from the guest rooms. He owned a lot of real estate in the city and was wealthy. Every day at four-thirty, he would come here. He would have a glass of wine and talk to her."

"Catherine speaks?" Hank asked.

Mr. Thomas shook his head. "No, but it is clear that she listens."

"You have talked to her?"

"Oh yes, many times. The first time was when Mr. Ackerman senior passed away; he left specific directions that I was to tell her when he passed. I was a young man and I was afraid to talk to her but I did. She cried when I told her."

"Is this room suite rented to guests?"

"There is only one guest who stays here, Benson Ackerman. As I mentioned to you before, he is the chairman of the company. He's the son of the original owner," Mr. Thomas explained.

"Does he know about Catherine?"

"Yes but he seldom says anything to me about her. Years ago, I suggested to him that we should remove her mirrors from the guest rooms because accidents happen to them. He said she would be upset if she couldn't look for the lieutenant in the guest rooms. So we didn't move them."

"I'm surprised more people don't know about her," Hank commented.

"She appears so seldom in the rooms that our staff doesn't see her. When people ask I won't say anything if I judge they are asking for the wrong reasons."

Hank asked, "What do you mean by the wrong reasons?"

Mr. Thomas hesitated. "You know…if they are a reporter, writer, or some nut job."

"Just so you know, I don't have any motivation other than I would like to know more about Catherine," Hank clarified.

"I believe you. I told you what I know. However, there's a retired schoolteacher who volunteers at the historical association. She knows a lot about Catherine and her family. Her name is Mary King but she is selective about who she talks to, so you may not have any luck with her. Tell her I told you to call. She knows me."

"I will. How often does Catherine come here?"

"She's here all the time," Mr. Thomas answered. "There've been times when I've been here and she'll appear on her own. Let me see if she will appear for us." He turned to a mirror and inquired, "Catherine, are you there?"

In a few seconds, the mirror started to brighten up. Hank stepped back a little.

Catherine appeared, wearing the same blue dress. She had a radiant smile and looked happy. Behind her in the background were flowers and green grass; it was a calm and serene scene. She was carrying a basket of colorful flowers.

"Hello Catherine, it's good to see you. I would like to introduce you to Mr. Hank Johnson. He is a friend of mine."

She smiled at Hank.

Hank was a little nervous and tried to calm himself. He said, "Mrs. Richardson, it is a pleasure to meet you."

She nodded back.

"I'm sorry; at this moment, I'm caught at a loss for words, but let me say this: You are lovely!" said Hank.

She smiled.

"Catherine, Mr. Ackerman will be coming soon. I spoke to him today."

She nodded in understanding.

Mr. Thomas said, "I can't stay long because I need to get back to my guests. Catherine, it was good to see you."

Hank agreed, "Mrs. Richardson, it was a pleasure."

Catherine smiled and then disappeared.

A few moments later as they were walking to the elevator, Hank said, "She is an attractive woman."

Mr. Thomas replied, "One of the prettiest women I have ever seen."

"I would agree."

They returned to the lobby and Hank had another drink with Mr. Thomas. Later he went to his room and ordered dinner. After dinner, he looked at the mirror. He wondered if Catherine would appear if he called for her.

He stood in front of the mirror and asked, "Catherine, are you there?"

Nothing happened; he called again this time saying, "Catherine, this is Hank Johnson. We met this afternoon. Are you there?"

Nothing happened. Disappointed, he grabbed his coat and went for a walk. As soon as the door closed, Catherine appeared in the mirror.

During his walk, Hank thought about everything he had learned about Catherine. He wanted to learn more about her. He decided to call Mary King at the historical association.

CHAPTER 19

THE NEXT MORNING, HANK CALLED the historical association and left a message for Mary King. That afternoon he got a call.

"Hello, this is Hank Johnson," he answered.

"Mr. Johnson, this is Mary King. You left a message for me to call you." She spoke with a Southern accent.

"Yes, I did. Thank you for calling. I wanted to ask about Catherine Richardson."

The line was silent.

"Ms. King, are you there?"

In a serious tone, she replied, "Yes. Why are you calling about Catherine?"

"I have stayed at the Barker and I saw her in a mirror."

The line was silent again.

"Did I lose you?" he asked.

In a serious tone, she replied, "No, I'm here. I don't provide information over the phone about Catherine."

"Okay. May we meet and talk?"

She continued in a serious tone, "I would need some information first. Let's start with what you do."

"I am the chairman and chief executive officer for Johnson Construction."

"You are not a reporter, writer, or an investigator." Her question came across as a statement.

"No."

"Is your name Hank Johnson or Henry Johnson?"

"My mother named me Henry but I prefer Hank."

Another pause. "How did you learn about me?"

"Mr. Thomas at the Grand Barker Hotel recommended I call you."

"Mr. Johnson, let me think about this," Mary answered.

"That's fine. I'll be in New York next week on Tuesday. Can we get together for lunch on Wednesday or Thursday?"

Mary said hesitantly, "I'll call you and let you know if I can make it."

"I hope you can. Thank you and goodbye."

"Goodbye," said Mary and she hung up.

Hank wondered about Mary. She seemed like a serious person. He pictured her as a gray-haired, stern old woman. He thought meeting with her might be a bad idea.

Over the next few days, Hank didn't hear anything from her. He was getting ready to leave for the airport on Tuesday morning to fly to New York when he got a call from a New York number.

"Hello, this is Hank Johnson."

"Mr. Johnson, this is Mary King. We talked last week." Her voice seemed cheerier than she was last time they spoke.

"Yes, how are you?"

"I'm fine, thank you. I'm available for coffee tomorrow at three-thirty if that's good for you?"

Hank replied, "That would be fine. We can meet at the Barker."

"I would rather meet somewhere other than a hotel. Down the street from the hotel is Blanchard coffee shop."

Hank recognized the name. "Yes, I know the place."

"I'll see you there at three-thirty," she confirmed.

"Thank you for calling," said Hank.

That afternoon, Hank flew to New York. He stayed at the Barker but room 613 had already been taken. On Wednesday afternoon, his meetings ran long and he was late getting to the coffee shop. He rushed in and there were three women sitting at different tables.

The first woman to his left was a slender pretty blonde who was fashionably dressed. He ruled her out because he was sure Mary was much older. The second woman was young, probably in her late twenties. He ruled her out because she was too young. The next woman had shoulder-length gray hair pulled into a ponytail. She was wearing black round-rimmed glasses and was reading a book. She looked like a retired schoolteacher. Hank murmured to himself, "That's Mary."

He walked up to the woman and asked, "Are you Mary King?"

The woman looked up at him, annoyed then grumbled, "No, I'm not."

He had guessed wrong. Embarrassed, Hank replied, "I beg your pardon. Sorry to bother you."

He heard a voice behind him say, "I'm Mary King."

He turned and it was the pretty blonde. He walked to her and smiled widely, "Mary, I'm Hank Johnson. It's a pleasure to meet you."

Mary had a nice smile and had lovely chocolate brown eyes. Her hair was almost shoulder length with slight curls. Mary reached out her hand. "I'm pleased to meet you as well."

"I'm sorry I'm late. Everything today took longer than I expected."

She smiled. "That's okay. I've only been here a couple of minutes myself."

A waitress carrying a pot of coffee walked up. "Would you like coffee?"

Mary said, "Yes, please."

"I would as well," said Hank.

The waitress poured them coffee and left.

Hank said, "Thank you for meeting with me. Judging from the questions you asked me on the phone, you're cautious about discussing Catherine."

Mary nodded. "I am, because there are too many crazy people in this world and I have talked to several of them about Catherine. I try to weed them out before I meet with them in person."

"Why did you decide to meet with me?"

"I called Mr. Thomas and he said you were a nice man. I also looked you up on the internet. You didn't look like a serial killer or anything."

Hank laughed, "Thank you for that."

She smiled and said, "That came out the wrong way. I meant from seeing your picture on the internet and from what I read, you seem to be a normal person. You are a successful person according to what I could find."

"It's been a busy life. I have to tell you, though, I was expecting someone entirely different."

She laughed. "You were?"

"Yes, Mr. Thomas told me you were a retired schoolteacher."

"That's correct; I'm a retired history teacher."

"In my experience, retired school teachers aren't...." He paused as if he was searching for the right words. "Please excuse me if this is inappropriate since we just met, but in my experience, retired schoolteachers aren't as pretty as you are and not nearly so fashionable."

"Well bless your heart! That is so nice of you! Thank you for the compliment." She was smiling and her eyes sparkled.

"I can tell by your accent you aren't from New York. Let me take a guess—I would say South Carolina."

"You're close. I'm from Georgia."

Hank commented, “I love the southern expression ‘Bless your heart.’ My mother used it often. She was from the South.”

Mary added in a joking tone, “Oh yes, a Southern woman can use it to deliver any message with grace. Such as ‘Bless your heart, did your momma drop you on your head when you were a baby?’”

They laughed.

Hank said, “When I came home on leave from the Army, my shaved head looked like a potato. My mother saw me and said ‘Bless your heart, your hair looks awful! Are you going to keep it that way? I hope not!’ Whenever I hear that expression, I think of her.”

Mary laughed. Hank liked her laugh.

Hank went on, “My mother had a unique way of giving some sugar with the sour, if you know what I mean.”

“I do indeed.”

Hank inquired, “So how did a Southern girl end up in New York?”

“When my husband died a few years ago, I decided to move here to be with my daughter. She works for an international fashion company and travels a lot, so I often have a large home to myself.”

Hank nodded. “My wife also passed away. It was three years ago from cancer.”

“I’m sorry. Jimmy died from a heart attack.”

“Life is so damn short,” said Hank as he shook his head.

"It is."

There was a long, awkward pause.

Mary asked, "Do you have children?"

"Yes. I have a daughter and she has two girls. I love my grandbabies and spend as much time with them as I can. I have a few pictures if you don't mind seeing them."

Mary grinned. "Not at all."

Hank proudly showed her pictures of his family on his phone. "You mentioned a daughter; do you have other children?"

Mary shook her head. "Just one daughter."

"Do you have grandchildren?"

"Not yet, but I hope for some. I have some pictures of my daughter." Mary showed him pictures too. As Mary talked, Hank thought she came across as intelligent and unlike what he thought when he first talked to her, he found she was happy and outgoing.

"I hope I haven't bored you with my pictures," she said.

"Not at all. Seeing pictures of a person's family is a good way to get to know them."

"I agree." Mary changed the subject. "Now Mr. Johnson, how did you come to know Catherine?"

"Please call me Hank."

"Okay, Hank. How did you come to know Catherine?"

"I was staying at Barker recently and saw her in a mirror. I was startled at first but as I learned more about her, I have become intrigued with her story. How did you discover her?" he asked.

"My daughter moved to New York from Atlanta a few years ago. I would come to visit her during my summer break. When my daughter traveled, I was alone. As a history teacher, I love all the stories that are out there. I spent a lot of time at the historical association reading about the city. I made friends with a woman there who did some research on Catherine. We became good friends. Her aunt worked at the Barker and told her about Catherine. My friend introduced me to Mr. Thomas, who let me see Catherine in one of the rooms. My friend also knew Jacob Dawson and she introduced me to him a few months ago. Jacob is the grandson of Howard Dawson, who was Catherine's brother. My friend at the historical society moved to California and she gave me her file on Catherine."

"Would you mind sharing some of Catherine's story with me?"

"Why do you want to know?"

Hank said, "I enjoy history and stories like this. I loved history in high school. I thought in college I would continue with it along with engineering. The first day of my freshman American history class, the professor listed five books we would have to read that semester. I dropped the class that day."

Mary agreed, "Yes, they piled the reading on me as well."

"I guess the real reason I want to know about her is because her story is so sad. They get married then he goes to war. He ends up missing. She goes there looking for him and dies there. I didn't know people traveled to Europe during the war."

"Yes, it was dangerous, but people did. Did you know during World War One, the English Channel ferries actually continued to go back and forth between England and Europe? One ferry actually rammed a U-boat intentionally."

He laughed. "See, that's what I find interesting."

"I do too. Now let me tell you a little more about Catherine."

Mary told Hank the story. She told him everything she knew about Catherine, Harrison, and their families.

Hank asked, "Does the Dawson family know about Catherine being in the mirror?"

"Not that I know of."

Hank enjoyed the story and he liked what he saw in Mary. As he listened, he wanted to learn about Catherine but he also wanted to learn more about Mary.

It was getting close to five o'clock and Hank asked, "I'm starting to get hungry. Do you have plans for dinner?"

"No, but I'm not dressed for dinner."

"You're not? To me, you look lovely in that sweater and skirt."

Mary smiled. "Thank you, but it's not nice enough for dinner."

"How about dinner tomorrow evening and you can continue your story?"

Mary's smile widened. "I would like that."

"How about seven o'clock at Bellisarios?"

"That works for me."

Hank smiled, then stood. "Mary, it has been a pleasure."

"For me as well." She shook his hand. "I look forward to tomorrow."

They left together. He watched as she walked away, thinking about what a nice meeting he had with her. She was smart, outgoing, had a good sense of humor and a positive outlook. He had met her because of Catherine but his interest was now more in Mary.

CHAPTER 20

THE NEXT DAY, HANK COULDN'T get Mary out of his thoughts. During his meetings, he would think about their discussion. Hank was anxious about their dinner and decided he needed to be better dressed. He left the building site early and bought a tie and shirt.

He arrived for dinner ten minutes early. Promptly at seven, Mary arrived. She was wearing a red dress with a low neckline, pearls, black pumps, and carried a black designer purse. The maître d' escorted her to the table and she smiled as she approached. Hank stood to greet her.

She said, "Good evening."

"Good evening to you." He helped her with her chair. "I love that dress!" he said then sat down.

"Thank you! I love your tie."

Hank grinned. "Thank you! I bought it today."

"If a man buys a tie for a dinner, it must be an important dinner," Mary stated with a smile.

"It is important. I want to tell you how much I enjoyed our conversation yesterday. I thought about you a lot today."

"You thought about me or our conversation?"

Hank was caught. "Ahh, well, is it okay if I thought about both?"

A small grin appeared on her face. "Absolutely! A girl always wants to be thought about."

"That's good. Now have you been here before for dinner?"

Mary shook her head no.

Hank declared, "Their seafood is exquisite and they're known for their desserts."

"I had a busy day and missed lunch so I'm starved."

Hank suggested, "Let's start with some wine."

They ordered wine then dinner and started talking about their lives. The time flew. They finished dinner then ordered dessert and coffee.

Mary observed, "We have been gabbing here all evening and haven't said one word about Catherine."

Hank agreed, "You're right. I got so caught up with the real woman I forgot about the one in the mirror."

"Did you want to talk about Catherine?"

"Yes, but I don't want to talk about her so much that you feel neglected."

She smiled. "Not at all, I have had a wonderful time."

"Me too."

"So let me give you more information on her." She picked up her bag and pulled out a brown leather notebook. She opened it then placed some old black and white photographs on the table.

"These photos I got from Jacob Dawson. He is the grandson of Howard Dawson, Catherine's brother. This is a wedding picture of Catherine and Harrison. They were a handsome couple; don't you think?"

Hank examined the photo. "This is the woman I saw; she is beautiful. He certainly looks the part of a West Point Army officer."

"Yes he does. Now these photos are of Douglas Dawson, her grandfather. Catherine loved him dearly. The first one is at Catherine's wedding and the others are with his motorcars. He loved cars and was one of the first in the city to have one. Jacob Dawson has three of Douglas' cars in his collection."

"He was a handsome man but his clothes don't look like a New York gentleman. They look Western," commented Hank.

"Yes, I think so too."

Hank said, "I thought most men of that era had a mustache or beard."

"I read in Catherine's diary he didn't wear them because his wife said they tickled her."

"Her diary?"

"Yes, I have Catherine's diary."

Hank was flabbergasted. "How did you get that?"

"Jacob Dawson loaned me her diary, all of Harrison's letters to her, which her mother saved, plus Douglas Dawson's diary. I also have Douglas' lab notes, an ancient red leather bound book on glassmaking that is in Latin, numerous books, and his letters to Howard Dawson."

"Wow!"

"Oh yes, it is quite a collection. When I first met Jacob, I told him I was a history teacher and I was interested in Catherine's story. He said he would give me access to all his family files. I had to sign an inch-thick set of legal documents before Jacob would lend the collection to me. All the material will keep me busy for years."

"Have you read much of it?"

"I have read Catherine's diary and a few letters. Reading all the material will take a long time. I remember one letter from Douglas to Howard, which was heartbreaking. Douglas searched for Harrison's grave after the war in Germany but couldn't find it. He pleaded with Howard to look for it when times improved there. I don't know if Howard ever did."

Hank looked down. "That is sad."

"Yes, it is. I have also read a couple of Harrison's letters. The letters clearly showed his deep love for her. The letters were sweet, but at times he also described the horrors he saw in the trenches."

"Their story is fascinating to me."

"It is a great story," she replied.

"Have you been to Catherine's room at the hotel?"

Mary was surprised and asked, "What? Catherine has a *room*?"

"Yes, Catherine has a room at the hotel in their grand suite. Mr. Thomas took me there. Ten mirrors are in the room and she appears in them. The first owner of the hotel met with her there every day at four-thirty."

"No kidding, she has her own room? None of the material I've read in the files ever mentioned that Catherine has a room. I thought I would be teaching you about Catherine, but now you're the one teaching me."

"Maybe we can have Mr. Thomas take us to her room."

Mary lit up. "I would love that."

"I'll call him in the morning and ask. Oh geez, I forgot. I'm supposed to fly home tomorrow."

She shrugged. "That's fine. We can do it next week."

Hank thought for a second then asked, "I really don't have anything pressing at home. I'll stay over. Do you have plans for this weekend?"

"I don't. My daughter is away in Europe and won't be back for two weeks."

"Are you sure I'm not imposing on you or interrupting any plans you have?"

She studied him for a few seconds then asked, "Hank, exactly what are you delicately probing for?"

Hank was honest. "I'm sure there must be a man in your life somewhere."

"No there is no man in my life and I have no plans for this weekend. Now what about you, are there women in your life?"

"Yes, my daughter and my granddaughters."

Mary laughed. "I don't believe they're the only ones. You are handsome and other than being from Tennessee, I haven't found any real problems with you so far."

"What's wrong with being from Tennessee?"

"My mother told me to watch out for men from Tennessee because they're smooth talkers."

"Smooth talkers?" Hank chuckled.

"Yes."

"Do I sound like a smooth talker?"

She teased him, "I can't tell yet, but I'm keeping my eye on you."

Hank smiled and said, "That's good to know."

Mary asked, "So you aren't seeing anyone?"

"My daughter has introduced me to a couple of women but there's nothing serious."

"I bet they're younger women," she stated with confidence.

"What do you mean younger women?"

"Younger than I am."

Hank shrugged. "I don't know how old you are."

"I'm sixty-two."

"So am I."

"So, does she want you to see younger women?"

"My daughter is younger so the women she knows are younger."

Mary looked at him. "How about you? Do you prefer younger women?"

"Mary, when I saw you I thought you were much younger. Knowing that you're my age is a good thing."

"Are you sure?"

"Why wouldn't I be? I think you're beautiful."

"Thank you! I hope you mean that." She blushed.

"Of course I do. I thought you were from the first moment I saw you."

"See, there's some of that smooth Tennessee talk." She laughed.

Hank laughed as well. "So tomorrow, I'll talk to Mr. Thomas about you seeing Catherine's room. I'll call you to confirm. May I have your cell number?"

"Yes." Mary wrote down her number and gave it to him.

"Also tomorrow, we can make plans for the weekend. I haven't been to a Broadway show in years. Would you like to go?"

Mary nodded. "Absolutely." She gathered her purse. "Thank you for a wonderful dinner!"

Hank smiled and said, "You are welcome. I had a good time."

They stood and walked to the front door. Hank leaned in and gave her a gentle kiss on the cheek. He helped her into a cab then walked back to the hotel.

CHAPTER 21

The next morning Hank called Mr. Thomas and asked if Mary could see Catherine's room. Mr. Thomas agreed she could see it during the manager's reception and Hank called Mary to tell her.

At four-thirty, Hank met Mary in the lobby. She was wearing a figure-flattering, tailored grey suit with a maroon blouse and gray sling-back heels, and carried a maroon purse.

Hank said, "Good afternoon."

"Good afternoon to you."

"Every time we meet, you are always wearing the nicest clothes," he complimented her.

"Thank you! It pays to have a daughter in the fashion industry who also wears the same size you do. I'm so excited to see Catherine's room."

Hank nodded. "Let's see if Mr. Thomas is ready."

They walked to the reception area and Mr. Thomas was there talking to a guest. He saw Mary then said, "Mrs. King, it is good to see you again."

"Mr. Thomas, it's good to see you too."

"Please both of you call me Cecil. So are you ready to see Catherine's room?"

"Oh yes, I have been thinking about it all day," said Mary.

Cecil led them to the elevator and using his special key he took them to the penthouse floor. He unlocked the grand suite and let them in.

"Now isn't this elegant! I always wondered what a penthouse suite looked like. Do you think I could move in?" asked Mary.

Cecil laughed, "I would have to check with the owner. Now over here is Catherine's room."

He unlocked the door.

Mary looked around, "This is wonderful! No wonder she comes here." Mary walked to the window, looked out on the park and said, "It is such a fantastic view of the park. I know Catherine loved going there. In her diary, she wrote about how much she enjoyed promenading through the park with her family on Sundays. She wrote several pages about being with Harrison in the park on the day of their engagement party. She was so in love with him."

As she spoke, Cecil reached out and touched Hank's arm then nodded to a mirror. Catherine was there.

Mary continued, "That day in the park, she and Harrison went to a garden by the water fountain. They had lemonade and they kissed in the garden. She described it as romantic and sweet."

Cecil said, "Mary, there's someone to see you."

Mary turned around and was surprised to see Catherine.

Cecil said, "Catherine, this is Mary King; you met her some time ago."

Catherine nodded her head.

"I didn't know you had Catherine's diary," stated Cecil.

"Oh yes, let me explain how I got it."

She turned to Catherine. "Catherine, let me tell you why I have your most personal possession, your diary. Your brother's grandson, Jacob Dawson, lent the diary to me. He has allowed me to read your diary and some other materials about your family. I have and will treat them with the greatest respect."

Catherine nodded.

Cecil said, "Catherine, you remember Hank Johnson."

Catherine smiled.

Hank said, "It's a pleasure to see you again."

Behind them in the other room, there was some noise as if someone was entering the suite. Catherine disappeared.

An older man in a brown suit and white shirt walked in slowly with the aid of a cane. He had thinning grey hair and gold, round-rimmed glasses.

The man asked, "Cecil, is everything okay?"

Cecil's demeanor changed; he was clearly nervous. "Yes Mr. Ackerman, everything is fine. I wasn't expecting you till next week."

"I decided to come early. Who are these people?" He gestured at Mary and Hank angrily.

"Mrs. King and Mr. Johnson are here to see the suite," Cecil replied.

"Cecil, you know I don't like people coming in here."

Cecil bowed his head, "Yes sir, please accept my apology but Mrs. King is a friend of mine and I wanted her to see the grand suite." He looked at Mr. Ackerman and said, "Please let me introduce them to you."

Mr. Ackerman abruptly replied, "Maybe some other time. I'm tired from traveling and I would like to be alone and rest."

"Of course, Mr. Ackerman."

Mr. Ackerman turned and left.

Hank whispered, "Did I get you in trouble?"

"No, everything will be fine. We need to leave."

Cecil escorted Hank and Mary to the elevator.

Mary said, "Cecil, thank you for letting me visit her suite."

"You are welcome. I'll come down to the reception in a few minutes after I have checked on Mr. Ackerman."

Once in the elevator, Mary reflected, "Did you notice how pretty her dress is? I love that deep sky blue color."

"I do like her dress." Hank changed the subject. "I hope I didn't get Cecil into trouble with Mr. Ackerman."

"Maybe Mr. Ackerman is tired from his trip."

"Hopefully."

They got to the lobby and enjoyed a glass of wine as they waited for Cecil.

Ten minutes later, Cecil returned. He looked upset.

Hank asked, "Are you okay?"

Cecil gave a brief smile, trying to assure them all was well. "Mr. Ackerman is angry. He is afraid someone will take her away."

Mary suggested, "Maybe I should talk to him and assure him we won't tell anyone."

"I did that."

Hank asked, "Can you patch it up with him?"

"Mr. Ackerman has a bad temper and he gets upset easily. I had to agree not to let anyone else in Catherine's room without his permission. I left so he could calm down. He will be in a better mood in a bit."

Mary smiled timidly. "Thank you again for showing me her room."

Cecil said, "You are welcome. Mary, Catherine seems to respond to you well. I think she likes you."

Mary's smile widened. "I hope she does. I have the greatest respect and admiration for her."

Cecil stood. "I need to see to the other guests then I need to check on Mr. Ackerman and make sure he has everything he needs. It was a pleasure seeing you again. Do you have plans for dinner?"

Hank answered, "We do; as a matter of fact, we will be late for our reservations if we don't hustle."

CHAPTER 22

After talking to some guests for a few minutes, Cecil took the elevator to the penthouse floor. He knocked on the grand suite's door but there was no answer. He waited and knocked again. No answer. He let himself in. The door to Catherine's room was open. He walked up to it quietly and heard Mr. Ackerman calling for Catherine.

"Catherine, are you there? This is Benson. I need to talk to you."

It was quiet for a few seconds.

"Please Catherine, are you there?" pleaded Mr. Ackerman.

A few seconds passed then he said, "There you are. I'm so happy to see you again. You look lovely. I would like to talk to you if you don't mind. I'm a little tired from my travel today so I think I'll sit while we talk."

He heard Mr. Ackerman slowly pull a rocking chair across the oak floor.

"Do you remember when I used to sit here and talk to you for hours? I miss talking to you. I would come to New

York to check on my properties and I could always count on you to be here. You helped me with so many problems I have faced over the years. There's one I need your help with now."

Mr. Ackerman paused as if he was thinking or gathering his strength.

"I'm sorry I haven't been here for a while. I have some bad news to tell you. I have a small brain tumor that is inoperable and is terminal."

Cecil gasped quietly as he heard the news.

"I have seen several specialists and they all say the same thing. They can't do anything about it. It is small now but they say it will grow. Right now, I only feel some weakness in my left hand but over time, it will get worse. The doctors say I need to cut back on my travel."

Mr. Ackerman paused. "No Catherine, please don't cry! We knew someday something like this would happen. Somehow, I was hoping you would be released from the mirrors and we could be together before I passed."

The tone of his voice went higher and louder. "Please, please don't go! I know I shouldn't be saying these things to you. I know you are a married woman."

There was a pause for a few seconds then Mr. Ackerman, his voice softer, said, "I know you don't like it when I say these things but I love you. You know I do. When I met you as a teenager the first time, I fell in love with you. You were so beautiful then and you are now. I have tried to find someone else I could love more than you but I haven't. I have had two wives, but looking back now, I never really loved either one. I always wanted to be here with you. When my parents divorced and my mother moved my sister and me to Chicago, I hated being away from you. I looked forward to my summer school vacation and holidays so I could be with you."

He paused for a few seconds then continued.

"My sister, as you know, lives with me in Chicago. I promised my mother that I would take care of her. She was born disabled and is now in bad health. I need to be there with her until she passes, which according to the doctors won't be long. I want you in Chicago with me. I don't know how many months or years I have left but I want you to be with me. Now I know this is new and you don't like change but I need to do this."

He sounded out of breath and there was a pause as he gathered his strength.

"I promise you won't have to stay in Chicago long. We will return to New York. We will discuss this over the next few days. I'm sure this is the best for everyone." He paused. "I'm too tired to talk anymore about it today. I'll talk to you tomorrow. Good night, sweetheart." Another pause. "I love you!"

Cecil heard Mr. Ackerman take a step and he quickly returned to the front door. He yelled out, "Mr. Ackerman are you okay?"

Mr. Ackerman walked out from Catherine's door and answered "Yes."

"I'll be leaving soon and I wanted to see if you need anything."

"Thank you, I'm fine."

Mr. Ackerman paused for a few seconds as if he was considering something. "Second thought, there is something I want to talk about if you have a minute."

"Yes sir."

"Have a seat here."

Cecil and Mr. Ackerman sat on a couch.

"Cecil, we have known each other for thirty years now."

Cecil nodded. "Yes sir, it will be thirty-one years in December."

"You have always done an excellent job here."

"Thank you, sir."

"My health is failing and I'll be cutting back on traveling."

"I'm sorry to hear that."

"Just because I'm not here doesn't mean you won't be taken care of. I know you plan to retire soon and when you do, I'll make sure you will continue to receive your current salary."

Cecil was surprised. "That's generous of you! Thank you!"

"However, there's one condition. You know we are building a new hotel. It will be the finest hotel in the country. I know you want to retire this year. I would like you to stay until the new hotel is finished. I need you to check on the progress of Catherine's new suite. It must be finished exactly the way I designed it. I'll move into the suite when it is finished. I need you to make sure this gets done because I don't trust anyone else."

Cecil nodded. "I'll make sure it happens. You can count on me."

"I need you to pack the ten mirrors in Catherine's room and send them to Chicago. I have locations set aside for them in my home. How many mirrors are left now?"

"Thirty including the ten here."

"The ten in Catherine's room, I want you to pack them carefully," Mr. Ackerman instructed. "I was thinking about using padded cases, like the ones used for shipping musical instruments."

"Yes sir. I know what you mean. I'll take care of it."

"Make the shipments in two separate trucks, in case there is an accident. Now one other thing…seeing those people today in her room worries me. We can't let anyone else see Catherine again. Please take the mirrors out of the guest rooms. Pack those mirrors in the same kind of padded cases and put them in a safe warehouse."

"Sir, you don't need to worry about the people today," Cecil assured him.

Mr. Ackerman was hesitant. "Are you sure?"

"Yes sir."

"That's good. However, I still want you to move the mirrors. Next week, you can start preparing for the move. I want this done quickly!"

Cecil nodded again. "Yes sir."

"Now you have a good weekend and I'll see you on Monday."

"Sir, you know I always stop in to check on you. So I'll see you tomorrow."

Mr. Ackerman laughed. "I know. I was trying to let you off the hook."

Cecil smiled. "I'll see you tomorrow. Good night."

CHAPTER 23

DURING DINNER, HANK AND MARY made plans for the weekend. Mary had always wanted to see the estate where Catherine and Harrison had honeymooned. It was open to the public and was a popular place to visit. The two decided they would drive to Long Island to see it on Saturday morning and then that evening go to a Broadway show.

On Saturday morning, Mary went to Hank's hotel. They met up, walked two blocks to a car rental, and picked up a car. Soon they were maneuvering through New York traffic on the way to the Hamptons. It was a great day for a drive on Long Island. The traffic was light and they made good time getting there.

The estate was now an upscale bed and breakfast. They toured the estate, walked the grounds, then strolled by the seaside watching the boats in the bay.

Mary commented, "Isn't this place gorgeous? I see why Catherine loved it here."

"It is. This would have been a great place for a honeymoon."

Mary nodded. "Catherine wrote a lot about her honeymoon and the estate. They had a wonderful time here."

Hank asked, "Have you been on the water much?"

"Not really," Mary answered. "Growing up in Atlanta, we went to the Gulf on vacation and went boating on the lakes nearby but not a lot. How about you?"

"My grandfather had a house on Lake Erie east of Cleveland. Every summer, I spent a lot of time there. He taught me to sail. As a kid, I would race small sailboats on the lake. I enjoy sailing. I rent a boat and go out on the lake a few times each summer. I have always wanted to own a sailboat but there always seemed something more pressing to do. I have been thinking about it more the last couple of years. Seeing these boats gives me the itch to buy one."

Mary sighed wistfully. "Sailing has always seemed romantic to me."

"It is to me too. The waves, the wind and the warm weather are a wonderful way to unwind. Have you ever been to Cleveland?"

"No, I haven't."

"Maybe you can visit and we can go sailing."

Mary teased him, "I'll have to think about that because I'm still trying to decide if you are a gentleman or not."

He jokingly choked. "You are still evaluating me?"

Mary continued to tease him. "Yes, I am. The reason for that is we were never formally introduced. My mother told me a man had to be properly presented to a woman.

He had to be presented by a family member or someone who was trusted. The other men in my life were properly presented. You showed up in a coffee shop and said here I am. For all I know, you could be a serial killer. We could go sailing and I might not return."

"Afraid I might get you out onto the lake and drop you in?"

She smiled, "Maybe."

"If you are worried about being with me in a sailboat on Lake Erie, would you consider a cruise?"

"You mean on one of those huge ships where people seem to fall into the sea mysteriously then someone cashes in on a recently purchased life insurance policy? No! I'm not interested. Also, don't say anything about going to some Caribbean island somewhere either; seems like Southern girls don't return from trips down there." She laughed.

Hank laughed along with her and said, "Maybe I should be the one who should worry. You seem to have thought about this a lot. Maybe too much."

They laughed.

Mary suggested, "Kidding aside, I would love to visit Ohio and meet your family."

"Maybe we can do that in the future."

"I would enjoy that." She changed the subject. "I want to thank you again for taking me to Catherine's room yesterday."

"I'm glad we could get in."

Mary said, "Last night as I was trying to sleep, I kept thinking of her. It's so sad that she's stuck in time. I have often wondered if I could help her in some way."

"How?"

She shrugged. "I'm not sure. Maybe finding her husband's grave."

"How would that help?"

"I don't know if it would help but I feel as if I need to do something to free her. I often wonder how much longer she'll have to look for him."

Hank reflected, "When you look at her, she doesn't look sad. She looks happy—almost as if she knows he will soon be there."

Mary thought for a moment. "According to her diary, she was ill when she learned he was a prisoner of war. She thought he was alive and would come home to her. There's no stronger force than faith. She had faith he would return and I think that's why she's here. I believe the key is finding Harrison's grave."

"Then what?"

She said, "I don't know, but without knowing where he is, she will keep looking for him. I have always wanted to go and search for him but I don't have the money to do it."

"I have the money."

"What?" Mary sputtered.

Hank repeated, "I have the money to help you search."

She laughed incredulously. "It could take a lot of money to do this."

"I have a lot of money."

"I couldn't ask you to do that." She shook her head.

"Let me suggest an idea. You are still examining me, right?" asked Hank.

She hesitated. "Well, we have only recently met."

"Since we can't be formally introduced according to Southern tradition, maybe we get to know each other by going on an adventure together," he suggested.

"An adventure? That does sound like fun," said Mary.

"We should go to Europe and look for him."

Mary's eyes lit up. "I would absolutely love to!"

"We could go anytime you want. I'm the boss so I control my schedule."

Mary offered, "Maybe we can start by going to Ohio first."

Hank agreed. "That's a good idea. If you survive a trip to Ohio, then maybe we can go to Europe." He laughed.

"Maybe you might not want to travel to Europe after spending time with me in Ohio," she countered.

Hank replied, "I seriously doubt that."

She asked, "No boats if we go to Cleveland, correct?"

"Yes, no boats." He chuckled.

"There's a lot of research I need to do before we go to Europe."

"That's okay with me. We'll go when you're ready."

Mary thought for a moment. "What happens if we can't find him on that trip?"

"I'm in no rush; we can always go back."

"We have some plans to work out together, don't we?" asked Mary.

Hank smiled. "We do."

"Now, we need to get back to the city and get ready for the show. Are you picking me up at my house tonight?" asked Mary.

"Only if you think I'm not dangerous." He laughed.

"I'm not sure of that yet but I have a gun and I know how to use it so I'll be safe there," she said with a wide smile.

Not knowing if she was kidding, Hank questioned, "You have a gun? Okay, good to know."

Mary's cell phone rang. She walked away a few steps and talked for a few minutes. She returned and she was smiling.

Hank asked, "Was that one of your boyfriends?"

"Are you jealous?"

"Should I be?"

Mary stated, "You should always be jealous."

"Then yes, I'm jealous."

"The call was from a friend of mine. She was calling to make sure I was okay."

"Why would you not be okay?"

"She knew I was going to be with you today. She wanted to make sure she didn't need to send the police or something."

Hank laughed. "Really?"

"Yes."

"I guess that's good she's checking up on you…but you are cautious about who you see, aren't you?" Hank said.

Mary replied, "Well you know we haven't—"

Hank interrupted her, "I know, I know. We haven't been properly introduced."

Mary laughed, "See, you're learning."

CHAPTER 24

THAT EVENING, HANK WENT TO Mary's home. He arrived early and waited outside for a few minutes. Her home was a restored and stately brownstone with a large welcoming porch. Hank rang the bell and Mary answered.

"I see you're right on time. Please come in."

Hank entered and she closed the door. "I wasn't sure if being prompt was part of the evaluation process so I've been outside for ten minutes. I didn't want to be early."

She giggled. "Being prompt is part of the evaluation process, not early and not late, right on time. You have passed another test."

"That's good; I want to be the teacher's pet." Hank leaned in and kissed her on the cheek.

She grinned, "You passed that test too. That was a nice welcoming kiss."

"What if it had been a real kiss?"

She scoffed. "Sorry, there would be points off for that."

"I'm doing my best to learn the rules."

"Now an important thing for you to remember is I can change the rules at any time." She waved her finger in the air at him.

He shrugged. "I figured that."

He looked around and said, "I love the decorating."

"Thank you! When I moved here, my daughter had recently bought it but there wasn't a stick of furniture except for her bed. I brought my furniture up from Atlanta. I love decorating. I'm always moving furniture around. From time to time, I'll test you on the decorating changes that I make. I'll be disappointed if you don't notice."

"Oh geez, maybe you should kick me to the curb now."

She looked confused. "Why is that?"

"I get into my little world and don't pay a lot of attention to things around me. I once came home from a trip to a garage door that was knocked in by my teenage daughter and I didn't notice it."

"Really?" She laughed, unbelieving.

"Yes, my daughter was learning to drive and mistook the gas pedal for the brake. She ran through the garage door. She and her mom pushed it back up. It had a big dent in it but I never noticed it. They quickly got it repaired then told me."

Mary laughed, "Sometimes we women do have to hide a few things from our men. In order to help you,

I'll give you some tutoring on what kind of decorating changes you need to look for."

"Please do. One of my fantasies has always been to be tutored privately by a pretty teacher."

"Now Hank! Let's not get ahead of ourselves here." They laughed.

He said, "We should get going, I would like to get a bite before the show if that's okay with you."

"I was hoping we would. I'm starved."

They left and got a cab to the theater district, then had a quick dinner and went to the show. They got back to her home at eleven. He walked her up the steps to the front door.

She exclaimed, "It's been a wonderful day! Thank you for spending it with me."

He agreed. "I've enjoyed it. Now tomorrow, we are having brunch right?"

"Yes, I know a place near the hotel. I think you'll like it."

"I'll meet you in the lobby at ten o'clock."

She nodded. "That works for me."

He looked at her for a second, deciding what he should do next.

She said, "You had better kiss me or you'll get points off."

He grinned. "That's what I had decided but it's good to have the teacher verify it."

He stepped forward, put his arms around her, and kissed her. It was a long kiss.

She pulled back from the kiss and whispered softly, "Now that was a good kiss!"

"I can do better."

She giggled. "That will be hard to do because you did a great job with that one."

Hank smiled, "I'll see you tomorrow at ten."

"Yes, you will."

Hank walked down the porch to the sidewalk. She was still standing on the top step looking at him as if she was thinking about something.

He said, "Are you going to stay outside?"

She grinned. "I was thinking."

"About what?"

She answered, "What a nice day I had and that I have kissed a few men in my life who were frogs. I don't think you're a frog."

Hank walked up the steps, took her in his arms, and kissed her again.

She pulled back from the kiss and said, "You are definitely not a frog. Not quite sure you are a prince yet, though."

"Maybe I can be a lord?"

She considered. "Lord Hank, maybe."

"I've never had a woman call me lord before. I like it."

"Oh Lord, what have I done?" she asked.

"See, you have it down already."

CHAPTER 25

Over the next few weeks, Hank and Mary spent a lot of time together. Hank met Mary's daughter Katie then Mary traveled to Ohio to meet his family. Hank traveled back and forth between New York and Cleveland often. Mary was happy with how the relationship was growing and agreed they should go to Germany.

Mary got the prison's name from Catherine's diary and she made a number of calls to Germany. She made an appointment with the Wittenberg prison camp military cemetery trustee. In order to get there before winter, they left for Germany in late September.

They arrived in Wittenberg, Germany mid-day on a Saturday—and by coincidence, it was Oktoberfest. They toured the town and enjoyed the celebrations. The people were friendly and the food and beer was plentiful.

On Sunday, they toured the area and located the prison camp cemetery. It was a clear warm day. They walked through the cemetery looking at the names on the headstones.

In the middle of the cemetery, there was a large headstone and on it were listed ten names. The fourth name read *Corporal Madrigal, 1st Infantry Division.* They looked at one another excitedly.

Ten grave markers were on the ground and each one was numbered but with no name.

Mary noted, "In one of Douglas Dawson's letters, he wrote that due to the large number of deaths during the winter of 1917-1918, men were buried in a mass grave. He said there were plans to separate the men. Maybe they did it."

"Wow! That would be great. Now if this is his grave, what do we do about getting him exhumed and moved home?" asked Hank.

"Geez, I don't know. I thought we would have to search more than this."

"So did I. I guess sometimes it takes time for people to do the right thing. It looks like they did."

Mary said, "The town government is responsible for the cemetery. Herr Muller is the trustee for the cemetery and we have an appointment to see him tomorrow at nine. We can ask him how we can move him."

The following morning, they went to the town administration building. A receptionist took them to the office of Herr Muller. He was in his late thirties with a reddish face and a full beard. A radio was playing soft classical music in the background.

"Good morning, Herr Muller," said the receptionist in heavily accented English.

"Good morning to you." Herr Muller spoke excellent English.

"I have some people from America to meet with you. I will let them introduce themselves."

"We spoke on the phone a few weeks ago. I'm Mary King from New York City and this is Hank Johnson from Cleveland, Ohio. I spoke to you about Corporal Madrigal."

"Yes, I recall. Please have a seat."

The men shook hands and the receptionist left.

They sat. Mr. Mueller asked, "How may I help you?"

"Yesterday, we visited the military cemetery; there is a large headstone with ten names on it and ten grave markers," Mary began.

"I'm familiar with the location." Mr. Mueller nodded.

"Each grave stone has a number and on the headstone, Corporal Madrigal is listed fourth. Is he buried in grave number four?"

"No. In 1936, money was available for improvements to the cemetery and a headstone was purchased for the mass grave. Ten names are on the headstone because those ten men died about the same time. Corporal Madrigal was the fourth man to die during that period. The bodies were never excavated from the mass grave. He may be in the mass grave or was buried somewhere else."

"I see. That's disappointing." Mary's face fell.

Hank asked, "Do the records show why ten men were buried in one grave?"

"No, the mass grave was dug during the Spanish influenza epidemic. The weather may have been poor or the men to bury the bodies weren't available. The prison death records only show the date, the individual's name, the prisoner's serial number, and their religion."

"Do you see in the future the possibility of disinterring the bodies and doing genetic tests to determine who they are?" asked Hank.

Mr. Mueller shook his head slowly. "There are no plans or funds to do that."

Hank asked, "Was there a cemetery record, a cemetery plot or map?"

"Yes. Those records were accurate early in the war. Each cemetery plot was carefully recorded. However, many of the records in late 1917 and 1918 were lost. Later in the war, so many died that simple wooden stakes with metal tags were used. The stakes eventually rotted away."

"Can you think of anything that might help us?" asked Mary.

"What religion was Corporal Madrigal?" Mr. Mueller asked.

"If you recall, the person we are looking for is Lieutenant Harrison Richardson. He took the identity of Corporal Madrigal so the other man would get better care," said Mary.

"Yes, I do recall."

Mary said, "According to what I read, Corporal Madrigal was Lutheran. Why do you ask about his religion?"

"The Lutheran church near the prison and the one in town kept in touch with the prisoners and visited them regularly. In the church records, they recorded the burial plot numbers of Lutheran prisoners buried in the military cemetery. I have seen these records and they have been useful in finding graves. Sometimes the soldiers were buried in the Lutheran cemetery if arrangements were made in advance."

"Now that's interesting!" commented Mary.

Mr. Mueller went on. "I have a list of churches, their addresses and telephone numbers. Let me make a copy for you."

Herr Muller opened a file and removed a paper then left the office.

Mary turned to Hank. "This is good news; don't you think?"

"Absolutely."

"We should go to the hotel and set up meetings with the churches," she said.

"Good idea."

Herr Mueller returned with the copy and handed it to Mary.

Mary said, "Herr Muller, thank you for your time and help!"

"I'm happy to help. Mr. Johnson, since you are from Cleveland, I have a question for you. Has the Cleveland football team improved any?"

Hank laughed, "They've had their ups and downs. Why do you ask?"

"I was an exchange student and spent two years in high school in Akron, Ohio," Mr. Mueller said. "The American family I stayed with loved the Cleveland team. I thought the Cleveland team lost too much."

"I grew up in Cleveland. It takes dedication to be a Cleveland fan."

Mr. Mueller said, "I suggested to the father of the American family he should consider changing teams. I suggested Pittsburgh because I heard they were a good team. He got mad at me."

Mary and Hank laughed. Hank said, "Yes, suggesting Pittsburgh would have been a bad idea."

Mr. Muller's smile faded. "Americans are serious about their football."

Hank grinned. "You're right about that."

Mary said. "Mr. Muller, thank you for your time."

"You are welcome. Please call if I can help you in any way."

They returned to the hotel. Mary set up appointments for the next day with the Lutheran churches.

The following day, they visited the Lutheran churches and met with the ministers. In each meeting, the minister was welcoming and checked their records.

Neither church had any record of Corporal Madrigal. Disappointed, Mary and Hank returned to the hotel.

Later that night, Mary's hotel room phone rang.

"Hello."

"This is Hank."

"Yes, Mr. Johnson," replied Mary in a serious tone.

"Oh, you sound so formal."

She kept it up. "Yes, until I know why you are calling, I will be."

"I see. You still don't trust me yet."

Mary, in a teasing tone, said, "You are still being evaluated but I have to say so far you're doing well."

"That's good to know. I was thinking about today. It was clear to me the Lutheran ministers visited the prisoners often and got to know them," Hank said.

"Yes, it sounded like they knew them well."

"Harrison came from a devout Catholic family, didn't he?" he asked.

She replied, "Yes."

"I don't think he would have changed his religion. Once he was there, wouldn't he still practice being a Catholic?" inquired Hank.

Mary thought. "Oh my! Of course; we should check with the Catholic churches. See, I knew there was a reason why I brought you! If you were here, I would give you a kiss."

The line went dead. She stared at the phone and wondered what happened. She hung up.

A few seconds later, she heard a knock. She quickly put on her robe and went to the door. She peered through the peephole and it was Hank. She opened the door.

Hank was standing there with a smile on his face. "I'm here for my kiss."

She laughed. "How did you get here so fast?"

"I was motivated. A pretty woman in a hotel says she wants to give me a kiss, I make it a priority."

She smiled, "Okay, you can come in and stay for a bit."

CHAPTER 26

The next morning, Mary made a few calls and eventually talked to a bishop. She learned the bishop was also a history buff and was knowledgeable of the prison war camp. She scheduled a meeting with him for that afternoon.

The bishop's offices were located in a modern building that also served as a grade school and high school. They arrived as recess was finishing and the grade school children were returning to their classes. The children were laughing, talking, and having fun. Mary and Hank smiled at the children's games and their excited German chatter.

A secretary escorted them to Bishop James Morgan's office. The bishop was in his sixties. He was thin, tall, and bald with a friendly smile.

In a booming voice with a slight Scottish accent, he asked, "Mrs. King, I presume?"

"Yes, and this is Hank Johnson; we are from America. Thank you for meeting with us."

"You are entirely welcome. Please have a seat." He gestured to the guest chairs.

They shook hands and he sat at his desk across from them.

The bishop said, "As I mentioned on the phone yesterday, I'm a history buff. You can tell from my accent that I have Scottish and German parents. My father was a doctor from Scotland. He was in the British Army and stationed here after the war. He met my mother, who was a history teacher. I grew up in Scotland and here. Now, getting to what you came here for. There was a prison camp here in both wars. In the first war, if the prisoners had good behavior, they could leave the camp, and they would attend the churches nearby. In World War Two, the conditions in the prison were harsh and the prisoners never left the camp. If I recall correctly, you asked about a Corporal Madrigal."

Mary answered, "Yes sir. We know Corporal Madrigal was sent to the prison in late 1917."

"Yes, I confirmed that. I called the parish near the prison and there is a record of a Corporal Tom Madrigal attending a Christmas service in 1917. Father Richard Hofmann administered it. Father Hofmann's ministry spanned from the Great War through World War Two then up until he passed away in 1970. In February 1918, he transferred to a position in Rome then he returned to Wittenberg in 1928. Now an interesting fact about the Great War was that some of the Catholic prisoners were buried in our cemetery. I asked my secretary to check this morning if we had any records of a Corporal Madrigal buried in any of our cemeteries. I'm sorry to say that we don't."

Hank said, "We know the approximate date he died. It appears he may have been buried in a mass grave."

The bishop said, "Knowing Father Hofmann, he wouldn't have permitted a Catholic man to be placed in a mass grave."

Mary asked, "As I mentioned yesterday, Madrigal was listed as Lutheran but the lieutenant was actually Catholic."

"Yes, it took me some time to get that clear. The parish survived without damage from the World War Two bombing and Father Hofmann's records are still there. He kept an extensive ministerial diary. If you would like, I could meet you there tomorrow afternoon and we could go through the records to see if we could learn more."

Mary got excited. "Thank you, we would like that."

"I have helped many families over the years locate their lost relatives. I enjoy doing it. I'll meet you at the parish tomorrow at one."

The following afternoon, they met with the bishop on the parish steps. The bishop walked with them through the chapel then to the rectory, which was behind the chapel. Books and ledgers were stacked from floor to ceiling along one wall. The bishop pulled out a book and brought it to a table. He said, "It says here on December 25, Father Hofmann had a service for the prison camp soldiers. Forty-six were in attendance and Corporal Madrigal is listed as attending."

He thumbed through the diary for a few minutes then said, "On January 14, Father Hofmann visited Corporal Tom Madrigal, who was gravely ill at the prison. He says the soldier asked for burial in the parish cemetery but as you know, we don't have a record of that. Now two days later, according to this, the soldier died of pneumonia. They didn't know it then but it was probably the Spanish influenza. Nearly a hundred townspeople died that winter and spring from it."

The bishop turned to a woman in the office and asked her something in German. The woman walked away quickly.

"I asked Johanna to go down to the files in the basement and see if Father Hofmann produced any documents during the week that Corporal Madrigal died. Would you like some tea while we wait?"

They had tea and got to know each other. About twenty minutes passed and Johanna returned with some documents. He studied them for a few minutes.

"This is interesting. This letter is from Father Hofmann to the prison commandant requesting Corporal Madrigal's body be released to the parish undertaker. This other letter is the approval from the commandant allowing the body to be picked up on January 18, 1918."

The bishop examined the documents. "This letter is to the stonemason requesting a headstone. There are several letters regarding the headstone. These are interesting! I need to go to the military cemetery and check something. Let's take a walk."

They walked out of the office and down through the cemetery. In the back corner surrounded by a tall, black iron fence was the military section. As they walked down the aisle, the graves were intermixed with British, Canadian, and German soldiers.

"What we are looking for is row ninety-six, grave number six."

Mary saw it first. Engraved on the stone was Lieutenant Harrison Richardson, 1st Infantry Division, American Expeditionary Forces. Born March 12, 1895 in New York City, New York. Died January 16, 1918. Mary stood above the headstone and started to cry. Hank put his arm around her.

Mary in tears, sniffled, "Lieutenant Richardson, you have finally been found."

Hank took pictures of the headstone.

The bishop said, "Now it is clear to me that Father Hofmann got to know Harrison when he was in prison and learned his real story. According to the letters, the headstone was paid for but there was no stone available due to the war. The order was misplaced or lost probably due to the overwhelming demand for headstones for the German people and soldiers. The headstone wasn't installed until Father Hofmann came back from Rome. He discovered the error and had the headstone installed in June of 1928. Let's check Father Hofmann's diary further and see if there is anything else written about Harrison."

They went inside. Bishop Morgan read more in the diary.

The bishop said, "Another note I see is on January 22, 1918. Father Hofmann wrote the weather had been poor for the past week and Corporal Madrigal's burial was delayed. He writes he had met Corporal Madrigal when he first arrived at the prison camp. He learned the man's real name was Lieutenant Harrison Richardson. According to the diary, Harrison gave the priest an expensive watch to pay for a decent coffin and a better headstone. I don't think there is anything else."

Mary concluded, "It makes sense to me now. Douglas Dawson came to Germany looking for Harrison and he spoke to everyone he could find who was at the camp but the person who knew Harrison and his story, Father Hofmann, had left for Rome. The headstone wasn't installed until after Douglas Dawson stopped coming to Germany."

There was a long pause as they thought about what she said. Mary broke the silence and said, "Bishop Morgan, you have been so kind to us. Thank you for your help!"

"You're welcome! Now, if the family wants to take the lieutenant home, we can help with that. We have done it many times over the years."

Mary looked at Hank for support, then back at the bishop. "We aren't sure what will be the next step. Thank you again for all your help!"

They stood and shook hands. Mary gave the bishop a hug. As Mary and Hank left the parish, Mary asked, "A mystery of nearly a hundred years has been solved. Now what do we do?"

CHAPTER 27

THAT EVENING, HANK AND MARY celebrated their discovery with a nice dinner. While they were having coffee and dessert, Hank asked, "Well, what next?"

"I have a couple of thoughts. First, I think we should tell Catherine that Harrison was found. We should talk to Cecil and see if we can talk to her. Second, I think we should talk to Harrison's family and let them know where he is."

"Do you think she'll stop looking for him?"

"Yes, I believe she will."

Hank said, "I think it will be incredibly sad for her."

Mary agreed. "I felt good about finding him but I feel sad now. Maybe we shouldn't tell her."

"When we started this, it was intended to help her move on."

Mary sighed. "I know, but it's still sad."

There was a period of silence as they thought about Catherine. Mary suggested, "Regarding Harrison, I think the situation is easier. I believe we should talk to the Richardson family and see what they want to do."

"I agree. Now, I have a question for you. Have you ever wondered how Catherine got in the glass?"

"Oh yes, I have thought about it many times and like a good fairy tale, only her prince, her lover can bring her back."

"I see you have given this some thought. You like fairy tales, don't you?"

Mary smiled. "Of course. Do you have a theory on how she got there?"

"Well, her family did own a glass factory and her grandfather was a glassmaker. Was there anything in Douglas Dawson's diary?"

Mary shook her head. "I haven't read it yet."

"I have also wondered how she got to the hotel."

"So have I."

They were quiet for a few moments then Hank asked, "Since we have finished early here, I have an idea. How would you feel about a few days in Paris, Rome, or London?"

A smile spread across Mary's face. "I have been to Paris with Katie to see a couple of her fashion shows. I have always wanted to go to London. Could we do that?"

"Sure, I can make the arrangements tomorrow."

Mary looked at him, smiled, and said, "I have finally made a decision about you."

"You have?" Hank was hopeful.

Mary grinned. "Yes, I think my mother would have approved of you."

"Even though I was born in Tennessee?"

She laughed. "Yes, I think she could have gotten over that."

"Does that mean no more tests?"

"Oh no! There will always be tests." She smiled then winked at him.

"Can you tell me what they are?" asked Hank.

"Nope, that is a woman's prerogative."

Hank sighed. "You are complex."

"Every woman is. I have been thinking about the arrangements for London and I have a suggestion." She paused and smiled.

"Sure, what do you have in mind?"

"You should reserve only one room for us."

Hank smiled and asked, "Are you sure?"

Mary smiled, "Oh yes, I'm sure."

Hank leaned over and kissed her.

CHAPTER 28

AFTER A WONDERFUL FIVE DAYS of sightseeing in London, they flew to New York and arrived on a Thursday. Hank called Cecil and asked to meet with him the next day. He agreed to meet with them at the hotel reception at four-thirty.

On Friday at four-thirty, Mary and Hank arrived.

Mary said, "It's good to see you again."

Hank and Cecil shook hands.

"It is good to see you too. I understand you have been in Europe and you have some news for me," stated Cecil.

Mary said, "Yes we do. I'm so excited. We found Catherine's lieutenant!"

Cecil was surprised. "I beg your pardon. You found the lieutenant alive?"

"No, I'm sorry. We found the grave of Lieutenant Harrison Richardson. No one knew where he was buried, but we found him."

"I knew he died there but I didn't know his gravesite was unknown."

Hank said, "Catherine's grandfather searched for Harrison's grave after the war but couldn't locate him, but we did."

"Why did you search for him?" asked Cecil.

"We believe Catherine is still looking for him. If she knew he had been found, maybe she would be freed from the mirrors."

Cecil nodded slowly. "I see. So you want to tell Catherine that he has been found."

"Exactly."

"Catherine would then not appear anymore…." Cecil's voice trailed off.

Mary asked, "Would it be possible for us to see her again?"

Cecil was agitated, "No! Catherine is in Chicago. Mr. Ackerman wanted her to be with him in Chicago."

Hank probed, "Cecil, is everything okay? You seem upset."

Cecil took a step back. "I don't think I should be involved with this anymore."

Mary asked, "Did we get you in trouble with Mr. Ackerman?"

"No, we are fine."

"Then what's wrong?" Mary asked.

Cecil was abrupt. "I'm retiring soon. I'll be dependent on the retirement money I'll be getting from here. I don't want to affect my retirement in any way."

Mary studied him for a second then asked, "Mr. Ackerman has known her for most of his life. Let me ask you a question. Does he have feelings for her?"

Cecil didn't say anything.

Mary answered for him, "That's it, isn't it? He loves her."

Cecil put his hands up, "I can't talk about this anymore."

Mary asked, "You're afraid if we talk to Catherine and she goes away that he will blame you."

Angrily, Cecil said, "Please, no more discussion on this! I can't and won't say anything else about this. Please excuse me; I have other guests to attend to."

Cecil walked away, leaving Hank and Mary to consider what they had learned. They left the hotel and went down to the coffee shop where they first met. They got a table and ordered coffee.

Hank said, "Mary, I think you are right about Mr. Ackerman and Catherine."

"Is it possible for a man to fall in love with a woman in a mirror?" asked Mary.

Hank replied, "Why not? She is beautiful. She doesn't age or change. She never complains. She is always there to listen to whatever he says."

They were quiet for a few seconds.

Hank pondered, "What do we do now?"

"We need to find out where Mr. Ackerman lives. We will appeal to him on the basis of his love for Catherine that she should be told about Harrison."

Hank replied, "Now remember, we're guessing that he loves her."

"You're right. We shouldn't start with that. We should appeal to him on ending her search that has gone on for nearly a hundred years. But what if he doesn't want to talk to us?"

"Once we know where he lives and he doesn't talk to us, we could break in and talk to her," said Hank, smiling.

Mary said, "I see. Now your criminal side is starting to come out."

"We could act as cleaning people or gardeners to get in."

She laughed. "You've been watching too much TV."

Hank offered, "Maybe we take him to court for kidnapping. He did take a woman across state lines."

"We could go to the press and tell them."

Hank shook his head. "Remember Mr. Ackerman provides a lot of income for my company. I don't want to upset him."

Mary concluded, "I think a woman could talk to him about this. I think I should talk to him."

Hank nodded his head slowly. "That makes sense to me. I'll find out where he lives and how to contact him. I can start that on Monday."

"Okay, let's start with that."

CHAPTER 29

Hank got the contact information for Mr. Ackerman. Mary immediately sent a letter asking to meet because she had information about Catherine's husband.

A week later, she got a call from Mr. Ackerman's assistant asking her to meet with him in Chicago. Mary set up an appointment to see him at his home the following week. Hank traveled with Mary there. The meeting was at Mr. Ackerman's estate in Lake Forest at ten on Tuesday morning. Hank stayed at the hotel to make some business calls and Mary drove out to see him.

His mansion sat on several acres and a security guard was positioned at the front gate. He checked Mary's identification and let her drive in. A maid met her at the front door and led her to the library.

Mr. Ackerman was sitting at his desk when Mary entered. He got up slowly, shuffled over to her with the aid of a cane, and held out his hand.

"Mrs. King, I am Benson Ackerman."

"It's a pleasure to meet you."

"I saw you once in Catherine's room in New York. I was tired that day. I'm sorry I was rude."

Mary smiled kindly. "No apologies are necessary."

"Please have a seat." They sat on a couch.

Mr. Ackerman said, "I understand from your letter that you found Catherine's husband's grave. I didn't know his gravesite was lost. How did you find him?"

"It is an interesting story. Her husband Lieutenant Harrison Richardson was with the American Expeditionary Force in France. During a battle, he changed identities with a man, Corporal Tom Madrigal, who was wounded. Lieutenant Richardson changed places with him because the man would get better care if he went to an officer's prison camp. Unfortunately, Harrison was sent to an enlisted men's prison and he died there. Before his death, he met a Catholic priest and told him his story. People after the war searched for him but they thought he was buried as Corporal Tom Madrigal. He was in a Catholic cemetery, not the prison cemetery, and under his own name. When my friend and I went to Germany, we found him with the help of a kind Catholic bishop."

"It sounds complicated," Mr. Ackerman replied. "Are you confident that it's his grave?"

"Yes sir. If and when we move him, we will do genetic testing to make sure."

Mr. Ackerman looked at her. "Are you related to Catherine or to her husband?"

"No I'm not," Mary said.

"Why do you have such an interest in Catherine?"

"I became aware of Catherine from a woman who worked at the historical association in New York," she answered.

"So you didn't learn the story of Catherine from Cecil?" asked Mr. Ackerman.

"No, I have talked to Cecil about Catherine but he is as protective of her as I am."

"Why would you be protective of her?" Mr. Ackerman wrung his hands.

"I know so much about Catherine and her family; I feel close to them. I don't want her to become a subject of the tabloids."

"Neither do I. Now we come to the crux of the matter. You want to tell Catherine about Harrison, is that correct?" Mr. Ackerman pressed.

"Yes."

"You think if she knows, she will be freed from the mirrors. What do you base that on?" he asked.

Mary answered honestly, "I base it on my own intuition and feelings. I want her to be able to move on so she can be happy."

He countered, "She is happy. I see and talk to her every day."

"Mr. Ackerman, don't you think she is still looking for her lieutenant?"

"No."

Mary thought about what he said then asked, "Mr. Ackerman, I don't know you and I don't want to offend you, but do you really believe that?"

"Maybe at first that's what she was doing but I think there are other reasons why she is here."

"Is one of them to be with you?" Mary asked gently.

"Yes."

Mary paused for a moment, then asked, "Mr. Ackerman, do you love her?"

Without any hesitation he said, "Yes, I do. I'm sure you think I'm crazy for saying that, but I do. I have known her for over sixty years. When I first saw her, I was a teenager. I fell in love with her instantly and I still am to this day. She's as beautiful now as the first day I saw her."

Mary nodded. "I agree, she is. Mr. Ackerman, you've been married, haven't you?"

"Yes, I was married twice. I know what you're thinking. How could I marry a real woman but love a woman in a mirror? To be honest, it was hard. I thought being married would help me move away from Catherine but it didn't. Loving her and wanting to be with her ruined my marriages."

"Do you have any children?"

"No, unfortunately."

"Mr. Ackerman, don't you want her released from that glass prison?" Mary asked pointedly.

"Yes, but I want her to be with me. If she can't be with me then I want things to stay as they are now."

"I see."

"I know you think badly of me for saying that," Mr. Ackerman added.

"No I don't. I understand exactly why you feel that way. She has been a big part of your life."

"She has been the best part." Tears lined Mr. Ackerman's eyes. He looked down.

Mary stated, "I believe her love for her lieutenant was so strong that time stopped for her so she could wait for him."

"I want her to love me the same way."

"Maybe she would have if she had met you first. Mr. Ackerman, what do we do?"

He replied quickly, "I don't want to do anything. I want this to stay as it is."

"Don't you think she should know?" she pressed.

"Not if it means she is going to leave me. I'm old and my health is failing. Someone can tell her when I'm gone."

"So, you are saying that I can't talk to Catherine now nor will you tell her?"

Mr. Ackerman gave a brief nod. "Yes."

"Mr. Ackerman, I disagree but I respect your decision. You have taken care of her for many years now. I know you are trying to make the best decision you can. I think she would be happier knowing," Mary said earnestly.

"Every day I worry someone will come here and take her away from me. I'll be taking her back to New York where she wants to be. I stayed here to take care of my sister but she passed away last month."

Mary sat back. "I didn't hear about your sister passing; I'm sorry for your loss."

"Thank you. She was ill for a long time and now she is at peace. Once my new hotel is finished, Catherine and I'll be moving back."

"May I visit you in New York?" Mary asked.

"I would enjoy that."

Mary nodded, pleased. "Thank you for your time."

Mary drove back to the hotel and knocked on the door. Hank opened it.

"Who is this beauty knocking on my hotel door? Please come in," Hank said.

He kissed her then closed the door.

Hank said, "A good-looking woman coming to my hotel room, this is truly one of my fantasies come true."

Mary laughed. "You seem to have a lot of fantasies."

"Oh yes I do, and you are in ninety percent of them."

"I won't ask who's in the other ten percent." Mary looked at him out of the corner of her eye.

"No, you shouldn't go there." He changed the subject. "How did your meeting go?"

She shrugged. "He was nice to me but he isn't going to let us see her."

"Were you right? Does he love her?"

She nodded. "Yes, he does, in a kind but sad way."

"So we hit a dead end."

Mary agreed. "For now, we have. I'll contact him from time to time. He is moving back to New York once the hotel is finished. It will be easy to see him then."

CHAPTER 30

WITHOUT ANY ABILITY TO TALK to Catherine, Hank and Mary moved on with their lives. Over the next few months, they spent as much time together as they could. On a trip to San Francisco, Hank asked her to marry him. In June 2014, they had a wedding with their children, grandkids, and a few close friends in a garden at a Napa winery. Afterward, they honeymooned for two weeks in the valley.

On the last day of their honeymoon, they were having a picnic and some wine under some tall shade trees at the same winery in Napa where they were married.

Mary suggested, "I love Napa. Why don't we move here?"

Hank thought for a moment. "I guess we could."

"I also love our house in Ohio. We designed and built it together. We'll keep it and have one here too."

Hank laughed. "Plus we have the condo down in Florida."

"We will keep that too."

"And you want to still spend time in New York," Hank added.

Mary smiled and asked, "So you are suggesting that's too many places?"

"I think so. We will visit here when you want, but no home here," concluded Hank.

Mary nodded. "I can live with that. I was going to ask you about Catherine. The hotel is almost finished and Mr. Ackerman will be moving back to New York. I was thinking about seeing him. I feel like we have unfinished business regarding Catherine and Harrison."

"Yes, I thought about Harrison yesterday when we drove through the Presidio in San Francisco and the military cemetery there. He deserves to be back home," said Hank.

"I agree. I guess there's no reason why we shouldn't talk to the Richardson family about him and see if they want to move him home." She nodded resolutely. "I'll get that started when we get back."

They finished lunch and went to their hotel. Hank left for the golf range and Mary went to the pool. She had brought Douglas Dawson's diary. It was a warm day and she was sipping an iced tea as she read it.

After an hour of reading, suddenly, she sat up after reading a passage and exclaimed, "Oh my!" She took her cell phone and called Hank.

She asked, "Dear are you about finished there? I need to talk to you about something."

"Just about, is there something wrong?"

"No, I have been reading Douglas Dawson's diary. I have learned how Catherine got into the mirror. Please hurry back, it is unbelievable!" Her voice trembled with excitement.

"I'll be there in thirty minutes."

"I'll be at the pool."

Mary read the diary again to make sure she wasn't mistaken about the amazing entry. Hurriedly, scanning ahead, she learned as much as she could before Hank returned.

Hank arrived and found her at the pool. "Wow! You put that bathing suit on after I left. You look wonderful in it."

She grinned from behind her sunglasses. "Thank you! I thought you would like it."

"If I had seen it before I left, I would have stayed."

She laughed and said, "That's why I put it on after you left!" She kissed him then said, "Now, I have news for you. I have learned how Catherine got into the mirror. Douglas Dawson put her there."

Hank nodded. "I thought he might have been involved."

"He learned of a magical glassmaking process in Italy. A glassmaker in Murano whose wife died tragically used the process to capture her in a mirror. Douglas Dawson met him and the Italian glassmaker gave the instructions to him in a special red leather book. I have the book at home in my collection. Douglas used the process to capture Catherine. It seems when a person's ashes are added while the glass is being made, the essence of the individual is captured in the glass. The person is captured in the prime of their life and remains that way."

Hank thought for a moment. "It's like a time portal."

"That's a good way to think about it. Douglas' plan was to find Harrison then capture him in the glass as well. He wrote that he had promised Catherine they would be together. His plan was to melt down Catherine's glass with Harrison's ashes along with some special ingredients. Guess where he stored all the ingredients?"

"I have no idea."

"In his burial crypt." She looked triumphant.

"Really?"

"Yes, he designed the crypt and supervised the building of it. He felt someone in the future might find Harrison and he wanted everything available to make it happen. Somewhere in his documents, he signed a letter that gives permission to open his crypt to remove the ingredients. He put the ingredients into teak barrels so they would be preserved."

Hank thought for a moment, then realized something. "One thing that strikes me is that Mr. Ackerman will surely blow a gasket when he hears that Catherine's mirrors will have to be melted down."

"No, according to the diary everything is in the crypt. Let me read it to you. 'In the second room of the crypt, you will find teak barrels of Chinese blue obsidian stone, and a crate of blue obsidian glass. This glass is from the batch when Catherine's mirrors were made. All of this is required to make the capture glass for Catherine and Harrison. The following formula and glassmaking process must be followed exactly."

Hank said, "I'm stunned, I don't know what to say."

"I'm so excited about this. I've wanted them to be together since I first heard her story."

"Mary, let's not get ahead of ourselves here. A lot of moving pieces have to fall into place yet. Who do we use to make the glass?"

"Douglas Dawson said the man who gave him the process was Michael Musso. Maybe the family is still involved in making glass in Murano. We could start there. I've always wanted to go to Italy."

"I see." He smiled knowingly. "You want to go on another adventure."

She nodded. "Yes, we were successful before."

"Okay, I have a trip to London coming up. Let's see if we can go to Italy on the back side of that."

"I would love that! What a year I have had! A fantastic wedding, a honeymoon in Napa Valley, and now an Italian adventure."

CHAPTER 31

Mary researched Michael Musso and found his great great grandson was still in the glass business. His studio was in Murano. Mary contacted him under the guise of wanting to know more about Michael Musso for some research she was conducting on glassmaking. Mr. Vincent Musso was a gracious and friendly man who invited her to come to Italy.

Hank and Mary flew to Italy then traveled to the Murano Islands, which was a short distance from Venice. They easily located the Musso glass store. The Musso family welcomed them and treated them warmly. The family ran the store and the glass factory was operated by Vincent, who was in his seventies. After a tour of the store and the factory, Vincent invited them to his home.

It was a hot day and they drank sangria under large trees that overlooked the Venetian lagoon. There was a slight breeze, which was cool and refreshing. The lagoon was full of colorful sailboats and other vessels of all sizes.

Vincent asked, "Mary, how did you come to know my great great grandfather?"

"He was a friend of a Mr. Douglas Dawson. He was a famous American glassmaker in the early 1900s. I researched the Dawson family and I came upon Michael Musso."

"Yes, I'm familiar with Mr. Dawson. In my early years, I studied in America and I learned about him. He developed a glassmaking process that's still used today."

Mary nodded. "That's correct. Mr. Dawson met Michael Musso here in Murano and they became friends."

Vincent said, "Yes, there is a picture of them in my office."

"I would like to see that before we leave."

"Of course."

Mary asked, "Michael Musso had a book on glassmaking techniques. Are you aware of the book?"

Mr. Musso's face lit up, "Yes, there was a book that was lost sometime around his death. How do you know about it?"

"I have the book."

Mr. Musso got excited and started to gesture with his hands. "No, that can't be true! We have searched for the book for decades. How is it possible that you have it? This is not some kind of cruel joke, is it?"

Mary answered, "I can assure you this is no joke. I have it."

Mr. Musso's facial expression changed and his face darkened. He stated sternly, "I see now! You know how valuable that book is. You want to ransom it! How much do you want for it?"

Mary replied, "No, Mr. Musso, we aren't trying to sell it or ask you for money. The book belongs to the Dawson family in New York. Michael Musso gave it to Douglas Dawson. I'm sure if the Dawson family knew you wanted it, you could have it."

Mr. Musso was surprised and asked, "Seriously, you think I can have it?"

"If nothing else, I can copy the contents and you can have that," said Mary.

"I'm so excited but I need to ask you a few more questions to make sure. The book is bound in what, and what color is it?" inquired Mr. Musso.

Mary sat up straighter. "The book is bound in red leather."

"Do you know what the book allows a glassmaker to do?" asked Mr. Musso.

Mary replied, "Yes."

"You tell me so I can believe you really have it. What does it do?"

Mary answered, "The book described how to make capture glass."

Mr. Musso asked, "What is capture glass?"

She replied, "The process uses some special ingredients that can capture the essence of a person. A person can be captured in the glass."

"What are these ingredients?"

"I don't remember all the ingredients but the key one is Chinese blue obsidian stone."

"You are correct. What language is the book written in?"

Mary answered quickly. "Latin."

Mr. Musso shouted with joy, "Unbelievable! You have made an old man so happy!" He stood up and hugged them. "I have been trying to make the glass for the past fifty years. I have tried many times to recreate the formula but I failed each time. Now the book has come to me, like manna from heaven. So many things are going through my mind right now!"

Hank said, "Mr. Musso, there's something we would like to ask you."

"Of course, anything!"

Hank began, "We would like to tell you a story of a woman who was captured in the glass. She needs your help to be reunited with her husband. She has been waiting for him nearly a hundred years now."

"I would love to hear the story. Let me refresh our drinks with some much better wine. I would like to celebrate this occasion while I learn the story."

Mr. Musso left and went into the house. He came back with a couple of bottles of special wine. He opened a bottle and poured them each a glass. After a toast, they sampled the wine, which was excellent. Mary then told him the story about Catherine and Harrison. The story brought tears to Mr. Musso's eyes.

"What a sad story this is! Now my part of the story is you want me to help you produce new glass and bring this couple back together. Am I right?"

Hank replied, "Yes. Can you help us?"

"It would be an honor. However, the key question I have is how do we get the ingredients needed to make the glass? Genuine Chinese blue obsidian stone is difficult to get."

Hank explained, "We believe we can provide all the ingredients. Mr. Dawson left barrels of the blue obsidian stone in his burial crypt. He wanted everything ready when the day came. His diary says all the materials we need are there. We haven't verified it yet but we can when we get home."

"I have some blue obsidian glass from my failed attempts that we could use. I also have some Chinese blue obsidian stone here but not in a large quantity. Chinese blue obsidian stone is often faked because it is so valuable. It would be excellent to have stone that we know is pure."

Mary inquired, "Do you think it is possible for you to make the glass, and will you do it?"

"Of course I can do it, and it would be an honor. I can make two batches, one to use for Catherine and one for the Dawson family to pay them for the book. Blue obsidian glass is extremely valuable. Even the glass I made trying to recreate the process I sell for high amounts. The Dawson family will receive a lot of money. I would guess $50,000 American dollars or more for a small batch."

Mary gasped, "That's great news! We will start the process of getting everything ready when we get back home. I'll ask for permission to return the book to you. If I can't for some reason, I'll copy the contents for you."

Mr. Musso offered, "I would be happy to pay you for all your trouble."

"No, we aren't looking to make any money from this. Mary and I have taken this on as our personal project."

Vincent was surprised. "You two must be special because most people would want money for their trouble. That's kind of you!"

Hank said, "Mr. Musso, it will still take some time to get this completed."

"I understand. I have waited years for this. I'm in no hurry."

Hank said, "That's good. We plan to stay here for a few days. We will get started when we return home."

CHAPTER 32

On the trip home, Hank and Mary agreed on a plan to approach the Dawson family about the glassmaking book and getting permission to open the crypt. They were reluctant to be completely open with them on exactly why they wanted to give the book to the Musso family and for removing the glassmaking materials. They worried if people knew the true story then someone might want to stop their plan to bring Catherine and Harrison together. They decided to tell the Dawsons the Musso family wanted the book to make some special glass.

During the summer, the Dawson family stayed at their home in the Hamptons. The meeting was at ten on a Saturday morning.

They parked in the circular drive of a large, two story house on the water. A smiling Jacob Dawson greeted them at the front door. He was in his seventies, tall, tanned, and fit.

They stepped in and Jacob took their coats.

"Please have a seat. My wife stepped out for a while so I'm your host today. Would you like some coffee or tea? I have both on the coffee table."

Mary replied, "Coffee sounds good."

"I will take a cup too," said Hank.

Jacob poured them each a cup. They sat, drank the coffee, and talked about the weather.

Jacob inquired, "So you have studied the books and files. What have you learned?"

"We learned Douglas Dawson was a fascinating man with a colorful history," replied Mary.

Jacob chuckled. "Yes, my family has many stories about him and the things he did. He seemed larger than life."

Mary said, "Yes, he was. Another thing we learned was he made a trip to Murano, Italy early last century and he met a family there. The family has been making glass in Murano for over 300 years. The patriarch admired Douglas Dawson and the work he did in glassmaking. He gave him his prized book on glassmaking that describes how to make a special glass. The Musso family would like to make the glass again and would like to have the book back in their family. They have asked us to see if you would be willing to give the book back to them."

"Is it valuable?"

Mary said, "I'm not sure if it has any value to anyone but a glassmaker."

"Why is this glass so special?" asked Jacob.

Mary explained, “The glass is exceptionally pure and has a unique light blue color. It is called blue obsidian glass.”

Jacob questioned, “Why would the man in Italy give the book to someone outside his family?”

“We’re not sure why,” replied Hank.

Jacob thought for a few seconds and stated, “I have no use for the book. If someone could use it, then I’m fine with it.”

“Good, now there’s something else we learned,” Mary began. “Did you know that Douglas Dawson stored in his crypt some glassmaking materials?”

“No.”

Mary noted, “In his crypt there are barrels of blue obsidian stone, and a crate of glass. He hoped someday that someone with the right glassmaking skills would use the book and his materials to make the glass again. The Musso family would like to use the materials to make the glass. The glass they will make is valuable. By valuable, I mean up to $50,000. You can either have the glass or they will sell it for you.”

Jacob was excited. “That’s great news! The Musso family gets their lost book and I get some cash. Is there any other good news you have for me?”

Mary said, “There’s nothing else at this point. If you’re okay with giving them the book, I’ll send it to them.”

“That’s fine with me. I’ll have my attorney amend the documents you signed so you can send it.”

Mary said, "We will pay the costs for opening the crypt. I'll search the records and see if I can find Douglas' letter so we can open the crypt. If not, I'll have an attorney draw up a document for you to sign so we can proceed."

"As far as any costs, you can deduct it from the glass that will be sold. I would like to be there when the crypt is opened."

Mary said, "That's kind of you about the costs, and we will make sure you're there. Thank you for your time! I'll get back in touch with you soon."

"I look forward to it."

They stood, shook hands, and Hank and Mary left. As soon as they got into the car, Mary started talking excitedly.

"We did it. Now we have to get the Richardson family's permission to move Harrison home. I've been thinking about this. You know we will have to have his body cremated, don't you?"

Hank replied, "Yes. We need to do a number of things. We will have to get permission from his family, get the body dug up, do DNA tests, cremate his body, steal his ashes, take the ashes to Italy, and have the glass made. I'm sure there are some things I haven't thought of yet. You know we're getting deeper and deeper into this."

"Are you sorry you got involved?"

"No, getting into this led me to you."

She smiled. "That's true!" She took his hand and squeezed it.

"Do you think stealing his ashes is against the law?" asked Mary.

He chuckled. "Yes."

Mary said, "I was afraid you would say that."

"It's time to contact Harrison's family."

"I agree," Mary said. "I know from my research there are two grandsons still living. I'll call them."

CHAPTER 33

Mary contacted the Richardson family and spoke with two men who were retired and living together in Florida. Mary went to Florida to meet with them. They were living in a retirement village outside of Orlando.

Their home was a single story ranch with an emerald green, manicured lawn. The front door was open. Mary knocked on the storm door and two small, white dogs came to the door. An older man with short, grey hair and dressed in a blue Hawaiian shirt, khaki shorts, and white flip-flops arrived a few moments later.

He smiled, "You must be Mary. I'm Don, please come in." He opened the storm door.

Another man walked up smiling and said, "Hello, I'm Ron."

Mary did a double take because the men looked exactly alike and were dressed exactly the same down to the same style white flip-flops.

Ron said, "Before you ask, yes, we are twins."

"Well, you look identical to me!" Mary laughed.

Don said, "Yes, we look the same but we're different in a lot of ways. I'm known as the easy one to get along with."

Ron asked, "If you are so easy to get along with, how many times have you married?"

"Three so far."

Ron countered, "I was married only once."

Don said, "Yes, but your wife was an angel. She finally had enough of your crap and left you."

"She was no angel!"

Mary laughed. It was funny watching these two men squabble with each other. She interrupted, "Gentlemen, I'm here to discuss one of your distant relatives, Harrison Richardson."

Ron said, "We are excited to hear about him. Please have a seat. Can we offer you some sweet tea?"

"That would be wonderful, thank you!"

Mary took a seat on a chair and the two dogs sat right in front of her, staring at her and not moving. She looked at them closely and realized they looked identical. One sat with his head to the left and the other with his head to the right. Mary laughed to herself as she thought about the twin men and the look-alike dogs.

Mary told them the story of Catherine and Harrison without discussing the mirrors. The story brought them close to tears.

Mary asked, "With your permission, we would like to bring Harrison home. He will be cremated in Germany then returned here for burial in his family plot. There will be no expenses for you. Do I have your permission?"

Ron looked at Don and replied, "It's okay with me."

"Me too," said Don.

Mary breathed a sigh of relief. "That's good—thank you! You two are easy to deal with."

Don countered, "I'm the one easy to deal with. Ron is a grump most of the time."

"Let me ask your three wives about that," retorted Ron.

"You're jealous that women find me to be the handsome one."

Ron scoffed. "You look like me."

Don scoffed back. "I have better hair."

"No you don't!"

Mary couldn't remember now who was who. She interrupted again, "I think you are both handsome. Now I need to get going. Thank you for your time and the tea!"

"Mary, it was nice to meet you. Ron, it's your turn to walk the dogs."

"No it's not. I walked them last."

"No, I did."

Mary walked to the door and let herself out as the two men continued to squabble.

Within a few weeks, all the appropriate documents were ready and the process of removing Harrison's body had started. The twins provided DNA samples. Once the body was disinterred, DNA samples were taken. The tests proved they were related. The body was cremated and the ashes were shipped to Cleveland. Hank replaced

Harrison's ashes with fireplace ashes in case someone checked to see if ashes were actually in the vase. The fake remains were buried next to Catherine's grave in the Richardson family plot in New York.

After Mary found the documents signed by Douglas, she worked with the cemetery officials to open the crypt. The crypt was opened on a cold day in late November. Mary, Hank, and Jacob were there. It took the workmen nearly two hours to pry open the door.

Inside were two rooms. In the first room, Douglas Dawson's coffin was on a marble shelf and was dusty but otherwise well preserved. In the adjoining room, the barrels were stacked and in perfect condition. Ten barrels of stone were there. However, the crate of obsidian glass wasn't in the room, which was a surprise—and a huge problem.

Mary and Hank tried not to show their concern at the cemetery but the missing crate of glass was a large issue. They had hoped Douglas Dawson had all the ingredients, but now the only approach was to use Catherine's mirrors. They had no alternative but to get Mr. Ackerman's permission to melt down some or all of Catherine's mirrors.

Now the puzzle pieces were coming together. The barrels were shipped to the Musso family in Italy. The final piece was the mirrors. Mary sent a letter to Mr. Ackerman requesting a meeting.

CHAPTER 34

IT WAS A COLD AND rainy day in Chicago. The past few months were difficult for Mr. Ackerman because his health had declined faster than he expected. He could walk only with the help of a walker. He was anxious about meeting with Mary; he was afraid she was going to try to take Catherine from him.

The new hotel was only days from completion and Mr. Ackerman was preparing to move there with Catherine. He wanted to talk to Catherine about the move.

Mr. Ackerman entered her room using the walker and sat down. The walk to the room exhausted him and he took a few minutes to recover.

He asked in a loud voice, "Catherine, this is Benson. Are you there? I have some wonderful news for you. I know you're going to like it."

Mr. Ackerman waited a few seconds. "There you are! You are always so pretty!"

Catherine smiled.

"I'm starting to pack for our move. We're moving back to New York."

Catherine smiled and twirled around, obviously happy.

"I knew you would like that. The new hotel and your suite are almost ready. Like the last time, we will pack you safely and move you to New York. I know you like being there. I was hoping we would spend more time together here in Chicago, and we have. I feel we're closer than ever. Over the next few days, I'll tell you the plans about the move but it will be soon."

Mr. Ackerman's cell phone rang. "Catherine, please excuse me." He fumbled with the phone and then answered the call. "Hello."

The voice on the phone said, "Mr. Ackerman, you have a meeting today with Mary Johnson. I spoke to her and she is close by. She should be there soon."

"Okay, thank you." Mr. Ackerman ended the call.

"Catherine, I need to leave for a while. I'll be back after lunch and we can talk more."

Catherine disappeared. Mr. Ackerman slowly made his way to the elevator and took it to the first floor. He wanted to be in his office before Mary arrived. He felt self-conscious about the walker and he hid it behind his desk.

He had just sat when his maid knocked on the door then opened it. She asked, "Mr. Ackerman, are you ready for your appointment?"

"Give me a minute and then bring her in."

The maid left and Mr. Ackerman took a few deep breaths trying to recover. The maid returned with Mary.

He stayed seated. "Mary, it is good to see you again. Please have a seat."

Mary sat in front of his desk. "It is good to see you too. How have you been?"

"I have been better but you are looking well."

"Thank you."

"Your name has changed since our last meeting."

Mary grinned. "Yes, I got married."

"Congratulations!"

"Thank you!" She turned the attention back to him. "I hear your new hotel will be completed soon."

"Yes, I'm excited about it. I'm looking forward to moving," said Mr. Ackerman.

"I have seen it. It's outstanding! I know you will be comfortable there. As I told your assistant, I wanted to meet with you because I have some news."

Mr. Ackerman looked serious. "Last time, you told me about finding Harrison. What's your news this time?"

Mary took a deep breath. "I believe we have determined a way to bring Catherine and Harrison together."

Mr. Ackerman was surprised and asked, "How do you expect to do that?"

"I have discovered the process of how she got into the glass and who put her there."

Mr. Ackerman said, "Please tell me about it."

"Catherine's grandfather knew of a special glassmaking process and was the one who captured her in the glass. This was done so when Harrison returned they could be together."

"Her grandfather did it?" Mr. Ackerman asked incredulously.

"Yes."

"How did he plan for them to be together?"

"At first Douglas Dawson expected that Harrison would return from the war and he would be with her like you are today. However, when Harrison died in the prison camp, Mr. Dawson planned to bring them together using the special glassmaking process."

"Exactly how would that work?" Mr. Ackerman leaned forward, scrutinizing Mary's story.

Mary explained, "Mr. Dawson described in his diary how Catherine's mirrors would be melted down along with Harrison's ashes. They would then be captured in the mirrors together."

Mr. Ackerman was quiet and thought about what she said. "So Catherine's mirrors will be melted down in this process. Has this been done before?"

Mary shrugged. "I don't know, but I would assume Mr. Dawson felt it would work."

"So you aren't sure it will work."

"I'm confident Mr. Dawson knew what to do. Also, the glassmaker we will use—his family has done this process before."

"So you have found someone to do this?"

Mary nodded. "Yes."

"This sounds like an amazing process." He leaned forward pensively. "Tell me more about it."

"I don't know much about it. I know when a person is captured in the special glass, their essence is captured and they return at the age when they were the most vibrant in their life."

"A person returns young?"

"Yes."

Mr. Ackerman thought for a moment. "Incredible! So it looks as if I'm the one preventing Catherine and Harrison from getting back together."

"Mr. Ackerman, I wasn't implying you were doing anything wrong."

He looked at her quizzically. "But you need my permission to do this?"

"Yes."

"My answer is no. I won't do it."

Mary was surprised. "Why not?"

"My health is failing. I want her with me until I pass."

"Mr. Ackerman, I know you love her," she said, trying to get him to see reason.

His face changed. "You think I'm some kind of old fool who fell in love with a mirror, don't you?"

"No, I don't. I believe you genuinely love her. She is a beautiful young woman. You have taken care of her for decades now. I admire you for the kind of love you have given her."

"Do you really?"

"Yes," Mary said honestly.

"Thank you for that!" he replied. Mr. Ackerman paused for a few seconds then said softly, "Every night, I dream I'll be with her someday."

"I'm sure you do."

Mr. Ackerman inquired, "If a person comes back young and vibrant, why can't you put *me* with her after I pass?"

Mary was surprised. She hadn't anticipated this and she took a few seconds to respond. "Mr. Ackerman… you have put me in an awkward position here. I believe Catherine has been waiting for Harrison. Her grandfather promised her that they would be together someday."

He shook his head. "Her husband went away to war. He left her and didn't return. My father and I protected her and he loved her like I do. Since we have been here in Chicago, we have gotten closer. Why shouldn't I be the one to be with her?"

Mary hesitated. "Mr. Ackerman, I…I have to think about this."

He sat up straighter. "Mrs. Johnson, I'm a wealthy man. Pick any amount and I'll pay it."

Mary shook her head. "Mr. Ackerman please don't talk about money. I have enough money."

"Everyone could use more money. I could you give a hundred million right now. I can pay you even more at a later date."

The amount of money he was offering, stunned her. She said, "I want Catherine to be happy."

"She is happy now, and she will be happier when she's with me. I want desperately to be with her."

Mary put her hands up. "I know, I know. This is getting complicated. I need to think about this."

Mr. Ackerman pushed forward, trying to close the deal. "Let me be specific. I can give you one hundred million now. In two months, I could add another hundred million. I'm talking about a total of two hundred million."

Mary stuttered, "That's a lot of money."

"Yes, it is. Dreams are made with that kind of money."

She hesitated. "I need some time to think about this."

"I'll be in the new hotel soon. Let's get together in New York and discuss it."

"Yes…that will give me time to think through this." She was eager to change the subject. "I have one last question before I leave. In your heart, do you believe Catherine has been waiting for Harrison?"

Mr. Ackerman spoke honestly. "Catherine has been with my father and me for over sixty years now. I know she wants to be loved like everyone does. If I were with her in the mirror, she would want to be with me. She knows me better than she does Harrison."

Mary nodded briefly. "I understand. Thank you for seeing me. I'll meet you soon in New York at the new hotel."

Mary left his office. Mr. Ackerman was pleased about the meeting. He had the opportunity to be with Catherine, something he always wanted.

CHAPTER 35

Mary left Mr. Ackerman's home. Her mind raced from the conversation. She wanted to talk to Hank about what she had learned but he was traveling in Europe and would be hard to reach. The money Mr. Ackerman offered was staggering. She thought back before her marriage to Hank when she was living on a fixed income. She had enough money to cover her expenses, but never any extra. Since she and Hank got married, money was no longer an issue. Hank was generous and all the money was theirs, not his.

However, the money offered by Mr. Ackerman would put them into a different category of wealth. Mary thought about her daughter. She had never talked to Hank about this but she assumed his estate would pass to his daughter and his granddaughters. Mary didn't have much she could leave her daughter. This money could benefit her daughter and Hank's family. Why shouldn't she accept the money, she wondered? She spent the return flight almost convinced that taking the money would be a good idea.

She arrived at her home in Cleveland late in the afternoon. Her home was special to her since she and Hank had designed it together. Now that it was finished, it had exceeded all her expectations. One thing she loved was having her own office. She had designed it to be a cozy place to read and pursue her hobbies. On the top of her desk were materials from the Dawson family including Catherine's diary.

She picked up the diary and started to thumb through it. Catherine had written sweetly about her wedding night. She described how gentle Harrison was when they were together for the first time and how they discovered their sexuality together. Their honeymoon was like a fairy tale but sensual because of their shared sexual awakening. The short time they were together caused her to long for his touch again. Later in the journal, as Catherine lay ill in London, her last passages were about what their life would be like in the future since she knew he was alive. Catherine's diary clearly showed the love she had for Harrison. Shame filled up inside Mary. Why had she let her head be turned by Ackerman's offer?

Mary made her decision. Catherine and Harrison should be together. Somehow, she would come up with a plan to either convince Mr. Ackerman he should make the right decision or get around him in some way.

The next morning, Hank called her from Brussels. She told him about her meeting with Mr. Ackerman and her decision not to accept his offer.

Hank said, "I agree with your decision but I was hoping sometime in my life that I would be a kept man."

"A what?"

"A kept man—a man who is kept by a rich woman to do her bidding."

She laughed. "Has this been a dream of yours for a long time?"

"Yes," he admitted.

"Let me tell you, you are already a kept man. According to Ohio law, I own half of your property, so that makes me rich—plus I already boss you around, don't I?" she joked.

"Come to think about it, I guess I am. With that, I agree completely with you. Now how do we convince Mr. Ackerman?"

"I've been thinking about that," Mary began. "I think I should meet with him again and try to change his mind but I also think we need a backup plan. One approach would be to tell him we would use him instead of Harrison but still use Harrison. We would donate the money he gives us to charity."

Hank disagreed. "He's a smart man. He'll have someone make sure that he was used."

"Yes, you're probably right. We would probably get caught and you would go to jail for taking his money."

He laughed. "Why would I go to jail and not you too?"

"You know that orange doesn't fit into my color palate."

He thought for second then laughed, "Orange jumpsuits, I got it."

"One other thought I had was to get Cecil to help us," she suggested.

"The last time we met with him, he didn't want to get involved."

Mary said, "Yes, but he knows Catherine. I need to tell him we can bring Catherine and Harrison together but I need to plant the idea with him before Mr. Ackerman can talk to him. I know he feels positive about Catherine and I think he'll do the right thing."

Hank agreed. "That's a good idea! When do you expect to talk to him?"

"Well, I wanted to see when you would like to go to New York for a visit with Katie. I haven't seen her in a while and she'll be in town for a few weeks before the next fashion season starts."

"I can stop in New York on this trip if that's good for you."

Mary replied, "I'll call her. When you call back later today, I'll confirm it with you. I'll call Cecil too."

"I'll call you later today. Love you!"

"Love you too."

Mary immediately called Katie. She was excited about the upcoming visit. Mary also called Cecil at the hotel.

"Hello, this is Cecil Thomas," he answered.

"Hello Cecil, this is Mary Johnson."

Cecil asked, "Excuse me, but I don't remember a Mary Johnson?"

"Oh, I'm sorry. My name was Mary King; I'm married now," she clarified.

"Of course, of course, Mary from the historical association. I haven't talked to you in a while. Don't tell me—did you marry Hank Johnson?"

Mary was sure her smile came through in her voice. "Yes, I did."

"Congratulations! How are you two doing?"

"We are doing well. I live in Cleveland now. Have you been spending any time at the new hotel?"

"Yes, I have been making sure Mr. Ackerman's new suite will be ready for him. The hotel is outstanding and so is the grand suite."

Mary changed the conversation. "Cecil, there is a reason why I called. I would like to talk to you about Catherine."

"You should know she's still in Chicago," he said.

"Yes, I know. You remember we found Harrison."

"Yes, and I don't want to talk about him," he insisted.

"Yes, I know, but you should know we discovered the original glassmaking process that put Catherine in the glass. After Mr. Ackerman passes, which I hope is many years from now, we can bring Harrison and Catherine together in the mirrors."

Cecil was quiet for a moment. "Really?"

"Yes, it's exciting. I spoke to Mr. Ackerman about it."

"You did? When?"

"I visited him in Chicago yesterday. I'll be in New York later this week. I would like to see you and talk to you about this. I would like to describe to you how the process works and what we will need to do when the time comes."

"I would like that. It would be a nice end to her story. Mr. Ackerman takes care of Catherine until he dies and then she can be together with Harrison."

Mary stated, "What I want is for Catherine and Harrison to be together when the time is right for everyone."

"I would be happy to help, but I don't want to upset Mr. Ackerman."

"I know. May Hank and I stop by the reception on Friday to talk with you?"

Cecil replied, "Yes, I'll be here. My wife will be here too; I'll introduce you to her."

"I would love that! I'll see you Friday." She hung up.

Mary was pleased with the call but she felt a little guilty that she held back some of the story.

CHAPTER 36

On Friday, Hank and Mary went to the reception at four-thirty at the hotel. Cecil was chatting with a guest when they arrived.

Cecil said, "It is good to see you again!"

Hank said, "You too!"

The men shook hands.

"I have been saving the Resiling for you." He opened a bottle and poured three glasses, handing them each a glass. "Congratulations to you two on your wedding. Here is to a happy and long marriage!"

They toasted.

Cecil said, "I have been looking forward to this conversation. I told my wife about it. She'll be here in a few minutes."

Mary asked, "So she knows about Catherine?"

"Yes, she does. Here she is now!"

An attractive African American woman walked up. She had shoulder length black hair, slightly curled.

She was wearing an expensive tailored black suit, a red blouse, black pumps, and a designer black bag.

Cecil said, "Dear, this is Mary and Hank Johnson. Folks, this is my dear Elizabeth."

"It's a pleasure to meet you," said Hank.

Elizabeth exclaimed, "I've heard so much about you two. I'm so excited to hear you have a plan to bring Catherine and her lieutenant together. How did you ever discover how to do it?"

Mary said, "Before I tell you that, I have to comment on your outfit. It's so becoming on you. It looks like a Gordano to me, is it?"

She laughed. "Girl, you know your clothes! Yes, it is."

"My daughter works for Gordano. She is their chief designer and she lives here in New York."

Elizabeth was surprised. "*No!* I love their clothes but Cecil doesn't. He thinks they're too expensive."

Cecil snickered, "Every time she buys a new Gordano suit. I have to work another year!"

Everyone laughed.

"Cecil, you *do* have to pay for quality," Mary insisted.

Elizabeth said, "I tell him the same thing but he never listens." Elizabeth gently nudged him then asked, "What's the plan to bring Catherine and Harrison together?"

Over a glass of wine, Mary told them what she had learned in Douglas Dawson's diary about uniting Catherine and Harrison. She described the plan to use Mr. Musso in Italy to make the glass. At the end, Elizabeth said, "I want to cry. All those years and you are going to bring them together. You should be so proud. When do you think you will do this?"

Mary answered, "After Mr. Ackerman passes."

"That can't be soon enough as far as I'm concerned. I'll be glad when that cheap, mean, old bastard is gone," Elizabeth said with anger and bitterness in her voice.

Cecil protested, "Elizabeth, you shouldn't say that!"

"That old man took advantage of you for years. He paid other men here more than he did you, and you were the manager. He woke up finally and started to pay you better when you got that job offer."

"Elizabeth, he has treated me well."

"For years he didn't! I remember all those nights that you came home after enduring one of his fits of anger. The man always has to have his own way or he gets angry and spiteful. He's also a crook. You know he's bribed people to get his way for years then there was that man who mysteriously died in the elevator during the union problems. That old man is rotten to his core."

"Elizabeth, please!"

Elizabeth relented. "I know, I know. Mary and Hank, I'm sorry for venting a bit but Cecil was ignored for years. He has done a fabulous job here and he should have gotten more recognition."

Cecil pleaded, "Elizabeth, please let's move on. It's all in the past now."

"You're right." She kissed her husband gently on the cheek then said, "I'm excited for Catherine and I'm excited for us. I didn't want Cecil to have to worry about her after Mr. Ackerman passed. This is good for everyone."

Mary asked, "Do you think she's still in the mirrors because she's looking for her husband or to be with Mr. Ackerman?"

"For her husband. Mr. Ackerman owns her but he doesn't own her heart," stated Elizabeth.

Cecil argued, "How can you be so sure? Maybe she's here because of Mr. Ackerman."

Mary asked, "Cecil, what does Catherine wear when we see her in the mirror?"

"A blue dress."

Mary commented, "The dress she wears is the same one she had on when Harrison left for the war. She had the dress made especially for that day when they kissed for the final time on the dock. I know because Catherine wrote about it in her diary."

"I didn't know that," he replied.

"I believe if she was here for Mr. Ackerman, she would be in something special for him, not something special for another man," concluded Mary.

Elizabeth added, "That girl loves her husband the way I love you. When you left for the Army, I wore a certain dress at the airport. When you came back, I wore the same dress. Women do that. Do you remember?"

"Yes, I do remember. I loved that dress." He thought. "I think you're right about Catherine's dress."

"You know I'm right," said Elizabeth, and she smiled confidently.

Cecil grinned. "I also remember taking that dress off of you when I returned."

Elizabeth exclaimed, "Cecil, stop that!"

He grinned and said, "Well, I do."

"So do I!" She kissed him on the cheek. "Mary, I would like to be involved somehow when this happens. I don't know how, but I would like to be involved."

"I would like that. I like you, Elizabeth. I like your style. Let me ask you this: Have you ever been to a fashion show in Paris?"

"No, I've never been to any fashion show."

Mary leaned forward. "How would you like to go to Paris with me to see a Gordano fashion show? We would have front row seats. We will be so close to the runway, the models will almost have to walk over us."

Elizabeth's eyes lit up. "Really? I would love to go."

"I'll talk to my daughter and set it up." Mary nodded.

Cecil asked, "Hank, may I work for you after I retire? I'm going to need another job to pay for her clothes!"

They laughed.

CHAPTER 37

Weeks later, Mr. Ackerman moved into the grand suite along with Catherine's mirrors. Mr. Ackerman asked Cecil to meet with him in the suite.

Cecil knocked on the door and Mr. Ackerman yelled back, "Cecil, please come in."

He opened the door and Mr. Ackerman was sitting on a couch in the living room.

"Cecil, it is good to see you again."

"You too, sir."

"The suite looks great. Thank you for watching over this for me. I can't find a thing that needs attention."

Cecil was proud. "You're welcome! I have a few loose ends but every day the to-do list gets shorter. This was my last project for you and I wanted it to come out well. I'm ready to start my retirement."

"That's what I wanted to talk to you about," Mr. Ackerman began. "I need you for one last request. Cecil, you know my health is failing."

"Yes sir."

"I don't have much time left," he went on.

"I'm sorry to hear that."

"I would like you to postpone your retirement until after I pass."

Cecil was surprised and upset. "Sir, I have already delayed it. I can't delay it any longer. My wife and I have plans."

"I know I'm asking for a lot, but I need you," Mr. Ackerman pressed.

"Sir, can't you find someone else to help you?"

"Cecil, I can only trust you with this task. It's about Catherine."

Cecil hesitated. "What do you want done?"

"You know Mary Johnson, don't you?"

"Yes sir."

"She discovered the glassmaking process that put Catherine in the mirrors. The process can bring Catherine and me together. When it happens, I'll be in the mirrors as a young man with the woman I love. It's what I've been dreaming of for many years now."

Cecil was surprised. "Sir, did you say Catherine and *you?*"

"Yes."

Cecil thought about what Mr. Ackerman said for a moment because it didn't mesh with what Mary had told him. He asked, "What would you want me to do exactly?"

"I want you to make sure Catherine and I are brought together in the glass."

"Sir, I spoke to the Johnsons and I know they found Catherine's husband."

Mr. Ackerman anticipated what Cecil was about to say and took a firm stance. "I don't want it to be Harrison. I want it to be me. I deserve to be with her. I have taken care of her for years now. Catherine and I are closer than ever. Don't you think it should be me?"

"Sir, I don't know what to think," Cecil said honestly.

Sternly, Mr. Ackerman said, "Let me make it clear to you. If you want that retirement we discussed, then you will do this for me."

Cecil was angry. "Mr. Ackerman, that's not fair! I did what you asked; now you're asking for something else!"

Mr. Ackerman heard the anger in his voice and quickly changed his approach. He said, "I tell you what—I'll raise your salary twenty percent and you can start working part time now. You only have to work a couple of hours a day. I want you to stop in every day and check on Catherine and me."

Cecil thought for a moment. "A salary increase and a couple of hours a day does sound good. How about the Johnsons, are they okay with this?"

"I plan to talk to Mary about it. Besides, it's my decision." Mr. Ackerman shrugged. "Catherine is with me. She belongs with me."

"What if the Johnsons don't go along with it?"

Mr. Ackerman's face hardened. "They will. I'll get them to agree. I have enough money to get it done. If they don't agree after I die, then I'll have someone destroy the mirrors."

Cecil was surprised. "Sir, you don't mean that."

Mr. Ackerman raised his voice. "Yes by God I do! I know she loves me. She must be with me and *only* me. Do you understand?"

Cecil looked down at the floor. "Yes sir, I understand."

"Now that I know you are in my corner; I have some plans I need to complete."

"What kind of plans?"

"For one, I have someone in mind who will help you with this. He will be the person who will destroy the glass if it comes to that."

"Who are you going to use?" Cecil asked.

"Cutter."

Surprise lit up Cecil's face. "Sir, I don't like him. He's a thug."

"I know he is. I need a man like him for this job. He always gets the job done. I'll call him and make the arrangements. After I talk to him, I'll tell you how much to pay him and when."

"Yes sir. When do you expect to talk to the Johnsons about this?"

"I'll talk to Mary soon. Cecil, my friend, thank you! If you do this for me, it will give me great comfort. I'll make sure you are well taken care of."

"Yes sir, I know."

Cecil left the suite. Mixed emotions flooded through him. He was upset because he had to do another task but pleased he could ease into retirement. However, the plan Mr. Ackerman proposed seemed wrong to him.

He took the subway and arrived home as Elizabeth did. They met on the front steps and he gave her a kiss.

"Cecil, you look upset. Is anything wrong?"

"Yes, I spoke to Mr. Ackerman today and I need to discuss it with you."

She smiled. "Okay, let's talk as we make dinner."

They went in, changed into more comfortable clothes, and walked to the kitchen. As they got started, he told her what happened.

Elizabeth sighed. "That old bastard is doing it to you again. Cecil, here is the carrot, run after the carrot. Oh no, you are too close, let me move the carrot again."

"I kind of feel that way but this would be a great deal for us," he reasoned. "I get a salary increase and I only have to work a couple hours a day. His health is failing so I will not have to work much longer."

"But Cecil, what he is doing is wrong! He shouldn't be with her. It should be her husband."

"Elizabeth, why do we care?"

"Cecil, don't you dare say that! You think Catherine stayed in the mirrors to be with some old, mean man. No!"

"When he returns in the mirror, he won't be old. He'll be young again."

"Fine, he will be young again but I believe she has been waiting for her husband, not him," she pressed. "We should help her be with her *husband*."

"Why?"

"Cecil, what is wrong with you?! We should help because it is the right thing to do! Ackerman's money shouldn't make us change our beliefs. Honey, we've saved for our retirement. We were going to have a nice life down in Florida. We will be fine with what we have."

He sighed. "I guess you're right. I don't want Mr. Ackerman to destroy the mirrors. What do we do about that?"

Elizabeth recommended, "I think we should call the Johnsons. We can work through a plan together. Mary is planning to come here and we are going shopping. I'll call her. I don't care if we have to steal those mirrors; Ackerman isn't going to destroy them."

The next day, Elizabeth called Mary and told her what Mr. Ackerman was planning to do. Mary was alarmed. She said Hank would be traveling for the next week but agreed they should meet for dinner when he returned.

CHAPTER 38

Cutter stepped from the cab at the Grand Barker Hotel. The attendant stared at him then stepped back due to his imposing appearance. Cutter was a bald, black man who was 6'6 and over 275 pounds of muscle. He wore a handmade, black silk suit, and an open-collared shirt with a gaudy gold chain. His face showed the toughness of his business with several prominent facial scars. He had an angry and impatient look.

"Take me to Mr. Thomas," demanded Cutter in a deep growl.

"Sir, please ask the front desk and they will be happy to page him for you," said the attendant who was smiling but clearly nervous.

Cutter stepped closer and towered above him. He looked down on him and repeated his demand, "Take me to Mr. Thomas!"

The attendant looked up at him, swallowed hard and said, "Of course sir, please follow me."

He led Cutter to Mr. Thomas' office and knocked on the door.

"Come in," said Cecil.

The attendant opened the door then quickly left. Cutter stepped into the office and closed the door. Cecil was sitting at his desk. There was tension between them from past bad experiences.

Cutter growled, "Do you have my money and the other stuff I need?"

Cecil opened his center desk drawer and left it open. He removed three envelopes. One was a fat envelope with $10,000 in hundred-dollar bills. The second envelope had a set of keys for the warehouse where the glass was stored. The third one had a signed letter from Mr. Ackerman that allowed Cutter to remove the mirrors from the hotel when the time came. He pushed them across the desk.

Cutter stepped forward and took the envelopes, then placed them in his breast pocket. He asked, "I understand there are thirty mirrors to be destroyed, twenty in a warehouse and ten in the penthouse."

"That is correct."

"I understand my job is to destroy the mirrors if Mr. Ackerman calls me or if his attorney calls me. Is that correct?"

Cecil replied, "Yes."

"What is so special about these mirrors?" Cutter asked.

"There's nothing special about them. They are cheap mirror glass."

"Then why so much fuss over them?"

Cecil explained, "The mirrors belonged to woman friend of Mr. Ackerman's. Mr. Ackerman has a sentimental attachment to them. He doesn't want anyone else to own the mirrors after he passes."

"I got it. Now take me up to Mr. Ackerman," demanded Cutter.

Cecil replied firmly, "You know where he is. He is expecting you. The guard in the lobby will take you up."

Cutter demanded in a loud voice, "No! You will take me."

"No, I won't! I don't want to be seen with you."

"You think you are better than me?"

"I'm not a thug like you!"

Cutter growled, "You will treat me with respect or I'll kick your ass!"

"You will get no respect from me!"

Cutter hissed, "You will take me up or so help me I'll slash your throat right here." Cutter pulled a pearl handle switchblade from his pocket. He pushed the button with his thumb and it popped open. He stepped toward him with the blade in his hand.

Cecil picked up a revolver from the desk drawer and pointed it at him.

Cutter stopped and jeered, "Maybe when we were kids back in the hood you would use that, but you won't now!"

Cecil tried not to look afraid, "You know I will if I have to."

Cutter laughed. "What would you tell the police?"

"I'll say you tried to rob me. With your long police record, no one will care."

"You would never shoot that. You've become soft!" he spat.

"No, I have become smarter."

"You need me."

It was Cecil who laughed now. "I don't need you. I don't want to be around you. Trouble and death follow you!"

"You want me around when you need something done that nice people don't like to do."

"Years ago, I needed that, but times have changed."

"No, times haven't changed; my business is always in demand. Remember, it was you who introduced me to Mr. Ackerman, twenty years ago when he was having trouble with the union."

"Yes, I know and I have regretted doing it."

"I fixed the union problem."

"You killed a man!" Cecil said.

"There's no proof of that."

Cecil went on, "A man died in that elevator shaft and you were the last one to talk to him."

"I had a job to do and I did it. The union problem went away. I have fixed other problems for Ackerman over the years. He knows he can count on me."

Cecil shrugged. "I don't know anything about those. Mr. Ackerman is waiting for you."

"You remember this money is for half the job. You pay me the other half after I destroy the glass."

Cecil sneered, "I know the arrangement."

"I hope someday you will have to face me like a man!" Cutter stared at him.

Cecil shook his head. "You're not a man; you are a demon!"

Cutter stepped toward him and Cecil clicked back the hammer.

Cutter glared at him for a few seconds then growled, "I have more important things to do today than deal with you…but I won't forget this conversation. You should start carrying that gun all the time because you'll need it!" He turned and left the office.

Cecil put the gun down. He got up, shut the door, and locked it with shaking hands. Seeing Cutter brought back bad memories for him.

He went to the cabinet in the corner and took out a bottle of whiskey. He took a long drink right from the bottle. A cold shiver went up his spine just thinking about Cutter. He took another long drink.

Cutter walked to the security guard. The man ushered him up to Mr. Ackerman's suite and knocked on the door.

"Come in."

Cutter stepped into the suite. Mr. Ackerman sat on a couch.

"Please have a seat," Mr. Ackerman croaked.

Cutter walked over and sat next to him.

"I presume you have received your deposit?" Mr. Ackerman asked.

"Yes."

"Do you have any questions?"

"What is so special about these mirrors?"

"The mirrors are cheap glass. A woman I loved used the mirrors and I don't want anyone else to have them." This confirmed what Cecil had told him.

Cutter asked, "What happens if anyone resists when I come to take the mirrors?"

"No one will because they understand my instructions."

"But in case they do?" Cutter pressed.

"I'm paying you $20,000 to take care of whatever obstacle is standing in your way."

"Does that go for Mr. Thomas too?"

Mr. Ackerman was confused. "Why do you ask?"

"I don't trust him; he has gone soft. I want to know how far I should go."

"You go as far as you have to and take care of anyone who gets in your way. Do you understand?"

Cutter donned a wicked smile, "I understand completely."

"When and if this happens, it will be a call from me or my attorney. Is there anything else?"

"No."

"Thank you for coming to see me."

Cutter got up and left. Mr. Ackerman sat there and thought about his plan. He was confident that Cutter would do his part but he hoped it wouldn't happen. He was sure Mary Johnson would accept his money and he would be with Catherine.

CHAPTER 39

Hank and Mary flew to New York to meet Elizabeth and Cecil for dinner. After greetings, they settled in and ordered.

Mary said, “Elizabeth, thank you for calling me. We were shocked to learn what Mr. Ackerman was planning.”

Hank asked, “Cecil, do you think Mr. Ackerman is serious about destroying the mirrors if he doesn’t get his way?”

Cecil nodded. “He is absolutely serious. He has already lined up a henchman who will destroy the mirrors when the time comes. I know the man personally. He will do exactly what Mr. Ackerman tells him to do and nothing will get in his way.”

“Okay, then we will need to develop a plan to deal with this,” said Hank.

“I have a question first before we talk about any plans. How do we really know Catherine is waiting for Harrison?” asked Cecil.

Elizabeth said, "Cecil, we have talked about this. She has to be waiting for Harrison."

"She probably is, but what if we're wrong? Maybe she gave up hope for Harrison and she wants to be with Mr. Ackerman. I want us to do the right thing. I was wondering if the three of you would mind if I spoke to her about this and let her make the final decision?"

Mary nodded. "I think that's an excellent idea!"

"So do I," added Hank.

Elizabeth asked, "Cecil, would you want one of us to go with you?"

Cecil shook his head. "I promised Mr. Ackerman I wouldn't allow anyone in her room without his permission. I shouldn't break my promise."

Elizabeth asked, "When can you talk to her?"

"Mr. Ackerman is seeing a doctor tomorrow. He will be gone for several hours. I can do it then."

Mary said, "Wonderful! Let's plan to get together tomorrow evening."

Cecil grinned. "Let's have dinner at my hotel. I know the hotel manager and I think he can get us a free bottle of wine or two."

"That's fine with us. Now Elizabeth, I need to work out some details with you on our Paris trip," said Mary.

Elizabeth lit up. "I can't wait to go. I told my sister. She is so jealous and wants to go."

"That's no problem; we can take her too."

"Oh no! I'm not going to Paris with that crazy woman! Besides I want to hold this over her for a while."

They laughed. For the rest of the dinner, the four talked about the Paris trip and the details of the fashion show.

CHAPTER 40

THE FOLLOWING MORNING, CECIL WAS at the suite when Mr. Ackerman left for his appointment. He escorted Mr. Ackerman to the limo then returned to the room. At the suite door, he used a special, untraceable security card to enter. He went to Catherine's room and opened her door.

He asked, "Catherine, are you there? This is Cecil Thomas."

He walked to the window and opened the drapes. The room was flooded with sunshine. He turned to the mirrors and Catherine was there.

"Thank you for appearing. I hope you are well."

She smiled.

"Catherine, there is something I want to ask you. Before I do, I need to tell you some news. This will be surprising to you but I need you to help me make a decision about your future. I want to tell you these things and have you help me to make the right decision."

He walked up near the mirror, nervous.

"I know how you got where you are. We have your grandfather's diary and he explained exactly what he did to get you in there. He also explained how we could bring you and Harrison together."

A look of excitement washed over her face. She listened intently.

"First, are you aware Harrison died in a prison camp in Germany during the Great War?"

Her happy reaction faded. It was clear she didn't know. She sunk to her knees, covered her face, and started to sob.

"Please don't cry. There's more to the story that I need to tell you."

She dropped her hands but tears still ran down her face.

"Your grandfather promised you and Harrison would be together, didn't he?"

She nodded.

Cecil went on, "After the war, your grandfather tried to find Harrison's grave to bring him back. He searched for years but he wasn't successful. However, there is good news. Mary and Hank, who came here to meet you, have found his grave and have moved him here to the States. We can now bring you two together in the mirror."

She wiped the tears from her face and smiled.

"Now Catherine, here is the dilemma I have. Mr. Ackerman has been taking care of you for decades now.

He loves you. He would like to be with you instead of Harrison. He has told me that."

Catherine's eyebrows came together in an exaggerated expression of concern. She shook her head no.

"Is your choice to be with Harrison?" Cecil asked carefully.

She nodded.

"You don't want to be with Mr. Ackerman?"

She didn't move.

Cecil hesitated. "I take it you have feelings for Mr. Ackerman too?"

She looked down and nodded.

"Are these feelings similar to the ones you have for your husband?"

She shook her head, tears filling her eyes again.

"You love him like a father?"

She shook her head.

"You love him as a friend?" he clarified.

She nodded.

"You prefer Harrison be with you but you want Mr. Ackerman to be happy?"

She thought for a moment, then nodded.

"If only one man can be with you, should it be Harrison?"

She nodded vigorously and smiled.

"Now for the process to work, we will need to use your mirrors in the glassmaking process along with Harrison's ashes. We will have to melt down your mirrors. If it works, you will be together. However, there's a chance that you could be lost forever if the process doesn't work. Do I have your permission?"

She smiled and nodded yes. Cecil couldn't know for sure, but to him it seemed that she was at peace with being lost forever if she couldn't be with Harrison.

"Mr. Ackerman doesn't want us to do it now. He wants to be with you until he dies. You will have to wait a little longer."

She stood and shook her head.

"He will not allow it to happen now. There is nothing I can do."

She shook her head again and looked unhappy.

"Let me talk to my friends and see what we can do. I promise you we will try."

She smiled, grateful.

"I need to get going before someone sees me here. Thank you for talking to me!"

She smiled then disappeared. Cecil left the room, exited the hotel, and walked to the Barker.

Later that day, Mr. Ackerman returned to his suite. He went in to check on Catherine.

"Catherine, this is Benson. Are you there?" He walked up to the mirrors but she didn't appear. "Catherine, are you there?"

He studied the room. The drapes were open—he never left them open. "Someone's been here," he muttered. He called security.

"Yes, Mr. Ackerman."

"Can you tell me who has been in the suite today?"

"Yes, give me a second; I'll pull it up on the computer."

Mr. Ackerman could hear him typing.

"Mr. Thomas was there this morning at nine-thirty."

"Yes, he was with me," replied Mr. Ackerman.

"Someone else entered the room again at ten, but the card that was used doesn't have a name assigned to it. Some cards during the hotel construction had unassigned names. These were given to construction workers and other people involved in the construction."

Mr. Ackerman was silent for a moment. "Thank you for the information. You should make sure all those cards are deactivated."

"Yes sir, I will."

"Can you check the security tape for this floor and see who it was?" he asked.

"No sir. The security monitors for your floor will be activated in about a month."

Mr. Ackerman hung up, frustrated. Someone had been here and it worried him.

CHAPTER 41

THAT EVENING THE JOHNSONS ARRIVED for dinner promptly at seven o'clock and Elizabeth arrived about the same time. Cecil was at a table waiting; he stood to greet them and kissed Elizabeth. After the greetings, they sat.

"I was busy all day and didn't get a chance to call you. How did it go with Catherine?" asked Elizabeth.

Cecil replied, "I saw her and she wants to be with Harrison."

Elizabeth said, "I knew it."

"That's a relief; now we know for sure," Mary said.

"Let me tell you exactly what happened." Cecil told them everything he said and her reaction to it.

At the end, Hank asked, "So you didn't tell her Mr. Ackerman has threatened to destroy the mirrors if it's not him."

"No, I didn't see the need to burden her with that. Catherine doesn't want to wait. She wants to do it now. I told her we would try."

Mary asked, "Now what do we do?"

"I have been thinking," said Hank, "but it does involve a little deception on our part. I studied the glassmaking process in Douglas' diary. He described exactly how much of Catherine's mirrors in pounds we would need. I did some estimates on how many mirrors we will need. Cecil, how many mirrors are there?"

"There are thirty mirrors," Cecil answered. "Twenty are in storage and ten are in her room."

Hank smiled and nodded. "That's good. I did some calculations guessing the mirror's weight. I think we will need twenty-three mirrors. To be safe, we should switch out five mirrors in her room. I'll need to weigh some mirrors to make sure of my estimates."

Cecil said, "Those mirrors are a unique blue. Mr. Ackerman will notice five plain mirrors. How will we switch them out?"

"I thought I would talk to Mr. Musso in Italy. He might have some glass that would work for us," Hank said.

Cecil added, "Catherine only appears in one mirror at a time. If you walk along the mirrors, she will appear in each one as you walk. Mr. Ackerman always sits in the rocking chair near the window on the right. He won't notice if we use the same color mirror. We can easily switch the mirrors on a day when Mr. Ackerman isn't there."

Hank nodded, pensive. "That's good. Where are the other mirrors?"

"They're in a warehouse on Long Island," replied Cecil.

"We will need to go there and weigh the glass. Can we go tomorrow?"

Cecil agreed. "Yes, that works for me."

Mary asked, "So the plan is to steal the mirrors?"

Hank replied with a grin, "'Steal' seems to be such a harsh word."

Elizabeth said, "How about borrowing with no intent of returning?"

Hank's grin widened. "I like that."

"I still want to try to convince him he should do the right thing and let it be Harrison," Mary pressed.

Cecil warned her, "You can try, but Mr. Ackerman is used to getting things done his way and when he doesn't he can be a mean and vindictive man."

"Maybe I'll use the approach that you took," Mary started. "I'll get him to ask her himself. If he sees that she loves him as a close friend but not as a husband maybe he will change his mind."

Hank said, "It doesn't hurt to try. Now, I think we should switch the glass as soon as we can. That way we have it. If he agrees then there's no issue. Does everyone agree?"

Elizabeth said, "Yes."

Cecil said, "Yes."

Mary said, "Yes, I agree." She teased him, "Now if anyone goes to jail it will be you and Cecil. Remember what I told you?"

Hank laughed. "Yes, I remember, you don't look good in orange."

Elizabeth replied quickly, “I don’t either.”

“Well to be honest with you, I was going to hire a crew to get this done for us,” stated Hank.

Cecil smiled. “I like that.”

Hank said, “Cecil, you will still have to let the guys in. So you will be in the middle of it.”

“Oh crap, I guess I could get used to orange if I get caught. Would you guys come to visit me in jail?” Cecil laughed.

Elizabeth joked, “Only if it is a minimum security, country club type jail.”

Cecil smiled at his wife. “Elizabeth, thanks for sticking with me through thick and thin.”

Elizabeth laughed. “When we got married the minister didn’t say anything about visiting you in jail.”

CHAPTER 42

CECIL AND HANK WENT THE next day and weighed several mirrors at the warehouse. They verified the need for three of the mirrors in Catherine's room, but to be safe they planned to take five mirrors. Hank contacted Mr. Musso. He did have some blue obsidian glass that would work. He agreed to cut the glass to size, silver it for mirrors, and ship it to them by air cargo.

Hank made the arrangements with a construction crew to remove the glass. Two weeks later, the glass arrived from Italy and they were ready to have the mirrors swapped.

Mr. Ackerman had a doctor's appointment and would be out of the suite for the afternoon. As soon as he left, a construction crew arrived with the new mirrors. Cecil met them and told the security guard there was some maintenance required in Mr. Ackerman's suite. He led the men to the suite and the job was quickly completed. The crew left the suite and drove the mirrors to Long

Island. The plan worked without any issues. Mary then scheduled a meeting with Mr. Ackerman.

The meeting was on a warm spring morning. Mary arrived at the hotel early and decided to take a walk through Central Park. Central Park was beginning to wake up from winter. Daffodils were blooming and the trees were budding. Mary enjoyed her walk then returned to the hotel. The security guard escorted her to the suite.

Inside, Mr. Ackerman was sitting on the couch. He looked frail. "Good morning, Mrs. Johnson."

"Good morning to you," Mary said cheerfully. "It's a wonderful day today. I took a short walk across the street in the park. It is so scenic there. I remembered, as I walked, a passage in Catherine's diary about the day she and Harrison announced their engagement. I could envision them in the park together."

"So your point is you cannot see me in the park with her!" Mr. Ackerman shot back.

Mary backpedaled. "No, that's not what I was trying to say. I only meant that today in the park reminded me of the passage."

Mr. Ackerman impatiently asked, "Mrs. Johnson, let's get to the point. Have you made a decision on my offer?"

Mary was hesitant. "After considerable thought, I'm turning down your generous offer."

Surprised, Mr. Ackerman exclaimed, "You are? That's a large sum of money."

"Yes sir, it is," Mary conceded. "I'm here to make an offer to you."

Mr. Ackerman sat back. "Okay, I'm listening."

"I would be willing to bring you and Catherine together for nothing...if she agrees to it."

Mr. Ackerman grinned then lied. "Then we have a deal, because she's in agreement that we should be together."

Mary asked skeptically, "You have talked to Catherine about this?"

Again he lied, "Yes, I recently spoke to her about it because I knew we would be getting together."

"I don't want to offend you, but I would like to be there when you talk to her again about this."

"So you don't believe me? You think I'm lying to you?" asked Mr. Ackerman, his voice rising.

"No sir, but I believe the heart can change what a person understands. Please talk to her again. Ask her if she wants to be with Harrison or you. If she says she wants to be with you, then we will make it happen when the time comes."

Mr. Ackerman hesitated. "I don't want to upset her."

"I understand, but I think you will want to know how she feels. Imagine if you're together but in her heart, she really wants to be with Harrison," she implored. "You told me your marriages broke up because you wanted to be with Catherine. You don't want that to happen with Catherine."

"It won't. I know she wants to be with me."

"Then meet with her and ask her," she pressed. "If she agrees then you won't have to worry about this again. I'll make sure everything will happen the way you want."

"I'll talk to her."

"Thank you. I'll contact you next week and see what we need to do."

Mary reached over and shook hands with him, then she left.

Mr. Ackerman sat thinking about the conversation. He didn't want to talk to Catherine about this because she might pick Harrison. He felt frustrated.

He got up and shuffled to the bar. He poured a drink and quickly downed it, then he poured another. He sat at the bar and thought about Catherine, debating the situation. He knew that she loved him…but did she love him more than Harrison? He finished the drink and felt more confident. He wasn't giving himself enough credit, he rationalized. She had been with him for so many years that maybe she would want to be with him.

Using his walker, he got up and slowly scooted into Catherine's room. He called out for her, "Catherine are you there? I need to talk to you." He waited a few seconds. "Catherine, please I need your help."

A few seconds later she appeared. She wasn't smiling; her eyes were red and swollen as if she had been crying. She looked tired.

"I see you are still unhappy about something. I wish I could figure out what's wrong," Mr. Ackerman said.

Her sad expression didn't change and she wouldn't look him in the eye.

He continued, "We can talk about that later. I need your help with a problem. If there was a way that someone could be with you in the mirrors but the process was dangerous and you might be lost, would you want me to do it?"

She looked up as if he had caught her attention but she made no other movement.

He impatiently asked again, "Would you want me to do it?"

She was hesitant to answer and reluctantly nodded slowly.

"What if the only person you could be with was me, would you want to do it?"

Catherine looked down and didn't respond.

"I think I know what you're thinking," he went on. "I wouldn't be like I am now, which is old and sick, but when I was young and handsome."

Catherine didn't respond.

His voice rose as he asked, "Do you understand my question?"

She nodded without looking at him. She was afraid of hurting him.

The reality was starting to sink in. He asked his next question quietly. "You don't want to be with me?"

Catherine didn't respond.

"You've said before that you love me. Do you?"

She nodded.

"You love me but you don't want to be with me."

She didn't respond.

"Is there someone you want to be with?"

She nodded.

He hesitated to ask the next question. "Is it Harrison?"

She nodded.

Anger flashed up inside him. "I have taken care of you! I have protected and loved you for decades. I have wasted my life pining for you! Can't you see that you should be with me? I deserve to be with you!"

Catherine sobbed then disappeared.

He screamed, "Don't you dare leave me! You return now or else! If you will not be with me then you will not be with anyone. Do you hear me? You're either with me or nobody at all!"

She didn't appear.

He screamed, "This is your last chance! Return now or I'll destroy all the mirrors and you will be with no one ever again!"

She didn't appear.

Enraged, he left the room. He took out his cell phone and dialed a number. The phone rang a few times then someone answered.

"This is Cutter."

"It's time to destroy the mirrors. Come here now and remove them. You know where the mirrors are in the

Long Island warehouse. Take all the mirrors and destroy them now!"

"It will be done by six tonight."

Mr. Ackerman ended the call. Agitated, he started to feel lightheaded. He made his way to the couch and laid down. The pain in his head worsened and his vision was blurry. With great effort, he rose from the couch and tried to get to the bathroom to get something for the pain, but he collapsed. Before he passed out, he pushed the button on his emergency medical pager.

In a few minutes, he awoke and paramedics hovered around him. Faces swirled around.

A paramedic said, "I have a pulse but not much. He isn't breathing."

A different voice out of sight said, "Get him oxygen quickly. There's no telling how long he hasn't been breathing."

He felt a mask pressed to his face then he felt the cool air of the oxygen. His head hurt terribly.

Someone said, "Looks like he's had a stroke."

The paramedics got him on a gurney and into an ambulance. At the hospital, he watched a nurse inject something into his arm then his anxiety and pain eased away.

Soon he was sleeping comfortably and he started to dream. He was in Central Park sitting on a bench. Catherine was there in her blue dress and she was walking toward him with someone on her arm. It was an officer in an Army uniform. It must be Harrison.

They stopped in front of him and Mr. Ackerman stood to greet them.

The officer said, "Mr. Ackerman, I am Lieutenant Richardson. I wanted to thank you for the kindness you have shown to my wife all these years. You and your father took excellent care of her. Catherine told me she was never afraid and was always secure in your care. I wish there was a way to repay you."

Catherine said, "Benson, thank you for what you did. It is because of you that I am with my husband again. I have loved you as my closest friend and guardian for so many years. I watched you grow up and you were always there for me. Thank you for everything you have done and for giving up so much for me!"

She stepped forward and hugged him closely then kissed him on the cheek. He had always wondered what Catherine would be like in person. She was warm and smelled like the flowers from his mother's garden.

Catherine gently pulled away from him then she and Harrison walked away.

Mr. Ackerman woke and he remembered the call to Cutter. He had to tell him to stop. He had done the wrong thing. He knew now that Catherine and Harrison deserved to be together. Catherine loved him for what he had done, but he was now ruining it. His and his father's guardianship of Catherine would be thrown away because of his jealous rage.

Mr. Ackerman could hear people in his hospital room but he couldn't see them or speak. With all his strength, he tried to move his hands but found he couldn't. He kept trying for what seemed like hours. Slowly the room got clearer. He saw a nurse and he mumbled to her. The nurse came to him and leaned close.

He asked in a whisper, "What time is it?"

"It's nine o'clock in the evening."

"No! No! It can't be nine. Cutter will be done by now. I'm too late. I'm too late. I'm so sorry, Catherine. I'm so sorry!"

Sobbing, he tried to get up. The nurse was alarmed about his behavior and she gave him a shot. He fell into a deep sleep.

CHAPTER 43

Mr. Ackerman was in and out of consciousness for several days. The doctors wouldn't allow any visitors. After two weeks, he returned to the hotel suite in a wheelchair.

When he arrived, the first thing he did was wheel himself to Catherine's room. All of her mirrors were gone.

He started to cry softly. He heard a knock on the door and looked up to see Cecil.

Mr. Ackerman sobbed, "All her mirrors are gone! Catherine is gone!"

"Yes sir, I know. Cutter came back the day after you entered the hospital. He said the mirrors were destroyed and I paid him the rest of the money."

The old man shook his head bitterly. "In a jealous rage, I destroyed them. I'm such a fool. I should have let Catherine and Harrison be together. I destroyed their chance of ever being together. I'm so sorry."

Cecil walked to him, hugged him, and said, "Mr. Ackerman, I need to tell you something. The glass Cutter destroyed was mostly plain mirror glass. He only destroyed five of her mirrors. My friends and I took mirrors from Catherine's room and the ones from the warehouse. We put them in a safe place. We put fake mirrors in here that looked like Catherine's mirrors."

Mr. Ackerman's face lit up. "That is wonderful news!"

"There's more. The mirrors were sent to Italy. Two days ago, the Italian glassmaker used the special process to bring Catherine and Harrison together."

Mr. Ackerman breathed a sigh of relief. "Thank goodness! I'm so glad."

"You're not upset?" Cecil was relieved.

"No Cecil, you have saved me! In a mad fit of rage and jealousy, I did something I terribly regret. You saved her and me."

Cecil shook his head. "No sir, I wasn't the only one. Mary and Hank Johnson, and my wife were all involved."

Mr. Ackerman was relieved. "Thank God that I had someone thinking for me."

"Mary and Hank are in Italy making sure everything goes well. They will bring the glass back here. It will be weeks before we know for sure if the process worked."

"I can't wait till it comes back."

Cecil hesitated. "Mr. Ackerman, I would like to suggest something."

"Of course, what is it?"

"When the glass comes back we would like to put it in a museum across the street from Central Park. Catherine's family has an endowment there for a glass display. We think it would be the perfect place for Catherine and Harrison"

Mr. Ackerman nodded slowly. "That's a wonderful idea. The couple can have a fresh start. I'll check with the museum and add to the endowment so she and Harrison will always be safe."

CHAPTER 44

THREE WEEKS LATER, THE GLASS arrived at the museum. Instead of many mirrors, there was one large mirror in an impressive oak frame that had delicate hand-carved flowers. The mirror was in a special area that overlooked Central Park.

Every day for weeks, Cecil with Mr. Ackerman in a wheelchair, stopped by and checked on the mirror. They had coffee and sat in front of the mirror for a while.

One day, they were alone with the mirror. Mr. Ackerman dozed in his wheelchair and Cecil was reading the paper. The reflection in the mirror brightened and Cecil looked up to see Catherine smiling at him—and at her side was Harrison. Behind them in a country setting was a stone house with a wraparound porch with large shade trees. It was peaceful, beautiful.

Cecil nudged Mr. Ackerman. He woke up and he saw them as well.

Mr. Ackerman said, "Well my dear, I see you have found your lieutenant."

She smiled and squeezed Harrison's arm. Harrison removed his hat and bowed to them. It was a clear sign that he was thanking them.

Mr. Ackerman said, "You're welcome, young man. Now your job is to take care of her. She's waited for you for a long, long time."

On the other side of the mirror, Harrison squared his shoulders and turned to Catherine. He gently cradled her face in his hands and looked lovingly into her eyes. He said softly, "My darling I know you've waited so long."

Her voice trembled, her eyes filled with tears. "I wanted to believe my grandfather but I almost lost hope that you would ever return. I have been so lonely."

"I know darling." He carefully wiped her tears away then gently kissed her. "We will never be apart again." He took her hands in his and said tenderly, "Come and sit with me."

Catherine replied, "I would love that. There is so much I need to tell you."

He put on his hat then he and Catherine walked to their home. The mirror turned blank.

Now on Sunday afternoons during warm weather, if you look carefully you can see a couple in turn of the century clothing walking in Central Park. Some people say they seem to be promenading through the park...

and Catherine would agree with them. Catherine always loved Sunday afternoons, and she especially loves them now that her husband is with her.

The End

Made in the USA
Middletown, DE
22 February 2017